EPSILON

Library of Congress Control Number:
TXu 2-303-346

Printed in the United States of America: First Printing, 2022.
ISBN 978-1-7378376-2-6 (eBook)
ISBN 978-1-7378376-3-3 (paperback)

www.huckleberryrahrauthor.wordpress.com

Copy/Line Editor: Wes Imrisek
Developmental Editor: Angela Grimes
Cover Art: Getcovers.com
Formatting: R. L. Davennor

CHAPTER 1

"Jade, you can do this."

Mom's words were meant to encourage me, but they just stressed me out more than they helped. My jaw clenched. I tried to keep the rest of my body from following suit—it wouldn't help—though I couldn't stop my heart from beating faster. It'd been over an hour, and I felt like an idiot, perched like a statue on my hands and knees. The dew misted on my fingers, as if they were the grass needing a drink. I growled down at my wet digits. She prowled inside me; I could feel it. She would come out this time.

Failure was not an option. Today was the day. I was

going to become a wolf.

Focus on wolfy thoughts, Jade: the wind, trees, tasty squirrels, and yummy rabbits.

I strained and panted. My heart pounded, blood rushing in my ears. Sweat broke out on my forehead and my hands shook. Pushing, I tried to force the change. Tried…and, and, and…nothing.

A breeze blew across the backyard. The familiar scents of the trees and animals suffused my senses. A bird landed on a tree branch. Closing my eyes, I focused on that, listening to the rustle as it chirped and pecked. There were a lot of cardinals in the area. Imagining a red body amongst the green of the tree centered me and the shaking in my arms stopped.

Calm. Think calming thoughts, Jade.

I could master anything I put my mind to. Why couldn't I do this? My breath quickened and I focused as hard as I could on my wolf. Sweat pooled on my back even though it was cool this late at night.

This was within my grasp, wasn't it?

My limbs shuddered under me, and I collapsed onto my stomach.

Failure, again. Nose in the dirt, disappointment flowed through me. Finally, I rolled to my back and stared up at Mom, feeling defeated.

"Anything?" Mom asked, though she sounded more like an alpha figuring things out. "Did you feel any twinges?"

"No twinges. I just felt like an idiot…again. Frozen on my hands and knees on the wet grass, naked, in front of my mom, for nothing. This is really frustrating." Punching the ground with both my hands, I finally sat up, pulling my knees to my chest.

Mom leaned down and kissed my forehead.

Both animals paced in me, clawing for release, but I could only figure out how to let the panther free. If I relaxed just a little, she would flow through me like water. We had been trying for the wolf transformation at least once a week for two months, since I had first discovered I had a werewolf form.

In the beginning, every time I tried, I became my panther. My first lesson became suppressing the panther. It took some practice, but I mastered the lesson.

Now I had to focus on bringing out my wolf, instead. Apparently, she was shy.

"Do you want me to pull her out?" Mom asked. She could use her alpha skill to force my wolf out. She squatted next to me and gently placed a hand on my shoulder. My breathing steadied with her touch, part of the magic of pack.

Stubbornly, I kept telling myself if I felt the flow to wolf *one more time*, my body would learn it and figure out how to do it on its own. My own? Her own? My own! Gah! Why was this so hard? *Grrr!*

"Yes. I need to understand the transformation. I need to learn and remember the feel of the change."

Flopping to my side, I rolled to my hands and knees and stared down at the grass, wondering if there was any inspiration there. Nope, only the dew.

My mom, my alpha, reached out and put her hand back on my shoulder. After a minute, she gently touched my chin and lifted my face, forcing me to look at her. The brown in her eyes glowed and took over my full field of vision. It felt like she touched my soul as the alpha's command took over. She called to my wolf.

My back arched and my fingers shortened as my face elongated. Coarse fur sprouted through my skin along with sharp, thick claws. Pain, pain, pain…and then everything flowed. The change, once it started, felt natural.

The shifting of bones still hurt, but everything happened faster once my body understood what to do. Shaking, I looked at my hand…my paw…a wolf's paw. Any confusion about my identity after the transformation was gone.

I took stock of the parts I could see: black wolf legs and paws. Success! Yipping and bouncing a couple of times, I shifted my gaze up to my alpha with my tongue lolling out in a grin. My wolf had come out to play.

A sudden commotion in the front yard had us both turning. Luke, a pack member, came storming around from the front of the house. His trajectory: my mom. He didn't even appear to see me.

"Hazel, we need to talk. I just can't take my job and that

man. I don't know what to do." He pulled at his short, light brown curls. "I can't afford to quit, but I can't stay there."

Mom slowly straightened to a standing position, her auburn hair glowing in a ray of sunlight. Though she was a few inches shorter than Luke, she had a larger presence. Shaking with agitation, he focused on her eyes.

Daring move, Luke, especially with your alpha — but could be dangerous when you're angry and looking for a fight.

After a minute of staring Mom in the eyes, he trembled. He dropped his gaze and paced back and forth in front of her.

Mom reached out and put a hand on his shoulder. "Luke, it's going to be okay. Just tell me what happened."

"They put me with Derek again. And I just can't. Not again, he just doesn't *do* anything."

He froze, turning as if lost. He sniffed the air. "Blue cheese." He sniffed again. "Blue cheese anchovy pizza." When his rotation brought him face-to-face with me, his grey eyes were wild. He looked ready to shift.

Gently sniffing the air, all I smelled were the lilac bushes and the forest growing behind the pack house. *Thank Mondara I only smell the scents of nature.* Blue cheese and anchovy? A shiver ran through me at the thought. The description alone made me recoil.

Owen and I had eating competitions, challenging each other with weird toppings, but even we never tried anything that weird. *I mean, pizza is pizza, but that sounds awful. Whoever put that monstrosity together shouldn't be let loose with pizza toppings.*

Mom approached Luke and put a hand on his shoulder. He leapt a foot in the air, his head jerking to her. "The pizza, Hazel!" He trembled, his scent changing as he told his story.

"Luke, what *about* the pizza?"

He squatted. "That damn pizza, he brings it in and eats it every day. And he doesn't finish anything. Gods, why do I always get partnered with him? He's a waste of space. Do you know what he did? His great idea? He discounted a product by increasing the price!"

Mom turned to me. "Jade, honey, a bit of help?"

How does Mom think I can help? Oh, that's right... Shutting my eyes, I found my center of calm. After the confusion of the day it hid deep within me. I didn't know why I could share my calm; no one else in the pack could. *Focus, Jade, figure out your weirdness later!* Luke continued to mutter about work ethics and pizza. Tuning him out, I took one more breath, and as I exhaled, I released my own center, my calm, blanketing the backyard.

I heard a thump and opened my eyes to find Luke on his butt in the grass.

Mom squatted next to him. "Better?"

He nodded. "Yeah." His head fell back. "Oh, gods, what did I do at work? I was just so angry. I don't know why. I just..." He turned to me. "Thanks, Jade."

I hopped a bit with my front paws to acknowledge him.

Mom turned to me. "I can help Luke now; he'll be fine. Go for a run, eat, drink, and have some fun. I'll see you when you return. There will be food waiting." She winked at me. "Maybe some of this pizza Luke's gone on about." She chuckled at her own joke. "We can discuss other options for your wolf issues later."

My lip curled up from my teeth in a laugh but after a minute I headed out to run in the woods. The pain of the change was gone, but my desire to run was still intact. Stretching my legs felt great, though it wasn't distracting enough. I couldn't outrun my failure from earlier. Nothing worked. The only form I could call on my own was my panther.

We were out of options.

CHAPTER 2

"This campus is gorgeous; would you ever consider going here?" Piper's voice sounded dreamy. I smiled, watching her gaze around at the beauty of the landscape, her eyes shining with delight. My hope was that she could imagine herself as a student here.

Piper and I walked around the beautiful campus of University of Wisconsin — Whitewater. We had only recently made our relationship official and hadn't had much time to spend together, so I asked if she could join the family when we brought Owen to sign up for his classes. It was her first official look at a college campus. Being on my own with her left me equal parts giddy and nervous.

Most of the buildings on the campus encircled a few blocks of well-manicured land. The main class buildings surrounded a landscaped waterfall with flowers. As we crested a hill, a student worker in a purple shirt came into view, walking backwards as they guided a group of teens and their parents.

At Piper's questioning look, I said, "Campus tour."

Her face cleared and she nodded. As they passed us, I cringed.

"What's the matter?" she asked. "Don't you like tours?"

"What? No, tours are fine. It's the body sprays. It's overwhelming and fake. It all smells like alcohol and battling hell. Sweat-smell is normal, healthy, fine, but these perfumes are too much. Especially when there are two or three of them, and that group had…a lot." Sneezing, I shook my head to clear my nose.

"Is it worse now that you have two animals?"

"Maybe. Or maybe they were wearing too much. Count them, at least ten teens in that group. I think they were competing for best, or worst, smelling."

Piper smiled. "How will Owen survive living in tight quarters with a bunch of them? And how did he end up here anyway, didn't you say he didn't want to continue school after graduation…*if* he graduated?"

Rubbing my nose, I obliterated the last of the fake scent. "True, his graduation was a bit of a shocker to all of us. But

Mom made him apply to a bunch of places his junior year, and Alejandro, José's dad, works here. Win-win really."

"Has he decided on a degree path?"

Scrunching up my face, I harrumphed. "After deciding he didn't want to be the pack chef—"

Placing her hand on my elbow, Piper said softly. "He never wanted that, hon."

"—he realized he liked helping me and Sarah with our panther training. He's leaning towards being a personal trainor…you know, so he can help Dad with his torture plans."

Her head swung around as she laughed, taking in the buildings. "Would you consider this campus?"

The modern buildings, interspersed with wide paths and carefully tended lawns, exuded a sense of peace. However, despite the loveliness of everything, I knew it wasn't quite the right place for me.

I squeezed Piper's hand. "No, I don't think I'll apply here." Seeing the tour group ahead, I steered Piper up a hill. My nose needed a break. "I want to study biology or another pre-med path. This is a great campus, but it's more focused on education and business. I don't think this is the right fit for me. What about you? Do you think you could see yourself here in a couple years?"

Sliding my arm around her shoulders, I kissed the top of her head. Some of the spiky auburn mess tickled my nose. *I wish her self-confidence matched her sassy hair!* Piper stood only a couple inches shorter than my five foot seven, but you'd never know it. She usually slouched into herself, making her seem smaller. *This summer we're working on that confidence I know is brewing in there!*

While Piper and I meandered around the campus, Owen and my parents attended the official campus tour and class registration.

Sarah, my best friend and panther pack-mate, had also joined us on this college visit, but she'd stayed with the rest of my family. Sarah was considering this campus, too. It had the benefits of being small, it was close to home, and the faculty and staff had the reputation of caring for their students. She told me she hadn't decided on what she wanted to study yet. Just finishing our sophomore year in high school, that was completely normal.

Piper brought me back to our conversation. "I might want to come here. If I go to college," she mumbled. Until moving here, her dad had been a lone wolf and they had moved a lot; she wasn't used to staying in one place and planning for the future. "It seems great, except for the big hill in the middle of campus. That must be fun in the ice and snow," she joked. Her eyes widened and she stopped dead, staring. "Look, they have a campus food truck."

The only person who focused on food more than Piper was my brother. I snorted. Then my stomach grumbled and we headed to the food truck. After checking over the menu, I ended up with a cheeseburger with the works and fries. Piper got a plain burger with fries. We each chose a soda, and then we sat at a round outdoor table to eat.

Sitting at the table's bench by the waterfall, I gazed at it, amazed by its beauty. Bordered by the school's pathways and lined with rocks and flowers, it lulled me into relaxation. The natural aroma of the flowers comforted me after the cloying scents of the touring students, and the sound of the water trickling through the rocks filled me with tranquility. Even the sound of voices from a passing tour group harmonized with the ambience of the waterfall.

Taking a big mouthful of the burger only added to my feeling of well-being. By the second bite, juices flowed down my chin and threatened my snarky T-shirt. I quickly leaned over to save it from food stains. Today's snark read, "If you say gullible slowly enough it sounds like orange." Laughing with her mouth full of fries, Piper tossed me a few napkins.

After wiping myself down, I asked, "What do you want to study when you go to college?"

"*If* I go to college, you mean."

Once again, she avoids the question.

"You're smart enough," I countered.

Staring at me, she took a big bite of her burger and chewed slowly. After swallowing, she sipped her soda. Sighing, she said, "Maybe, but I don't know. And then there's the cost. My family doesn't really make enough. I may be smart, but not smart enough for a scholarship. I don't want to owe that much."

"There are ways. Like a two-year tech college with transfer credits. It costs less, and then you wouldn't have to pay as much. So, what would you study if you did?"

Piper sighed, her shoulders slumping. She slowly lifted her eyes, almost like she was ashamed. "Maybe art or history."

That doesn't tell me anything, not really.

"That's really cool." Smiling and nodding, I channeled every ounce of cheerleader I had…which wasn't much.

"No, that's really: 'Would you like fries with that?' Or: 'do I want to become a teacher?'" She dropped her gaze to focus on eating her fries.

New tactic time. She's finally opening up.

"Fast food and teaching wouldn't be your only options. What do you really want to do?" Reaching down to take another bite of my burger, I found it was gone. *Huh, when did that happen?* I looked around. *Did it fall?*

While I searched for my burger, Piper played with the last of her fries. "Maybe teach," she replied, "but I'm not sure. I've never loved that idea." She looked up, her face brightening. "I do like the idea of solving things, maybe doing crime solving. I kind of like CSI. Or art. I may work blowing glass with Luke as an apprentice." She blushed, like she was worried I would mock her interest. Chuckling, she added, "And you already finished your burger, stop looking for it."

Feeling sheepish, I moved on from the food. "Piper," I said, grinning, "I think that is one of the cooler things

I've heard. If you like crime scene investigation, then that's what you should study. I'll help you with the math, too. And glass art? That's amazing!" My smile blossomed into a full blown grin.

Scooting around the table to sit next to her, I gave her a quick kiss and a longer hug.

She pulled away, her eyes searching my face. "You don't think it sounds dumb?" Her voice was a low whisper and she bit her lower lip. I could hear her heart beat faster with her question.

Shaking my head, I rested my hands on her shoulders and met her stormy blue eyes. "No, I don't think it sounds dumb at all. I think CSI sounds amazing. You don't have to worry about me laughing at your interests. I'll support you, even if you believe it's a silly idea. And this isn't silly, it's great."

She smiled and hugged me. Letting go, she said, "Okay, enough about me. I want to talk about your two forms." *Oh, great! I know where this is going.* "You've been avoiding this talk with me because we've always been around other people. Have you figured out your wolf?" Her eyes narrowed at me, and her scent changed. I could smell her concern for me, the scent calming, like herbal tea.

I grimaced. "Sort of."

Piper furrowed her brow. "What does that even mean?"

Twisting a napkin between my hands, I spun away to hide my frown. I didn't want her to see my frustration. *I don't want to ruin today with my failures.* "Okay, so, if I'm with Mom, she can get the wolf out of me. So far, alone, I've only been able to access panther form."

Piper tilted her head, narrowing her eyes at me.

My shoulders drooped. "Mom, being my alpha, has some power over me and my wolf. She can call any of her werewolves to wolf form if she wants. I just need to figure out how to get to my wolf form without her. So far, it's been a big bust. I try, but I just end up kneeling in the grass, human, cold, and embarrassed. It isn't me at my best."

"Have you tried mindful meditation?" she asked with a tiny snort.

I punched her arm lightly, but finally smiled. Since early May, mindful meditation had been the big buzzword around the kids of the pack members. We were all done and over it. Talk about a losing battle, teaching a bunch of rowdy kids how to calm themselves, but the adults seem desperate to try anything.

"No. But I need to figure out *something.*"

"Do you feel different when your mom is there to help?"

"I don't know, maybe. When she's with me, I just kind of let myself go. I let her take over. She tells the wolf to come out, and she comes out."

Piper slipped her hand into mine. "Maybe that's it. You're trying too hard. Maybe you need to try switching to a more relaxed manner. Instead of trying harder, try thinking about one part of your body, maybe your nose or your toes. I don't know, maybe that sounds dumb."

"That…" I paused to think. "That actually makes sense." Sliding back to her, I threw my arm around her shoulders to give her a quick squeeze. "That's a good idea. Like, a really good idea. I'll try it next time."

Staring into my eyes, she mumbled, "You tend to think about a lot of things too…much." Her hands slowly came up to the sides of my neck and she pulled me down for a kiss. Leaning in, I deepened it, energy surging through me as I grasped her hips. After a few minutes she pulled back with a smile. "See, relax, like that." Laughing, I had to agree with her.

We cleared our food detritus and continued our walk. My phone vibrated. I pulled it out of my pocket and read a text from Owen saying, "Done."

We needed to head back towards the car. "Looks like time is up here on this fancy campus."

"Do you think I could watch?" she asked, as we walked back to the car.

"Watch?" I was pretty sure I knew what she was talking about, but I wanted her to be specific.

She blushed a light pink and stared at her shoes. "Could I watch you transform into a wolf, or panther?" She looked up and waved her hands, speaking fast. "I mean, now that I hang out with the kiddos during the full moon runs, it's cool that I've seen you as a panther and Dad as a wolf, but I've never seen the transformation."

The spicy scent of her nerves prickled my nose and her heart rate sped up. Her face turned the color of a ripe tomato.

"You do know that a transformation starts with me getting naked, right? Or is that part of it?" I teased. It was worth it. Her face somehow went a brighter red.

"No!" she all but yelled. She sputtered, unable to get words out for a few minutes. It was cute. Once she got herself under control, she continued. "That is so not the reason, Jade. You can't think that of me, oh, my gods! I mean…yeah, but no…you can't, goodness, no, that isn't it…"

As she babbled, my smile grew. Pausing, her jaw dropped and eyes grew wide. And then, her blush of embarrassment turned into a glare. She hit my arm hard. *Ouch.*

"Jade! I can't believe you!"

She walked away faster than I could catch up with my usual amble. As I trotted after her, she suddenly stopped and spun around, lost. "Which way?" she asked softly, eyes wide.

I caught up, laughing under my breath and threw my arm around her shoulder, then kissed her cheek. "Yes, you can watch my next attempt. I'll talk to Mom and tell her about your suggestion. She'll be there, so I'll go wolf no matter what. Now, let's go this way to get back to the car, unless you want to hang around campus a little longer."

She relaxed and huffed a laugh back at me. She slid her arm around my waist.

We were walking, laughing, when we saw the car. My parents, Owen, and Sarah were all standing outside of it, probably waiting for it to cool down. The doors were open, and they were talking.

"Man, your dad and brother could be twins," Piper said, not for the first time. "Except for the hair."

She wasn't wrong. They were similar in size and build, lean, muscular, and athletic. The biggest difference being Dad's hair was as black as mine with some grey coming in, while Owen somehow had bleach-blond hair. They were both a pinch under six feet tall with brown eyes.

She sized up my family and then looked at me. "You know, if you had your mom's hair color, we'd almost match. Is her wolf that shade of red?"

"Yep. Just like I match my animals. They're as black as my hair, too. It isn't always that way, but it is for us."

"Me, too," said Sarah, who had obviously heard us as we walked up. "My panther is as black as I want my hair to be."

She came over and bumped shoulders with me. Sarah was gorgeous. Tall and athletic with dark terra-cotta skin and long, flowing dark brown hair. Her eyes were so dark they were practically black. She was almost as tall as Dad and Owen.

Smiling at her, I nodded. "In panther form, we're almost identical."

She smiled back. We had been friends long enough that our smiles probably matched.

"Did you get all the classes you wanted?" I asked Owen once we reached the car and piled in.

"I don't know, I have a lot of general education classes,

gen ed." He said the last in a way that made me wonder how many times he had heard 'gen ed' that day.

He belted himself in, then turned back to me. "They aren't really for my degree. They called them breadth, versus depth, classes. I guess everyone has to take them." He sounded bummed. "I don't know what I'd hoped for. This year sounds a lot like high school: math, English, history, and then some classes that are degree specific. I guess it'll be cool. I get to meet new people, which will be the best part."

He perked up for that last bit.

"That, and Alejandro works here and is available if you ever need a pack mate?" I asked.

"Yeah, that part's cool, too. On your days off, you could come down with him and hang out with me," he added with a goofy, hopeful smile.

"Maybe," I said. "Sleep in and do nothing, or hang out with you? Why would you want your little sis hanging out with you anyway? You'll have friends in, like, a minute."

"A day of Dad's training, or hang out in college classes," Owen countered with a knowing smirk.

Damn, he has a point.

"Did you see there's a food truck?" Piper asked. She and Owen had bonded over food. She might be tiny but ate like a trucker. When she was given free range in the kitchen, people were afraid. At first, Piper hung out in the kitchen a lot because her mom was a great cook. Eventually, people noticed that she and Owen did more damage in there than good. Both in physical destruction, as well as food eaten. They were like a herd of elephants.

Owen perked up. "Really? I didn't see it. How was the food?"

"Pretty good. I think it was the same as inside the building, but it was more convenient. Pretty cool that it was right there, outside."

"Right on. That's what I am talking about." And suddenly, eyes wide, brows dancing, Owen was excited again.

During the ride home, Piper, Sarah, and I mocked the latest pop music sensation on the radio when a news announcer cut in. "The Amber alert from Joliet, Illinois, for a missing child is now canceled. Five-year-old Penelope Anne has been found and will be held in foster care until family can be located."

Navigating to a web page on my phone in search of the story, I asked Piper, "Do you know anything about that report?"

She nodded. "Yeah, my dad's been following it. I guess the car was found last Monday on the side of I80. Her parents were inside, dead. It's really weird. Apparently, they were attacked by some sort of wild animal while still seat-belted into the front seats."

My dad spun to face us. "They were attacked by wild animals in their car?"

Piper nodded.

"And your dad didn't inform us?"

I could smell the fear ooze off her as she froze in place.

Dad shut his eyes. "Piper, I am not going to eat you. I just need to explain how the pack works to your dad. This is the kind of information that needs to be shared."

He took out his phone and dialed a number. "Greg? It's River. Tell me about this girl down in Joliet…Uh-huh…. Yep. Got it…Okay. One last thing—next time, tell me right away. Okay…" He hung up and turned to Mom.

Mom watched the road, tension radiating off her. She spoke quickly and quietly. "We should go check things out. I have a friend who lives down there, Kira Johnson. She should have space to put us up."

Dad checked his watch, then turned to Mom. "It's Saturday. The parents were attacked on Monday. Just under a week. I'll call Tyler, give him a heads up, then call my assistant and let her know I'll be working remotely for the week."

Tyler was a pack member who worked for Dad. His family had been attacked by a lone wolf, and though he had been bitten, his daughter hadn't. That was good; bitten kids needed extra care. It wasn't easy to blend the violence of an animal with the tenderness of kids. In any event, Tyler would understand the urgency of the situation.

Gods, I hope she wasn't bitten!

"I want to go," I said. "If this is a case of a kid being turned and losing her parents, maybe even seeing the attack, I think I could be helpful."

"If she gets to go, I want to go, too," Owen said.

"This isn't a field trip," growled Dad.

"Why not?" I asked. I gave my mom a purely devious look. "We never go on vacation as a family. Why not all of us go? We could even bring some of the rest of the pack and make it an even bigger affair."

She groaned. "How about we just go as a family? I don't really see a reason to bring more of the pack to Joliet. It isn't like we're going to a travel hot-spot. If you really want to do something more spectacular with the full pack, plan it in a group email, and make sure you find a date and a place everyone agrees on."

She switched lanes, merging towards the exit to Madison. "You'll need to budget, plan, and make reservations. It will be hell, and in the end, anything that goes wrong will be your fault. But, hey, if you want a pack vacation, have at it."

I rolled my eyes and she chuckled. But in the end, at least I got myself on the roster to meet this girl. Instinct told me I could be helpful, especially with my ability to help calm the people around me.

Mom growled again as someone tried to cut her off. "I'll call Kira about staying with her. If she can't put us all up, we'll get a couple of hotel rooms. We'll leave at seven tomorrow morning. Sarah, Piper, I'll drop you both off at home. I'm sorry, I know the three of you were planning a slumber party, but that's canceled. Jade, Owen, pack for a week in Joliet, just in case."

CHAPTER 3

Coffee mug steaming between my hands, I basked in the peace and quiet of six in the morning.

Owen trudged in. His eyes weren't completely open yet. He grunted at me, something along the lines of "morning." He shuffled over to the coffee pot and poured himself a full mug, adding a splash of milk and several scoops of sugar.

I arched an eyebrow. "Want any coffee with your sugar, bro?"

He grunted again and sat across from me at the table. After a few minutes of drinking his sweet sludge, he started to animate. Lifting his head, he scowled at me. "How are you up this early every day?"

Yawning, I took another gulp of liquid energy then raised the mug in tribute.

He snorted.

Down the hall, the shutting doors and running water told me the rest of the household had woken up. Dragging myself from the table, I filled some travel mugs with coffee for the road.

Mom appeared first. "Everything ready to go?"

Drinks prepared, I wiped down the counter and cleaned out the coffee maker. "Coffee is. I figured we'd stop for food."

She took stock of the mugs. "Sounds good. Grab your bags and let's head out."

Owen and I piled into the car. Owen took the middle bank of seats and I took the back, as usual. He clutched his pillow and looked ready to pass out despite the coffee.

My plan for the drive was perusing one of my favorite books. It was one I had read over and over since I was young, and my current copy was wearing out: *Slathbog's Gold*, the first book in the *Adventurers Wanted* series. The other books in the series were packed for when I finished this one. It would be nice to read about Alex figuring out what made him special since I couldn't figure out what made me different in all of my research.

As I crawled into the back, I found a huge tome lying on the back seat. It was brown and smelled leather-bound. It had a gold-embossed wolf howling at the moon emblazoned on the front. In peeling gold letters, the title read, The Werewolf Encyclopedia. I reached out a hand and gently touched one finger to the cover. The book looked like it would crumble but was solid and heavy with history.

The front doors of the car opened, jarring me from my contemplation. I jerked my hand back.

"Oh, good, you found the book."

My head snapped up. Mom stared at me through the rear-view mirror. "A werewolf encyclopedia, Mom? What is this, really?"

I could've used a book like this six months ago.

"It isn't as fragile as you're acting, for one thing. I asked my parents to send it to me. I knew there were more books out there than we own. They must've kept it when they moved up north."

My eyes darted to the book and then back to her. "Do you think it will be in here?"

"I don't know, hon, but I hope so. I remember reading something about it as a kid."

Growling, Owen pushed himself up from his pillow. "What are you two talking about? I'm trying to sleep here."

Gazing between Mom and Owen, I wasn't sure where to start. Finally, I shrugged. "Haven't you noticed I'm different?"

He snorted. "Since you were born, sis."

"No, I mean it. I'm dominant to you, but you don't have to drop your eyes to me."

Owen frowned. "Now that you mention it, yeah, that is weird. And then there's that calming thing you do…. Okay, yeah. So, you think some crusty old book holds the answers?"

I just shrugged.

Mom started the car. "A little light reading never hurt anyone."

Owen's eyes bugged out. "Light?" He flopped back down on his pillow.

Hope surged through me. I buckled in and picked up the book. *Maybe I'll find the answers within.*

The drive to Joliet took just over three hours. As I paged through the book, I found four sections: a description of rites honoring the gods, Mondara and Sonnara, a history of werewolves, their folklore, and classifications. An instant desire to dive into the book and absorb everything overtook me. *A treasure trove of information.* I practically vibrated with need. Carefully, I turned to the end and paged through the classifications.

My whole life had been spent studying werewolves. I knew more than most wolves in the pack. If I wasn't destined to become a healer, I could have become our historian…we didn't have one of those. I looked up. "Mom, Dad, we should have a historian in the pack."

Dad turned and gave me an appraising nod. "Not a bad idea, pumpkin. It isn't something I've heard of, but it seems obvious now that you say it."

I flashed a smile and returned to the book. Classifications began with the alphas and dominant wolves. It included details I knew and some new theories I'd never considered. "Hey, Dad, did you know that part of the pack hierarchy is based on our own choice? I mean, some want to be higher and aren't; it isn't *all* choice, but desire plays a role in dominance."

Owen's groggy voice floated up from the middle seat. "No way, really? Then why am I so middle of the pack?"

"Desire is just part of it. There's a theory that the wolf side has a bit of precognition. They know what the pack needs and fills those roles. This book is spectacular."

Everyone went silent as I continued to read. We stopped just before the Illinois border for a quick drive-through breakfast. I put the book aside while I ate, not willing to harm it.

Between bites, Mom asked, "Did you learn anything more?"

Trying to calm my nerves, I took another sip of soda before answering. Trees flew by the car as I thought about the amount of information in the book, and everything I'd read. There was a new category of wolf that I thought fit, but by giving it a name I was giving myself a label. If I was wrong, I'd have to start over, but if I was right...

Steeling myself, I swallowed and drank some soda. "The book talked a lot about dominant and submissive wolves, and of course the zeta wolves, the ones who are just changed and too new to be classified. But you were right. There was a fourth classification of wolves in that section. There wasn't a lot on them, but what I read seems to fit."

Owen slowly turned to me, eyes wide. "Really? There's another classification? What is it?"

Licking my lips, I locked gazes with him. Talking to him was easier than talking to the car at large. "Epsilon. From what I read an epsilon wolf stands outside of the hierarchy. There's a folk story of one who single-handedly calmed a raging army. They were the peacekeepers and the healers in times past. At one time they were more common, but a rogue wolf, crazy and wild, went on a rampage years ago and took most of them out. It's why no one has heard of them. They're rare…like, *really* rare."

"Whoa, but Jade, that's you. Is there anything else about what funky skills you'll develop?"

"Not yet, but I'll keep reading."

Mom let out a pleased sound. "I knew I'd read something that reminded me of your abilities. It's been so long since I've read that book. I must've only been ten or eleven. Those stories were always so sensational. Well, now we have an answer. An epsilon wolf…my daughter. That's just amazing."

As we approached Chicago, the flow of traffic got thicker. But before hitting the big city, we took an off-shoot interstate that led us towards the suburbs. Next thing we knew, we were in Joliet, famous for a big jail and a lost kid.

We navigated to a small side street lined with stunning historic homes, stopping at a grey house set back a bit from the road, hidden behind mature trees and picturesque flowering bushes. Mom pulled in, and we finally got to get out of the car and stretch our legs. Three hours was a long time to not be able to move for a car full of wereanimals.

A woman in her forties with short, light brown hair opened the door of her house. She bounced a bit when she saw my mom and some crazy blue and purple chunks of hair flashed from under her professional hair style. *Awesome!* She skipped down the stairs and gave my mom a huge hug. She was about an inch or two taller and a bit thicker. Not fat, just thick; she looked fit. Unlike most norms, she wasn't wearing any weird body lotion or perfumes. I had tensed just in case, prepared for the inevitable headache.

"Kira, these are my kids, Owen and Jade. You know River," Mom said.

I mulled over everything I'd heard about Kira. She and Mom had known each other most of their lives. They'd gone to grade school together. Her uncle had been part of the pack. Though Kira wasn't a werewolf, she grew up knowing about werewolves and had spent some of the full moon nights with the other kiddos watching movies and eating pizza. When she reached the age she could decide, she chose to stay a norm. She figured she could support the werewolves without becoming one.

Kira pulled back and surveyed us with a bright smile.

"Wow, you brought the family! Let's get inside, get you freshened up and settled. And then we'll discuss how we can meet this girl."

When we entered the house, I gaped at the grand staircase in a polished dark wood. I dropped my bags, circling, taking in the beauty of the historic house. Off to the left was a living room and to the right a dining room. I could see a door through the dining room, which I assumed led to the kitchen.

Kira turned to us. "Okay, everyone find a room; there should be enough. We can meet in the dining room to discuss details for tomorrow."

Snatching up my bag, I ran up the stairs and found a huge room. It had a slightly stale smell, so I knew it wasn't Kira's. A massive bed shoved against the far wall took up a third of the space. I threw my bag on a chair, placed the encyclopedia on the desk in the corner, and then flopped down on the bed to test it out. I sighed. *Heaven.*

A few minutes later, Owen knocked on the door frame. "Everything okay in here?"

"Uh-huh, all good. Very comfy. Find a room?" Flipping onto my side, I faced him.

Owen pointed down the hall. "That one, across the hall and two doors down. Mom and Dad are across the hall from me. You all set?"

I nodded, and we headed down the stairs. Before we even reached the dining room, I heard the adults deliberating without us.

"Do you have an idea?" Dad asked.

"I do," said Kira. "My firm is representing her, so I can get you in to meet her. I was actually going to call you, but you beat me to it. The story felt like one you should be brought in on. Anyway, I'm hoping, if we're all correct, I can get her placed with you, even though you live out of state. She's originally from Santa Fe, but we can't find any living relatives, which in this case is both bad and good."

"I can probably find a way to link our families," Dad said. "I've got some great IT people who can create connections, if you think that that will help."

Kira hesitated, looking a little shaky at the obvious illegality of it, but then nodded. "If you could find a way to make her a second cousin of yours, that would make the placement much easier."

I found myself nodding. *In the end, if this girl's been bitten, being placed with the pack would be best. Kira has to know that. But knowing that and accepting the law being bent aren't always the same thing.*

Dad grabbed his phone and typed. "I'll get this all started, and if we are wrong, I can get it cleared before anyone finds the trail."

"What's everyone talking about?" Owen asked, grabbing a cookie from a plate sitting at the center of the table.

The adults looked at him, but for a moment, no one spoke. Seeing the tension on everyone's faces, I jumped in.

"Think about it, Owen, this Penelope Anne may have been attacked by a werewolf. Her parents didn't survive, but if she was bitten, then she may be a werewolf. If that's the case, we need to get her into the pack and protected before anyone else figures out what happened to her or gets hurt. What if she bites someone?"

Smiling at Dad, I continued. "Dad is going to create a back-story connecting her to our family. That way if she ends up being a werewolf, we can get her placed with us."

Owen nodded. "Got it. So, tomorrow we'll go and meet her. If she's a werewolf, we all act like family and go from there," he summarized. "What do you do if this girl is scared of us and refuses to even get close?"

"We'll cross that bridge when we get there. The biggest part of the plan is just getting in a room with the girl and finding out if she is a werewolf," Mom said and got to her feet. "When I was a kid, there was an eight year old boy who'd gotten bitten by a rogue wolf. Our pack tried to help him, but the wild violence of the wolf was too much for him. He didn't make it to his teen years. We didn't have an epsilon in our pack."

Kira stood and headed for the kitchen. "There is a lot to discuss, I'm going to grab lunch fixings."

Over meat and cheese sandwiches, we came up with different ways to approach a five-year-old and hopefully not scare her. Kira knew the girl, and we hoped her familiarity would work to our advantage. She thought we should just go in and be friendly. The girl needed niceness in her life.

Kira believed the trickiest part would be getting her out of the foster family's house right away if we confirmed her status as a werewolf. When a child got placed into a new home, family services considered it in the child's best interest to leave them placed there for continuity. Unfortunately, as a werewolf, she increased our exposure the longer she stayed with the humans.

Owen, having finished two sandwiches, bounced a bit in his seat. "Tomorrow will be fun."

Dad turned to him. "You're not going."

Deflating, he asked, "Why not?"

"This isn't a family field trip. Mom and I will go, and Jade is coming because hopefully she can calm the kid down, if she's scared. You will stay here. We don't want to overwhelm her."

I could almost taste Owen's disappointment. I had to get my blocks up. Being home over the summer had made me lazy.

Mom reached across the table and placed her hand on Owen's. "You can take a walk, see if you can find a park. Find a place for training. If this goes as planned, we'll need to stay here for a few days. It would be wise to get a good lay of the land."

Though Kira knew the area, she didn't know what we needed as well as Owen did. Owen's shoulders dropped and he grabbed another cookie, obviously relaxed as he gave Mom a smile. "Fine, but it's still not fair."

That night, I stayed up late reading as much as I could find in the book about epsilon werewolves. There wasn't much; some stories about taming savage beasts, which I translated to mean "calming," and other stories about epsilons being great healers, which I also figured involved calming.

A line from the final story haunted my dreams: "My hand, as my nose, became a conduit of understanding."

CHAPTER 4

The next morning, we all dressed nicely, as if going to court, except for Owen who lounged in pajama bottoms in front of the TV. We wanted to impress the people at the social services. We also wanted Penelope Anne to see us as nice people and be comfortable with us. I put on a pair of black slacks and a light blue silk button down. I pinned my wild curls up in some semblance of order and even applied a bit of make-up. It wasn't great, but I looked presentable. I wanted to be able to blend into the background.

I took a selfie and sent it to Sarah. She sent back

a thumbs-up.

My parents made it clear I was only being included because of my ability to calm people, which I now knew was my epsilon ability. *I wonder if it works on norms?*

We piled into Kira's car, and she drove us to her office downtown. Security poked and prodded us before leading us to a meeting room. Penelope Anne would arrive later with the social worker. Kira offered us water while we waited.

Tapping her fingers on the table, Mom fidgeted with her ring. "Remember, Jade, stay quiet, let Kira do the talking. This is her office, her domain. She knows what's going on," Mom said…again.

I kept my voice neutral. "I get it." I wasn't going to be the cause of more stress. Mom was repeating herself, but if she needed to do it to help herself stay calm, I wasn't about to stop her. I took another drink of water and tried to radiate my epsilon calm. *I can't believe I have a name for this!*

They both smiled at me as their shoulders dropped a few inches.

Better.

Kira came in. "The others are on their way up. It's go-time." She vibrated with energy. This was obviously her specialty. She smelled of hope and dread. I wasn't sure, but I didn't think she liked the social worker.

I could smell the social worker before she got to the door, and I wasn't sure I would like her, either. She wore enough perfume that it made me sneeze twice. I feared my nose wouldn't work to identify the girl as a werewolf. Even worse, it was a cheap scent used to cover up the odor of cigarettes. Yuck!

My parents looked at me sympathetically.

Kira gave me a concerned look. "Will you be okay?"

Nodding, I forced my mind to put the scents into boxes, where they belonged. "Yeah. I'll be fine. It's just so much."

We all faced the door and I tried to focus on the two coming in. Kira handed me a tissue to wipe my eyes. I hadn't realized they were watering that much.

The door opened. In walked this little slip of a girl with brown curls so dark they were almost black. She had pale, sea-green eyes and rosy cheeks. *She really could be related to me.* She looked up at me and a jolt ran through me, like we had an instant conversation.

She paused at the door and took in all the adults. She saw my mom and dad; again, her eyes showed some sort of recognition, probably the wolf in them. Her gaze shifted to Kira and she had a little wave for her. Finally, her gaze flew back to me. A penetrating stare. Once more, I sensed she recognized me, somehow, as someone who could help.

After a minute, her head rocked up to her social worker. She slipped her hand out of the social worker's grip and ran over to me. She jumped into my lap and curled into a ball, tucking her head under my chin. She smelled of the sun and wind and of kid. She also smelled of fur and claws…werewolf.

"Hi, Penelope Anne," I whispered so softly I wasn't even sure Mom sitting next to me could hear. "I'm Jade."

I wrapped my arms around her as if I had done it a thousand times and hugged her close. Her heart beat so fast I thought she would start to vibrate.

"Shhh," I said loudly enough for everyone in the room to hear, "it's okay, love, I'm here for you."

I tried to radiate calm. At that, she raised her head and gave me a tentative smile. She tucked back in. Her shoulders dropped and her breathing evened out.

The social worker tilted her head as she studied the two of us. "I see you already know our young Penelope Anne." Her brows furrowed. She smelled confused, though it was hard to smell through her perfume. I didn't think anyone had told her of potential family.

Penelope Anne whispered softly to me, "I keep telling her to call me Pebble, but she says that's a silly name."

Mom looked over, squinting, trying to concentrate on the whispered words. Dad didn't even flinch.

"Pebble, her name is Pebble," I said loud enough for Mom, but no one else. I had my head down in the young girl's curls, hiding my voice in her hair.

"Yes," Mom said, taking the lead for the family and looking up at the social worker. "Hi, I'm Hazel Stone, this is River, my husband, and my daughter, Jade. And you are?"

"Hello, Ms. Stone, I'm Janice Dotson, and I'm a state social worker. I've been working with Penelope Anne since she was found. She's been staying with a local foster family. Because of some issues there, they are asking that she be removed immediately. We didn't know she had friends or family close by, otherwise we would have called you in."

"Issues?" Kira asked, opening a manila folder in front of her and shuffling through the pages. "I haven't been informed of anything." Frustration spiked off her. I wiggled my nose to avoid sneezing again.

"The issues happened last night. We wanted to double check with the foster family before bringing anything up officially. However, if the Stone family is familiar with Penelope Anne and can prove a family connection, maybe we could get this settled without the bother of an investigation." She sounded hopeful, but I could smell her reluctance. She didn't want to investigate the foster family.

"I could stay with Jade?" a tiny voice asked from my lap.

Everyone took a second to look at her before the meeting continued.

Kira fisted her hands on the file folder and her mouth tightened. "I understand the simplicity of your suggestion, Ms. Dotson, but can you elaborate on the complaint, please? I wasn't given paperwork. I do expect that paperwork after this meeting." Eyes narrowed, she pierced Ms. Dotson with her gaze.

Ms. Dotson responded in a rush. "Of course. It seems there was an altercation between the child and two of the family members. The family's oldest son and the father say

Penelope Anne attacked them. Penelope Anne has denied the attack. The family has three other foster kids and one additional biological child, a second son. They would rather not have any other disruptions in their home."

She gave a good run down of the complaint, but didn't really explain anything.

"Pebble, dear," Mom said, focusing on the young girl.

Dad looked confused for a second, but then cleared his face.

Focused on my mom, the social worker seemed to have missed my dad's confusion. Her eyes grew wide at the mention of the girl's preferred nickname. Her smell became citricy with hope. She seemed to really want an easy solution for this foster family.

"Did you attack the people at this house, hon?" Mom slid out of her chair to squat next to my chair as she spoke with Pebble. She emoted enough love and care that Pebble relaxed and reacted with all the trust a five-year-old had to give. She uncurled and gazed at Mom with a smile.

"I didn't mean to. The boy came and scared me at night when I was supposed to be sleeping. His dad was there, too. I got really scared." She didn't say more, she just stared back and forth between me and Mom.

I wasn't sure what more she wanted to say, but I just held her, letting her know she wasn't alone anymore. I understood her terror of being rejected.

"Did they say anything to you or try to touch you?"

Mom asked.

Wide-eyed, Pebble shook her head. "They were being quiet. I should've been in bed, but I was hungry." She wrung her hands and bit her lips. "I went to the kitchen. He grabbed my shoulder. I got really scared, and I don't know what happened." Looking up at me, she took a shaky breath and I squeezed her tight. "The next thing I knew, it was cold and dark and there were bars around me. I couldn't get out of the cage until morning." She ducked her head against my chest for a moment, then faced out again. "Then, today I came here. Am I in trouble? Am I going to jail? I didn't mean to steal the grapes."

"They put you in a cage?" Dad asked. He sounded flat, calm. I knew that voice, he was livid.

The anger pouring off my parents was thick enough to almost choke me. I took a sip of my drink to clear my throat, but I still couldn't breathe. I, too, simmered with the idea of caging a person. Of caging this sweet girl I held. How could they?!

I felt her quiver with all our emotions. Crap! I froze. Taking in a deep breath, I radiated as much calm as I could…for Pebble. This tiny girl didn't need more trauma.

Her gaze shot to me, worried that she had done something wrong.

"No one is mad at you, cuz," I said, deciding to take the next step in our decision that we were keeping her.

"Cuz? As in cousin?" the social worker asked.

"Yes," Dad said definitively. He turned cold eyes to the social worker. "Please keep me informed as to the action you *will* be taking against the family regarding the matter of this cage. The assault on our young cousin is intolerable."

Kira opened the folder and handed a piece of paper to the social worker connecting Penelope Anne, Pebble, with my family. "I believe you will find everything you need here. We can put a case together against the family. I can't believe you've let this go on, Janice. This can't be the first report you've gotten." Kira's face was flat and her scent had turned minty with frustration.

Ms. Dotson's scent turned spicy even through her perfume. "I don't like the implication of what you're saying. I have gotten no other reports like this. At this point, we just have the word of Penelope Anne, a five-year-old girl."

A coldness took over the room at those words. Pebble curled into an even smaller ball in my lap. I could sense the wolf waking in Mom. Whereas Ms. Dotson was trying to cover all bases, we could smell the truth in Pebble's words. She had spoken no lies. Her story may have been condensed, but it hadn't been false.

Mom's voice came out husky with the influence of her wolf. "Are you implying that Pebble made up this story? That a five-year-old would invent being put in a cage?"

Ms. Dotson blanched; even a norm could feel the weight of an alpha. "No, of course not, I was just explaining that we shouldn't jump to conclusions. We will, of course, take young Penelope Anne's words very seriously. We will look into the practices of this household. There will be a surprise inspection. Ms. Johnson and I will work together to ensure that every child at that house is safe."

Kira eyed the social worker doubtfully. She cleared her throat. "Back to the matter at hand and the current placement of Pebble."

Ms. Dotson picked up the paperwork and gave it a longer look. Her lips twitched on the verge of a smile. "I was wondering. She looks so much like your daughter. I'm so glad that she has family, assuming you want to claim her. We haven't found any other family, and if you don't take her, she will end up in the system, bouncing around from foster family to foster family." The social worker painted a bleak picture, though possibly an accurate one.

"This is why we came, Ms. Dotson; to fight for our young relative. When we heard this case on the radio, we knew that we had to come. Someone had to fight for her and her future," Mom said. "I'm not sure what the next steps are in this process, but we're hoping we can keep her with us. She's so young and so scared. We really want to start to rebuild her world and the safety *she* deserves."

The social worker evaluated us, and then the paper in front of her. "It's against procedure to let you take her home without double checking the paperwork, however, at the moment we don't have any other place to send the girl." I could smell the lie on Ms. Dotson, she was worried about

Pebble for some reason, but since I wanted Pebble with us, I kept my mouth closed.

"If it helps," Kira jumped in, "they're staying with me, and will be until everything is figured out. I'm on the books as a foster home, though I usually don't take in kids with my schedule. The Stones aren't a flight risk. You can spend time making sure everything is as it should be."

Ms. Dotson's shoulders dropped and her smile finally became natural as she relaxed. A vanilla scent wafted from her, cutting through the perfume, letting me know just how happy she was with this new development. "I don't know if that will work. I'll pass it by my boss and get back to you," she said as she straightened up her papers.

I suppressed a snort. *What a liar. She's delighted.*

Once the social worker left, Pebble lifted her head and looked at me. "Do I really get to go away with you?" Her voice trembled, scared and unsure. Though she had attached herself to me, she didn't really know me yet.

"Yes, and if everything goes as we hope, maybe you'll become my little sister one day."

"Jade," Mom warned, "you are jumping quite a bit ahead." But she smiled. Mom turned to Kira. "Is this room private?"

Kira nodded. "You four can talk here for a few minutes safely."

Mom returned her gaze to Pebble and gave a warm smile. "Pebble, my name is Hazel, and this man is River.

And as you probably know, you're sitting in Jade's lap. We have a son, Owen, at Kira's place. I know that's a lot of names, but you'll have time to figure it all out. We are all nice people, and we hope you like us."

Pebble wrinkled her nose. "Does everyone smell funny like you? I mean, Kira smells normal, but you two smell like me, and Jade just smells weird."

I groaned and rolled my eyes skyward at the same time. Dad snorted, and Mom laughed.

"We'll finish this conversation at Kira's home where we can figure everything else out in relative privacy," Mom said.

That was easier said than done. It took a few hours to get everything approved and the paperwork checked over and signed. On the way home, we picked up ribs and mac and cheese for dinner. I smiled to see Pebble bounce with excitement. "Oh, I love mac and cheese!"

When we got to Kira's house, Pebble met Owen.

"Why Pebble?" Owen asked.

"My dad always said that my eyes looked like river pebbles," she said simply.

"I see it," he said.

"You smell like me and your parents." Pointing at me, she added, "But Jade smells weird, almost like water and trees. It makes me want to nap."

Owen laughed good-naturedly. He knelt beside her. "That she does, little Pebble, that she does. But don't tell her that, she still thinks she's normal. As to why *anyone* would want to be normal, I have no idea. If you want to know the truth, Jade is mostly cool."

Pebble smiled at him as if they were sharing a secret. And just like that, he had won her over.

After we ate, we moved into the living room. There weren't enough seats, so I sat on the floor with Pebble and Owen.

Since Pebble had decided to adopt me first, I started off the conversation. "So, Pebble, did you see what or who bit you?"

Her eyes got big, she shook her head in denial, but before she could say anything, I continued, "Because, it was a werewolf, wasn't it?"

"What?" she asked with wide eyes and a shaky voice. "That can't be true. I told people it was a big wolf and they said that wasn't possible because I would've been eaten all up and I wasn't even hurt."

She paused and looked at her hands as if searching for the injuries. Quietly and shakily, she said, "They said if I had gotten bitten, there would have been an owie. No owie, no bite. They told me I was making things up, and if I lied, I would get in big trouble." It sounded like she was repeating what adults had told her several times.

I pulled her into my lap and gave her a big hug. "Pebble, we believe you. When you get bitten by a werewolf, you get the power to heal yourself quickly."

She stared at all of us. We all nodded and smiled. I could smell her emotions take over as she started to cry.

We let her cry it out. No one had believed her for days. I wanted to growl. *It's almost like psychological torture.*

After a few minutes, her cries turned to sniffles, and then she hiccupped. "You really believe me?"

I smiled. "Yes."

Her small face shifted to each of us in turn as everyone said "yes" to her. Tears gathered in her eyes. "Am I a monster?" she asked softly.

That word! Why does everyone always automatically go to that word?

I shook my head quickly. "No," I said with all the authority I could muster. "You are, however, a werewolf. But so are most of the people in this room. A monster is someone who hurts others for fun. You don't do that, do you?"

"No," she said swiftly.

"Well, there you go, not a monster. You just have the ability to turn into a wolf."

"Can you turn into a wolf?" she asked.

I paused at the question, debating my answer. Sighing, I finally said, "I can."

"Why are you so weird-smelling?"

Giving her a squeeze, I huffed out a small laugh. "I wish I knew. I can turn into a wolf and a panther."

Her mouth turned into a perfect 'O'. The spicy scent of her shock quickly spread through the room.

"I'll show you someday soon, but I'm also able to calm people around me. It's that third bit that I think smells weird."

Her eyes were so big, and every time I mentioned something new, they just got bigger and bigger. I hoped they wouldn't pop out of her head. I kissed her forehead and let her take it all in.

"You're a werepanther?" Kira asked.

I had completely forgotten she didn't know all the gossip. Yesterday when we arrived it had all been about Mom and Pebble, not about family news.

I looked up at her. "Yeah, last spring break I went to Florida and was bitten by one."

Kira just looked at me, baffled.

"There are werepanthers? Are there *other* wereanimals? Or vampires? Or fairies?"

Mirth bubbling out of me, I asked, "Why is it every time someone hears about wereanimals, they automatically go to other paranormal creatures? As far as I know, no." I shifted my gaze to the couch where my parents were sitting. "Mom?"

She just laughed and shook her head.

"Wait, and you can turn into both?" Kira's eyes grew to the size of saucers.

"We're getting off topic," said Dad.

I suppressed an urge to roll my eyes. *Of course, his focus is unbeatable.*

Pebble, still sitting on my lap, yawned, and put her head on my shoulder. Cuddling her close, I kissed her forehead.

"We need to find a room for Pebble," said Kira.

She froze. "Can I stay in Jade's room tonight?"

She was so scared, and for some reason I was her safe place. The room I had chosen had a queen-sized bed, but I wasn't sure she would want to sleep with a stranger, no matter how attached she was to me.

Kira seemed to think about it then said, "I can put an air mattress on the floor of your room, if the two of you don't mind."

"I don't mind," I said.

"Me, either," Pebble added. I smiled down at her and patted her head.

We got Pebble set up in the bedroom and I stayed in the room until she fell asleep.

Once I got back downstairs, I joined the conversation.

Dad's voice was a low rumble. "Hazel, you know that the lone wolf who attacked her family is still out there, but I don't know how we can track it. I know it needs to be taken care of, but it isn't your responsibility to take care of all of the rogue wolves in the world."

This was an old fight between Mom and Dad. Mom always felt responsible for the rogue wolves. Wolves who had attacked and killed people, not just wild animals. Dad didn't.

"Why do you think the wolf attacked the parents but left the daughter?" Kira asked.

This had been bothering me as well. *Why leave a five-year-old by the side of a busy interstate alone? And how did no one see any of this go down?*

"I wonder if the parents were wolves, and he was somehow punishing them. Let them see their daughter get turned, and then kill them," Owen said.

Man, he has a devious mind.

Sitting down on an open chair, I shook my head at him. "Do you think the rogue wolf stayed in this area? The family is from the south. They were only coming up here for a family vacation."

Dad huffed. "You can't make assumptions. There's no way to know if the rogue wolf was from here, from Santa Fe, or just driving through. 180 goes from the Atlantic to the Pacific. They could be from anywhere. Trying to track it down is as close to fruitless as we can get. Unless—and until—we hear of other attacks, I don't know what else we can do about it."

Mom sighed. She slumped in her seat. "You aren't wrong."

Dad looked shocked at her words.

Mom laughed tiredly. "Don't look so surprised that I'm agreeing with you. We have a lot on our plate. First, we have to stay around here long enough to gain custody of Pebble and start the adoption process. Jade was right about her becoming her little sister one day; that would be the best and safest course. Then, we need to get Owen prepared for college. Next, we need to start discussing Jade's future educational plans. She's taking a lot of AP classes; she may graduate early. She has to start applying to colleges. What about college tours?"

She closed her eyes and took a deep breath, letting it out slowly. It had been a long day. Her fingers flipped up with each item she listed. "Then there's Pebble. We bring her home, show her around so that she's comfortable with the house and the area, set up a room for her, and finally introduce her to the pack." Her eyes opened and she turned to Dad. "That reminds me, we need to call a pack meeting a week from Sunday. Can you send out the email tonight?"

Dad nodded and took out his phone.

Mom's eyes slipped from Dad up to the ceiling as if she could see the little girl sleeping. All of us followed her gaze. "On top of all of that, we need to get Pebble integrated into our lives, get her trained as a new werewolf, and figure out if we should register her for public school. Is she safe? Do we need to homeschool for a year or two? Is she capable of keeping the family secret? And if it is homeschool, who will be her teacher?"

With a tired sigh, Mom's gaze returned to Dad. "So, you see, we have a lot on our plate right now. Running after a rogue wolf doesn't seem like a high priority to me. So, yes, dear, I agree." She ended with a sweet smile and leaned over to give Dad a quick kiss. Then she crumpled back onto the couch with a tired groan.

"Gross," Owen said, and laughed. "Get a room."

Dad raised an eyebrow. "You know, after all of that, I'm thinking chasing a rogue wolf sounds like the easier task."

CHAPTER 5

We were stuck in Joliet until the the social worker called. We planned to have a lot of fun, touring the big city and getting Pebble comfortable with all of us.

Kira grabbed two mugs from the cupboard and poured coffee. It was early on the third morning while everyone else slept. "Did Pebble crawl into bed with you again last night?"

Watching her motions, I nodded when she waved the sugar, but held up my hand to stop her from adding too much. "Yeah. That makes every morning. Her P.J.s were damp again, and she smelled of fear. She's having nightmares; it's the only explanation. But none of us can get her to talk about them. Or maybe she isn't able to talk about them. All I know is she's calmer when she's in the bigger bed with me."

Setting the mug down in front of me, Kira nodded. "I'll try to get her to tell me tonight. She's known me longer. It could be the foster family, the attack on her family, or whoever bit her."

Nodding, I sank into the vat of warm coffee. "I wonder if the person who bit her also killed her parents."

Kira shrugged. "When she was found on the side of the road, she wasn't bitten, so no, that can't be the case. She had to have been bitten before. Possibly days, weeks, or even longer. Maybe she'll be able to tell us some day."

Dread washed through me at the idea of the time Pebble had spent being a werewolf. It was unfair she'd been bitten so young.

Kira got up, grabbed her bagel from the toaster and spread some cream cheese on it. "Do you want one?"

I shook my head. "Nah, I'll eat later. Will you be joining us today?"

"No. I have to work again."

We sat in companionable silence for a few minutes; she ate while I sipped my coffee.

"Well, I'll be late if I don't leave now. Have fun today." Grabbing her purse and phone, she headed out the door.

I cupped my warm mug and turned my phone on. It had been a few days and I wanted to fill my friends in

on what had been going on. I started a group text with
Bevin, Sarah, and José. Bevin and José's mothers had been
attacked by the same lone wolf that had attacked my dad
back when they were all in college. They'd all followed my
mom back to Wisconsin and raised their families together.

Though Bevin and José were a bit older than me, they
were two of my closest friends.

True to form, Bevin was up.

You're going to be a big sister? he asked.
Crazy, no?

Absolutely crazy! I can't believe your
parents are going from hearing a news
story to adoption in three days. I mean,
I can, they have to, but wow. She's five,
and has a doggie?

Looking up towards the room where Pebble slept, I smiled
at his euphemism. We were trained young to be careful what
we put into a text. My fingers flew over the keys.

Yeah, crazy! I can't imagine what
she's going through.

She's going to have to be homeschooled,
Bevin predicted.

Ya think? I mean, she tried to keep
the secret from us.

Kids bite, Jade. Can you imagine? She
gets into a fight with another kid who's
mean and she bites them? Dang, that

would be horrible!

I hadn't thought about that. I bet my parents have. I wonder who'll stay home and teach her. I mean, she's only five, school can be held off for another year. This is so much!

My mind whirled with all sorts of new thoughts. Who in the pack was available to homeschool her, and could we trust non-wolves? Would she accidentally bite a norm?

José joined the conversation. Dude, you two need to learn the love of sleep! A five-year-old with a doggie? Well, hell, that's a new one! What kind of brute does that to a kid?

Is Hazel going after the R? Bevin typed, using shorthand for "rogue" like we'd been taught.

No, believe it or not, too much is going on at home.

Too much? Like what? José asked.

Just school, Pebble, the usual. P meeting coming up about it and everything.

What, not about you? Sarah chimed in.

I sent a crying laughing emoji. Then an eye rolling GIF.

Footsteps above let me know others were awake. Love you all, gotta go.

Everyone said their goodbyes. I missed my friends but knew that being down here for Pebble was important.

Now that people were waking up, I made a new pot of coffee and started cooking bacon and eggs—close to the limit of my abilities. Those smells brought everyone down fast.

"Morning, all," I said with extra cheer.

Dad scowled at me. "Stop being chipper."

"Don't you want a home-cooked meal?" I asked, bouncing up to him and kissing him on the cheek.

He glared, but I could smell his citrusy amusement.

I filled a plate with bacon and eggs and placed it in front of him with a smile.

His mouth twitched and he grabbed my wrist, pulling me down to give me a kiss on the cheek. "Thanks, pumpkin."

Mom came down, hair wet from a shower, hand in hand with Pebble. "Are you breaking Dad with your morning pep?"

"Yep."

She grinned. "Good for you."

I handed her a plate of food, a mug of coffee, and set a serving down for Pebble as well, whose shoulders were near her ears, but was smiling happily at all our exuberance. Finally, I sat down with my own food.

After a few bites, Mom asked, "Plans for the day?"

"I'm going to get in a run, then read that book you gave me. There's so much to learn."

Now that it was summer, Dad's torture system, er, training, had amped up. After I'd become a werepanther, I had been attacked by two different pack mates who believed I shouldn't be part of the pack. Dad decided then and there that all new wereanimals needed to learn how to fight and gave us training schedules. During the school year, homework took precedence, but now that it was summer nothing held Dad back from his scheming.

Owen stuffed a big bite of eggs and bacon in his mouth, washing it down with coffee. "If I can use the car, I'll take the rugrat to a water park I found."

Nodding, Mom stood to clear her plate. "I think I'll join you two. Leave these two here to be boring."

Pebble squealed and ran to find a suit. Thankfully, a swimsuit was one of the few items she did have.

Friday morning, the call came informing us we were free to leave Illinois. We had passed the background checks and the state felt we were safe to take Pebble home with us. They had set up inspections throughout the year to make sure she was being treated well.

Pale sea-green eyes looked up at me. "Do I really get to come home with you?"

I smiled down at this mini-me. "Yes. You get to come home. They'll come and see how well you're adjusting to life at our house. Make sure you're safe." I tapped her nose. "But I'm not worried."

My smile grew as she bounced.

Owen came out of the house with a bunch of bags. After loading them into the car he swung Pebble up into a hug. "Hey, kiddo. Ready for the drive home?"

Her eyes widened at that word. She mouthed the word 'home' and nodded at him, giggling.

He put her down. "Go get into the car. Make sure you buckle yourself in. I'll be checking, so do a good job."

He turned to me. His face lost a bit of its bright cheerfulness and grew serious. "I hope we pass all those home inspections and get through the adoption process. I like her."

"Me, too, bro. Me, too."

When Pebble saw our house a few hours later, she stared at it wide-eyed. "Is this a hotel?"

Owen gave her a jovial smile. "No, scamp, it's home."

Pebble knew werewolves existed, but nothing about them. We still weren't sure what to tell her. She didn't know about our pack, or that our home was the pack house. She would be learning a lot at next Sunday's pack meeting.

There was an extra room across the hall from mine that we set up for her. She had her own bed, a dresser, and a closet. The room even had a small, attached bathroom with a toilet and sink.

She walked in and took in the furniture. Turning around, she pointed at my door. Her eyes widened and her hands shook. "Where does that door lead?"

I crossed the hallway and opened the door. "My room. I'll be your neighbor."

Putting my hands in my pockets, I winked at her.

She looked around some more but seemed a bit disappointed.

I knew why. The room was pale yellow and boring.

I knelt and took her hands. "Want to go to the hardware store and get some paint?"

Her eyes grew. "Really? Can I help pick the color?"

I couldn't stop the laugh from escaping and neither could Owen who stood in the hallway. "Pebble, you can choose whatever colors you want. We'll paint the walls and, if you want, the furniture. This is going to be your room now."

Her jaw dropped in utter astonishment. Her emotions were so strong they flooded the room. Even with my blocks up, I could taste her shock.

That afternoon, we headed out to a hardware store and let her pick out paints for the bedroom walls, furniture, and bathroom walls. For her room she chose a pale green. For the bathroom a pale blue, and for her dresser a royal purple.

She asked if her bed frame could be painted to match the dresser. Apparently, she liked purple.

When we got home again, Sarah came over to meet Pebble. She would be helping out, and we figured the sooner they met the better. Sarah plopped onto her butt on the floor and held out a hand. "Hi! I'm Sarah. I'd like to be your friend."

Pebble, eyes wide, hid behind my leg for a minute, but held out her hand all the same. "I'm…I'm Pebble."

"Can I see the colors you choose for your room?"

"Sure!" Pebble bounced. Her excitement at redecorating was infectious.

Sarah checked out the colors. "Green and blue for the walls? Where's the pink?"

At first, I sensed Pebble's worry that she'd done something wrong. After she realized Sarah was teasing her, she answered, "I used to like watching those shows with my mom, you know, where they fixed houses? We watched them a lot. I liked trying to come up with my own colors. I thought this would be pretty."

Sarah gave her a quick hug. "I agree."

"Dinner!" Dad yelled.

The three of us headed to the dining room for pasta.

Dad passed the bowl of saucy pasta around. I served myself and Pebble.

While I was waiting for the cheese and red pepper flakes, Mom got down to business. "Pebble's family had been planning a one-week trip to Chicago, so she has some clothes, but really only about four outfits. Tomorrow we need to have one group go out shopping while a second group paints."

Mom hated shopping; we all hated it. I watched everyone dig into their dinner to avoid volunteering.

When my eyes settled on Sarah, she just stared back and shook her head in disgust at all of us. She liked shopping. Leaning over, she whispered, "Taking a five-year-old out shopping will be fun. Not bad at all."

Sarah tried to catch Owen's eyes, but he was militantly eating. She huffed out an annoyed grunt. "How do any of you have clothes? I'll take her. Jade, will you come, too?"

I nodded, reluctantly. *Gods, I hate shopping. But I'll do it, for Pebble.*

Placing her hand slowly on the table, Sarah took a long breath. "You're all acting like this is much worse than it really will be. Tomorrow the three of us are going to have a lot of fun and buy clothes and lots of sugar."

Mom smiled a thank you at us before digging into her dinner.

The next morning, Mom gave Sarah and me a budget, and off we went. We bought Pebble outfits for the summer, fall, and even some winter clothing.

While we were out, Owen, José, Bevin, and my parents painted the rooms and furniture.

Once home, we washed all the clothes and put them away.

By mid-afternoon Saturday, Pebble had a place in the house all her own.

Early in the afternoon, I took her on a walk around the neighborhood so she would know her way around. Owen came with us. We showed her the library, grocery store, movie theater, and drug store. There was a local bakery within walking distance, as well. We went in and got three cookies, one each. Sitting outside the grocery store, a homeless man begged for money.

"Can we give him some?" Pebble asked, her big pale green eyes hopeful.

"Why?" asked Owen.

"Mom and Dad always said it was a nice thing to do."

I dug into my wallet, found a dollar bill, and then handed it to Pebble to put into the man's hat. When she hid behind my leg, I held her hand and went with her. I felt better not sending her close to a stranger alone. Owen stayed back, so it ended up being just the two of us. Ironically, as dirty as the man looked, he smelled clean. *Maybe he's just down on his luck.*

"Thanks," he said. His sign said he was out of work and had a family to feed. Pebble looked at the sign, brows furrowed. I didn't think she could read it yet.

She smiled at him and waved goodbye.

CHAPTER 6

Dad's training was never-ending.

First thing Monday morning, I ran around the indoor track in the barn behind the pack house. The gym inside the barn had all the equipment we needed, from weights in all sizes fit for growing wereanimals, to stationary bikes, stair climbers, even a few ellipticals, and the dreaded track circling it all. Living in the Midwest meant snow and high humidity, so frequent indoor running was a foregone conclusion.

During my pre-wereanimal years, I developed a hatred of running…and all things sports. Since becoming a werepanther, my dislike of running had dimmed; partly because I could now smoke everyone, including Sarah and Owen. While I had always been a bookworm, they had participated on sports teams. I wasn't sure why I was so fast, but it gave me a perverse glee that I tried to hide from them every time I smoked them in a run. I probably failed miserably.

After my warmup run, I trotted over to the weights. The machines helped for inspiration, but I wanted free weights. My weak arms became my focus. Bicep curls, triceps curls, and pushups—three sets of twenty for each workout.

Owen joined me, watching the last few pushups of my final set. "Why do you do boring pushups?"

Dropping down, I rolled to my butt, about to stand and grab my weights. "Because that's all I have to do, and they work?"

"But these are better." He started doing one-armed pushups.

"You have got to be kidding me." I threw my sweaty towel at him.

"Gross." He tossed it back.

I rolled away so he missed. "Not even close."

He laughed. "Try these." He made a diamond with his finger and thumb and did pushups with the diamond aligned with the center of his chest.

I did about ten before they hurt. "Easy." The word huffed out of me.

He chuckled. "Not bad. What about pullups?"

I groaned. "What is Dad paying you?" I flopped down, rolling to my back.

Owen grinned at me, his eyes sparkling. "What? You can't do them?"

Blowing out a breath, I rolled my eyes. "Fine." I forced myself up and trudged to the bar. Grabbing it, I managed thirteen pullups. "Satisfied?"

Dad's voice floated in from the doorway across the track. "I'm never satisfied."

Owen and I whipped around to face him.

Dad came up and grabbed our log sheets. "But you've probably done enough for today. Go, shower. You both stink."

After cleaning up, I went to find coffee and food. I could hear Pebble laughing at cartoons in the basement. Mom, already in the kitchen, looked up at me over the edge of her mug of coffee. "Do you want to try calling your wolf today?"

We'd discussed this enough that she knew I was equal parts discouraged and determined. She set down her mug and went to fill one for me while I thought about the question.

Once I had my liquid ambrosia, I added some milk and sugar and took a sip. *Heaven.* Her question finally registered in my brain.

Do I want to try finding my wolf today? I hesitated, but finally said, "Sure...yes. Piper had an idea or theory, or something. She was wondering if she could watch my next attempt."

Mom raised a dubious eyebrow. "That was her great idea?"

I lifted my mug and shook my head. "Nope, that

was not the idea. The idea was to focus on one body part transforming to wolf, like my nose or something. She thinks I've been trying too hard. Stressing myself out. Maybe if I focus on my nose, I'll relax enough to transform."

Mom stared down into her coffee thoughtfully. She finally looked back up at me. "She's probably right. Do you think she's ready to see you try to transform? It isn't pretty." She took a drink while I contemplated her warning. But she had more to add. "I mean, you do start off naked and all, but then all the body parts move, and crack, and shift… it gets ugly fast. I don't know. It might be too much for her."

"What if we also invite Sarah over?"

"That may help," Mom admitted.

"What I want to know," Owen said, joining us, hair wet from his shower, "is why Jade is the only one of us with two forms."

"How do you know she is?" Mom asked with a deceptively innocent voice.

Before last spring, none of us had heard of a werepanther, or any other werebeast besides a werewolf. When I returned from my trip to Florida after the attack and turned into a werepanther, not everyone in the pack liked the idea of a werepanther in a werewolf pack. A pack member who wanted to eliminate me before the pack could vote on my inclusion attacked me. I survived, but only barely. That attack led to me having two wereanimals.

There was a chance I could've become a werewolf

naturally, but I was pretty sure the attack moved up the change timeline. Chances were, there weren't any others with two wereanimals. Having one wereanimal was rare; you had to be born into it or bitten. Two was incredibly unlikely.

Owen stared at Mom with a large, innocent gaze. "Well, I don't. It's just…I want to be bitten. I also think Sarah should get a chance." Owen was a bit too quick with his answer.

My eyes narrowed at him. "Does Sarah know you're making these declarations for her? Shouldn't we figure out if my wolf form is even viable and stable before we mess around with you getting bitten?" I waved my mug in his direction. "You've already tried, haven't you? On one of the Aunt Allison days when I couldn't make it. You two have tried biting each other, but you haven't transformed into a panther."

His eyes grew big and blameless. His scent turned bitter with guilt, and his heart rate increased. "No. There's no way we would've done that without talking to Mom and Dad first."

I stared at him. *As if. I'm not buying your innocent act.*

Mom's eyebrow went up again. "Owen!" she snapped.

His gaze shifted back and forth between us, and then he caved. "Okay, fine, maybe we did try, but we need help. We both want what you have, Jade. It really isn't fair that you get everything."

A snort escaped me before I realized I'd reacted.

"Everything? With all the issues I'm having, why did you think this was a good idea?" I glared at him. *It would be a better glare with more coffee.* "I'm going to text Sarah and Piper. Hopefully, they can get here sooner than later so we can see if this new theory works."

"What are you talking about?" Owen asked, perking up.

Ignoring Owen, Mom said plainly, "If it doesn't, I'm not sure what else we can try. We've been trying for weeks and you haven't found your wolf without me. I hope this does work, but I don't want you to get your hopes up."

Bracing myself for the reality of the day, I nodded. I completely understood, but the words were still hard to hear. *I have a wolf inside me, but what if I never reach her on my own?*

Owen looked back and forth between us and shrugged. He got up to get food and caffeine.

Sarah arrived first and Mom sat her down to talk. They were sitting at the kitchen table together with Owen. I stayed at the island.

Tilting her head, Mom asked, "How long ago did you two bite each other?"

Sarah squirmed under Mom's penetrating gaze, somewhere between a Mom-stare and a teacher-glare, not fun. No one warned Sarah that Mom knew about the bites. At least, I hadn't told her.

"It's been, um…" She looked at Owen, who shrugged.

He had already suffered under this Mom-interrogation

enough times to not be as affected.

Owen took one last bite of his breakfast and then drew some of the pressure away from Sarah. "We tried about six weeks ago. We've been through two full moon nights," he admitted.

I gaped.

Mom growled. "And why in the name of Mondara didn't you tell me this before?" Mom got up and circled the kitchen. "You do realize, if something went wrong, we could have been exposed? Normal people could have seen you. Are you two trying to get us all revealed? Are you trying to 'out' weres?"

Sarah blanched, and Owen, well, Owen's smile was gone, but mostly he looked pale, too.

Mom grabbed my empty mug with a jerk and went to fill it. She growled, "What would you have done if one of you did change and attacked some innocent norm on the street? What would Dad and I have had to do then?"

She dropped a full mug of coffee in front of me and sloshed some milk into it. "Did either of you think about that? Someone reporting a large rabid animal on the loose. The whole town would go into lockdown mode, afraid of who would get attacked next!" She was practically spitting from fury. Her eyes glowed, and her voice got wolfy, husky and deep. "Damn it! This is not the type of thing you keep to yourselves!"

Owen's eyes grew to saucers. "Mom, we weren't being

that rash. We did the full moon nights with you. If anything crazy happened, you were there."

Mom handed me the sugar and a spoon and then spun on Owen. "First off, I didn't know to expect anything different. Second, what would I have done if you had gotten the taste of human blood? A rogue werepanther, Owen? I couldn't have controlled you both. There would have been only one option."

"Um." He blanched. "I guess I hadn't thought about you being overwhelmed. But Sarah and Jade were there."

"Yeah, you hadn't thought. Damn it, Owen, you have to either start thinking or tell me when you do stupid things. It's the only way I can help you as your alpha or as your mom!"

Sarah and I tried to turn invisible. She hunched her shoulders in a mirror of my motions as we looked anywhere but at Mom. My chances of success were much better.

Mom closed her eyes and took a few deep breaths. "Okay, this is what we're going to do: Jade's going to try Piper's method of becoming a wolf. If it doesn't work, I'll try to call both of you to your wolves."

She said that last bit to Sarah.

Then she turned to Owen. "As for you and your panther, only Sarah can trigger the change. She's the alpha werepanther around here. I'm hoping, if she can feel what it's like to have an animal called, she can translate it into helping you, *if* you have a panther in you."

She dropped down at the table with them, rubbed

her eyes and took a long drink of her coffee. She held her mug in her hands and breathed in the scent, as if it had a calming effect, then said, "If either of you have a second animal, we'll go from there. If you don't, I just don't know. I really don't know why you two didn't discuss this with me or River. You think what Jade is going through is romantic, but talk to her—it's difficult and frustrating. It's been months and she still can only call one form, not two."

Searching Sarah and Owen's sulking faces, I asked, "Do you feel one or two animals in you?"

"What?" asked Owen. His brow dropped and his mouth scrunched up.

"Do you feel a panther in you? I feel both my panther and my wolf in me. I can also feel when one is more present. Can't you feel your wolf?"

They were all looking at me like I was speaking crazy, even Mom. "Mom? You can't feel your wolf?"

Placing her mug of coffee down, she considered me. "Like a separate entity? No. When I want to switch, I switch, but it isn't like I can feel an animal inside. And with the pack, I feel a wildness in others, and it's that which I call out."

Staring at each of their faces, I tried to summarize as best I could. "Huh, that's weird."

Sarah's head tilted. "I'm not really sure what you're talking about either."

Piper arrived, saving me from trying to explain

anything more about my animals. I quickly dragged her down to the basement to meet Pebble. Afterwards, we all headed to the backyard. I stripped down. Piper turned around to give me privacy.

Sarah and Owen both laughed.

Piper stiffened in a way that told me she must be glaring at them.

"Piper," Sarah said, "if you have your back to Jade, you won't see the transformation, not to mention, she isn't shy. She probably doesn't care."

I remembered giving Sarah this same speech only a few months back. *Oh, how quickly they grow up.* For the most part, Sarah was right, but in this particular case I did get down on my hands and knees pretty quickly. Being naked in front of my girlfriend, my best friend, and my family pushed the boundaries even for me.

Once I assumed the position, Mom took over. "Okay, Jade, I want you to focus on relaxing. Just change your hand into a wolf's paw. Whenever you change, the first thing you do is look down at your paw to see which animal you've transformed into. Use that as your anchor."

It surprised me she knew how I checked which animal form I shifted into. Where had she picked that up? Interesting. Alphas apparently took in a lot of information.

Walking several feet away, Mom left me alone in the yard. I appreciated her thoughtfulness and confidence in me. If I did do this, it would truly be me on my own, not my alpha helping me.

Dropping my head, I thought about my first few changes. I imagined the wolf inside me wanting to come out and run and play. The panther needed to sleep while the wolf and only the wolf came out to run. I was trying to push her out. I strained.

My breathing grew rough.

It's not working.

I gazed up at Owen and Sarah. Looks of disappointment passed between them.

Piper's voice came to me, encouraging and bright. She gave me a big smile. "Jade, you're trying too hard. Think about your hand, and just your hand. Make your hand a wolfy paw."

Dropping my head again, I took a calming breath.

Focus on the wolf's paw. My hand had to become tiny and my nails long and sharp. I wanted to open my eyes and be a wolf, not a panther. *Be small, black, with wolf's claws. Concentrate on letting the change happen, Jade.* I tried to relax my body for the change. My shoulders dropped and my head dipped further towards the lawn. Breathing deeply, I imagined sharp claws in the grass and dirt. I intended to feel the ground beneath my paws. I centered on how the world appeared as a wolf.

My mind went to the feeling of running as my claws ate up the dirt.

A wave of weirdness struck. A nauseating dizziness

flowed over me as if I were being taken over by a new consciousness. A tingling erupted in my fingers and toes. My body began the shift. This feeling happened before. The last three times this occurred I had shifted into a panther. *Did I relax my hold on her?*

Since Piper never witnessed any of my transformations, anything she saw today would be edifying for her, even if, in reality, it turned out to be a failure. I breathed and my back arched. *Ouch!*

My bones shifted and cracked, popping. Piper gasped as my body made horrible sounds. I heard murmurs, probably Sarah calming Piper down and explaining what they were seeing. Then it was all pain, and I couldn't listen to them. Hands and feet shortening, face elongating and reshaping, fur growing, pain, pain, pain!

It was done. I didn't open my eyes.

No one said anything; they were silent.

Then Mom whooped.

I opened my eyes and looked down. A wolf's paw!

I let out a yip and reared a few inches, and my tongue lolled in a wolf's laugh. I trotted over to Piper. Her words alone had brought me over the hump at last.

She gazed down in shock.

Sarah tackled me in a hug. We rolled across the lawn.

Lying next to me, Sarah caught her breath. "That was amazing! I can't believe it finally worked. Come here, Piper; give her a doggie hug. Isn't she a beautiful wolf?"

Piper laughed and gave me a hug. I licked her face.

Mom came over and checked me out. "Nice work. Next thing we test is if you can transform between animals."

Her words sent a chill down my spine and I froze.

I slowly moved my focus up to her in shock. *Is she serious?*

Mom smiled grimly. "Yes, dear, I'm serious. Though, not today, and not with a crowd. This was a great start. Sarah, do you want me to see if you really have a wolf in you?"

Sarah's voice quavered as she said, "Yes, please."

Mom squared up to her, put her hands on her shoulders, and looked deep into her eyes.

I gently sniffed the air, searching for wolf-scent in Sarah. I didn't smell any wolf and I usually possessed one of the best noses for this.

Mom dropped her hands and shook her head. "I'm sorry, Sarah, I'm not feeling any wolf in you. My guess is you are a single wereanimal. I really think Jade is something unique. I'm not sure what is allowing her to hold two animals, but it is exceptional."

"What about Owen?" Sarah asked.

"You'll have to search him for a panther. I'll have to lead you through the process after Jade returns to human form."

"Can Jade try biting Sarah to see if her bite will give Sarah a second animal?" Owen asked.

Gazing up at him in shock, my tail tucked between my legs, and I backed away. *Why is he so invested in this?*

"I don't think Jade wants to bite Sarah," Piper said

quietly, reading my body language correctly.

I whined in agreement.

Mom watched me closely. "I don't think this is something we should jump into lightly."

Owen opened his mouth to complain.

Mom held up a hand. "I know you and Sarah have been discussing this for months, but it's new to us. Let's all discuss this over a meal. For now, Jade, go take a quick run. I'll leave some food out in the kitchen for when you get back, assuming Piper and Owen don't eat it all." She glanced at Piper, who had the grace to duck her head.

Before I could leave, the glass door slid open. "Hazel-mom, can I…could I…" Pebble poked her head out then ducked it down. Quickly, as if she were afraid, she asked, "Can I see Jade?"

Mom reached out her hand. "Of course, dear."

Pebble skipped out. "Oh, she's a wolf this time. Can I be a wolf with her?" Her scent combined a mixture of hope and fear. I whined and wagged my tail. *Everything and everyone is still so new to her.*

Mom's brows came together as she thought about the request. Giving Pebble a chance to run now would be a safe introduction to the area. It would also allow us to see her wolf. Mom growled low in her throat. "You don't all have to stare at me. I can feel it."

We all turned away quickly, except Pebble who stared at Mom with hope in her eyes.

Mom blew out a breath. "Sure, honey. Do you need help with the transformation?"

Pebble shook her head quickly. Our backyard had a few privacy fences up. She darted behind one and several minutes later we heard the cracking of bones, and the whining sounds a person made when they were in pain.

My tail tucked between my legs and my back hunched. Tucking my nose in my front paws, I whimpered quietly in a small echo of her sounds. When those sounds came from a five-year-old, they broke your heart.

The shift took time. A lot of time. We waited. We listened. We all hurt in solidarity with her. Finally, a small grey wolf trotted out and joined us. I nosed her and licked her face.

Sarah knelt in front of Pebble and gave her a quick hug. "You have the same coloring as Owen. Now you could be his twin. You definitely belong to this family, kiddo."

Pebble gave a tiny yip and licked Sarah's face. Then she trotted over to me, headbutting my side.

Mom released a burst of love, filling us both like the warmth of the sun. "Go, run, then come back and eat."

The four of them went inside while we ran.

Pebble needed to learn the boundaries of the property, so we ran the safest areas for her. Her tiny wolf body wobbled as she skittered around. Despite the rough start, she quickly got her paws under her. This obviously was not her first time furry.

I often used my runs to clear my mind and enjoy the freedom from human thoughts. Today, my head jumbled too full of human worries and questions to fully become a wolf. Then there was Pebble to think about.

Despite running with the small wolf, I couldn't stop thinking about how Owen wanted me to bite Sarah. Owen probably wanted me to bite him, as well. Would my bite even be a single animal bite? What had Sarah and Owen been thinking, biting each other? I could see Owen doing it, but Sarah? What could Owen have done to convince Sarah to go along with him?

Leaping over a fallen tree, I spun to watch Pebble. It took her a few tries to scramble over it, and when she got to the top, she did a small bounce. Losing her balance, she toppled over and landed on her side. Before I could run to her, she popped up, tongue lolling out as she trotted over to me.

We continued our run, and I continued my musings. Piper figured out how to get me to shift into a wolf.... Piper. Not me. Not Mom. Piper.

Would the shifting technique work again? I would try again and hope Piper had offered me the permanent key. It was kind of amazing how she had figured that out. What else would she discover to help us all?

We reached the stream, and we both drank deeply of the cool refreshing water. As she drank, she nosed a rock and overextended. With a "yip" of surprise, she fell tail over nose into the stream. After taking a second to make sure she was okay, I plopped onto my belly to watch as she splashed around.

Pebble darted out to me and back in. The second time, I knew what she wanted, and I waded in after her. We played for a few minutes before continuing our tour of the property, heading towards a running-trail near the house. Pebble got ahead of me and dashed across a sidewalk.

No!

Despite the sharp bark I let out, she didn't stop.

I took off after her. She streaked across a park. When I caught up with her, her nose was still pushed deep within a backpack next to a slide, finding whatever prizes the bag hid. I nipped at her rump and she jumped back. I shook my head and led her back, sniffing to make sure we were alone.

We weren't.

"Mom, look, dogs!"

With me nipping at Pebble's paws, we ran faster to get back to our property. I wouldn't feel safe until we crossed into pack territory. Once home, we shifted back and got dressed.

As soon as I had arms, I gave her a hug. "Pebble, honey, you can't cross sidewalks. You get into areas where norms are."

Pebble frowned. "Norms?"

"Normal people, non-werewolves. We can't let them see us. Once you crossed that sidewalk, it became dangerous. I know you don't know a lot about being a werewolf, but first rule, stay on pack land. Second rule, don't nose around in a stranger's backpack."

Her eyes widened. "But Jade, there was chocolate!"

"We have chocolate. You don't need a stranger's food."

She sighed and looked up. "Can I have some chocolate?"

CHAPTER 7

Pebble and I went into the kitchen and grabbed ice cream bars. She scampered back into the backyard to play and I sat at the kitchen table.

Owen dropped down next to me. "Did you try transforming into a panther?"

"Darn. I knew there was something I forgot." I turned to give him a wide-eyed innocent look. "Next time."

We both laughed.

"This is not a trustworthy sight," Mom said, joining us in the kitchen. "What are you two plotting?"

"Nothing, Mom," I said with a perfectly blank and

innocent face.

"I think I liked it better when you two fought all the time, before becoming wereanimals," Mom countered, eyes narrowing.

Sarah and Piper came in while Mom spoke. Piper sat next to me and Sarah next to Owen. *Interesting*.

"They're planning on trying the wolf to panther change," Sarah said, ratting us out.

I stuck my tongue out at her.

Mom's face became hard, then she gave one of her patented eyebrows raises. "Well?"

Owen and I both broke out laughing. There was no way to cover it up this time.

Dad came in, joining us for the first time for the day. It was Saturday, so he had slept in. "What did I miss our scamps getting up to this time?"

Mom's stare became level, then she shifted her gaze to Dad. "Later," she said. "We have other things to talk about. First off, Jade found her wolf this morning, without help."

Dad's eyes gleamed as he stared at me. "Did you, pumpkin?"

I nodded.

He engulfed me in a hug. "I'm proud of you. Can you do it again?"

Shrugging, I said dryly, "No idea."

Everyone chuckled.

"I'm sure she can," said Piper, slipping an arm around

my waist. *The ultimate supporter.*

"She'll try again in a few days. Once she can choose her shape consistently, then—" Mom shot a look between me and Owen, "—and *only* then, she'll try to transform between her two animals."

"She'll what?" Dad demanded. We all looked at him, surprised he was so behind in the news. Didn't Mom and Dad discuss this stuff before bringing their ideas to us?

"I figure, why not," Mom said sheepishly. She shrugged at Dad with a little smile.

"You know that's insane, love, don't you?" Dad gave Mom a weird look, brows furrowing, upper lip twitching up, and head slightly cocked.

"I do, but it would be remarkable, too." Her eyes sparkled.

I was shocked that Dad hadn't heard about this, but in complete agreement that the animal-to-animal transformation would be beyond amazing. I didn't know of any real application for it, though.

"What need would Jade ever have for that skill?" Dad asked. "I've been building her training program, including fighting. If you think that she would need this for anything, let me know and I'll build it in, but I can't see any necessity for this skill." He sounded hopeful, though.

"The only thing I can think of is if she were in one form and needed to switch because we were fighting and needed the other form." Mom stopped to think. "She runs faster in panther form. If she's out there as a wolf and needs to escape, it would be nice if she could go directly to panther to flee. Going to human and then panther would take too much energy and she would pass out, so yes, I would love if this could be a skill she could learn, train, and master." She seemed to convince herself by the end as much as Dad.

"Not to mention, can you imagine the shock value? Fighting a wolf that suddenly turns into a panther? It would be freakishly cool, and distracting. Dude," Owen exclaimed. "I so want to be able to do that, too." That last was under his breath. I wasn't sure if anyone but me and Sarah heard it.

"You want to do it?" Dad exploded. Or maybe werewolf ears heard everything. "What are you talking about? Jade is the only one with two animals."

Dad sounded more and more wary.

"Sarah, Jade," Mom said, "come over here. Put your hands on Jade's shoulders, look into her eyes to show dominance, and think about probing into her to find her panther."

Sarah followed Mom's directions. While Mom was showing Sarah what to do, she modeled it on me. With her hands on me, I felt her alpha power in her stare and my wolf looking up, taking notice.

Then Sarah took Mom's spot. She was more tentative, but her hands were strong and her presence that of an alpha. She looked me in the eyes, and my panther perked right up.

"Oh, my god!" Sarah said, her voice full of wonder.

"I can totally feel her panther. I could definitely pull it forward if I wanted to. I can feel it responding to me. That is so freaking cool!"

I smiled at her enthusiasm.

"This must be what happened last spring. I didn't even realize what I was doing."

"Perfect," said Mom. "Now, use that new skill to check out Owen."

At Dad's startled look, Mom continued, "Apparently, the kids have been trying to replicate Jade's 'coolness' on their own. I'm trying to figure out the extent and do some damage control. I'll explain more later."

Dad's scent changed to something spicy. "Jade's 'coolness?'"

I shrugged. "Could've fooled me."

Sarah went over to Owen and put her hands on his shoulders. She looked him in his eyes, and he immediately dropped his gaze.

"Owen," Mom demanded, "you can't look away."

Owen whined. "I can't help it; she's so damn dominant when her panther is present."

"I hadn't predicted that. Jade, go take up the position over Owen, see what you can determine."

What? Okay, I can do this. I'd been on the other side enough times.

I went over to Owen, put my hands on his shoulders and looked into his eyes. He started to look down, and I growled at him. I tried to be calm. Because I was an epsilon wolf, he didn't need to drop his eyes to me.

He stopped his visual descent, pausing for a beat. He blinked and settled his eyes squarely on mine. I probed into Owen, feeling like I was falling forward. Both my animals joined in; my wolf wagged her tail in greeting, Owen's wolf seemed to wag back. Owen's eyes grew wider.

"Jade, that isn't a panther," Owen squeaked.

"I know, let me figure this out. I'm new to this. Give me a second."

"Is my wolf's tail wagging? Does that even make sense? Jade, what the hell are you doing?" His voice sounded awed, or was that scared? I wasn't an alpha; I couldn't call his wolf out, but I could see him, and he seemed happy to see me.

Why can't he sense his animal like I can? What does it feel like to him?

"Give me a second!" I said. "Calm down." That wasn't how it worked, and Owen's raised eyebrow said he knew it as well as I did.

I kept going, trying to relax. Was there another animal there? I couldn't really feel another animal. I searched more, using my panther to help my search. I saw an old injury. When did he break his arm? Could that have been Piper's dad's car? I saw the seed that could be a panther but wasn't. Could a panther be pulled out? My eyes squinted and my head tilted as I considered the prospect of Owen being a panther.

I didn't know how long I stood there probing him, but

he finally pulled back. "So, is there a panther in me?"

"No, but I think there could be," I said. "There's a seed of something there. I think that first bite opened the door for a dual animal, but you aren't quite there yet."

"Jade, can you look more closely at Sarah and see if the seed is there as well?" Mom asked.

I was so distracted by everything I had seen in Owen, it hadn't even occurred to me how strange that question was.

Before I moved away from Owen, I quickly asked, "Did you know he had broken both arms at some point?"

I felt, more than saw, everyone in the room freeze.

Almost feeling like I was in a trance, I moved over to Sarah. I put my hands on her shoulders and looked into her eyes. Her panther immediately stared me down. It almost dropped me to my knee, but Sarah held me up. I felt her physically push the panther down.

Once the panther was under Sarah's control, I looked again with the wolf in the front of my mind. With the wolf in the lead, her panther couldn't drop me as easily. As we searched, *I searched*, I didn't feel what I had sensed in Owen. I wasn't sure what was different, but I knew that the seed Owen had wasn't within Sarah. After a few more minutes, I broke away and would have fallen if someone hadn't caught me and put me in a chair.

I trembled as someone pushed food into my hands. I ate my sandwich. *Food, good.*

After eating a few bites, my mind was clear enough to

answer. "I didn't feel a wolf in Sarah. I'm not sure what the difference is. I don't know that she couldn't have a wolf, but whatever Owen did wasn't enough. It may be because her panther is so strong, she would need a really strong wolf to bite her, but I don't really know. But, damn, her panther is strong. It wanted to swat me into my place like an errant child. Phew, please tell me we're done."

Mom brought me a glass of orange juice. "I know you're tired, and you don't have to do that again, but you have an interesting ability. I wonder how much you can tell from looking inside different people. Can you tell if anyone is able to have a second animal? Can you tell which of the kiddos will one day change?"

She brought me another sandwich and, after placing it on my plate, rubbed my shoulders. My tension eased. "I wonder how perceptive you are, and how much of that is what has led you towards medicine. This is really interesting." Eyes narrowing, she considered me. "I would like you to test out Piper, but it can wait."

At that, both Piper and I looked up sharply. I reviewed everything she had said, and slowly my brain caught up. "Let me eat more, and maybe finish my juice first."

"Is anyone going to mention my broken arm?" asked Owen.

"It isn't broken anymore." I mumbled over a BLT. I was halfway through my second before I realized I'd even started.

"It was probably when you were hit by a car last spring," Sarah mused.

My parents looked at all of us. Mom was the first to speak. "You were hit by a car?"

I quickly stuffed another bite of BLT in my mouth and was sad to note it was the last of the food on my plate. Sarah's face lost a bit of color. Owen shrank in his seat.

Before Owen could answer, Sarah turned to Owen, every bit of alpha in her stare. "You *said* you would tell them."

He wilted. "After Jade collapsed, it just didn't seem as important. Then when we figured out it was Piper's parents, I just figured we would let it slide."

Dad fell into an island chair, head falling into his hands. "Stop, before the story gets worse. Next there will be aliens."

Mom smelled of fur and wildness. "So, you were coming home from Allison's, you weren't paying attention, you crossed a street, and ran into a car?" She moved towards the table where Owen was sitting. Her fists hit the table. "Then, with a broken leg, you just limped home?"

Owen cocked his head. "No. My leg wasn't broken. That can't be when it happened."

Sarah and Owen looked at me.

I shrugged. "You were on the ground whimpering and your leg *did* seem messed up. When I investigated it, there was a cracking sound and then you ran off. I don't remember much more."

Sarah's brow furrowed. "I didn't hear a crack. I just saw you pet him, and he leapt up."

"Huh? The crack was loud. I mean, it didn't echo, but it was loud."

Now everyone was watching me. I shrugged, completely baffled.

Mom, still fuming, said, "This is why you tell me and your dad things right away."

Piper huffed. "You know, I never knew Dad hit a werewolf…or knew he hit anything. None of you tell me anything. Everyone knew, well maybe Mom doesn't know, but she probably does." Frustration oozed off her in waves, mixing with Mom's dissipating fury.

I sneezed and my eyes watered.

"Mom, can we get back to the animals?" I pleaded.

Mom gave me a half-smile. "What, you don't want to discuss medicine? Fine, back to your weird ability to sense animals…for now. But Owen, we will need to discuss your broken arm when it's just the immediate family."

He groaned and dropped his head in his arms.

Sarah took a sip of soda and then said to Mom, "That would make a lot of sense, about her ability to sense the inside animal, animal potential, and the medicine." She turned to me. "I could almost feel something wanting to pounce on you or swat you down. I've never felt anything like that before."

"Um, well, yeah. Your panther was not happy that I was playing alpha. She really wanted to put me in my place, until you held her down, and I could bring my wolf to the front."

Dad nodded.

Mom was watching me and him. "River, do you know what she's talking about?"

"You don't?"

"No." Mom snarled.

"It's a hippy thing, you wouldn't get it," I added helpfully with a smile.

"Huh." Dad thought for a minute. "This is fascinating. Yeah, I sense the animal in me. I feel my wolf. It helps me to understand what needs to be done."

I grinned at everyone's astonished looks. I got up and gave him a big hug and whispered a thanks. It was nice having someone else there to take some of the pressure off me.

"Okay, Jade, up for testing Piper?" Mom asked.

Turning to Piper, I gave her a huge smile.

She blanched but didn't back down.

Moving to her, I put my hands on her shoulders and looked into her eyes. "Just relax and stay calm, this is nothing, don't worry," I whispered.

A wave of dizziness hit me. She wasn't a wolf, but I was using whatever epsilon essence I could to get her to calm down. She gazed back at me and nodded. She took a quick breath and stood taller, shoulders back, head held high. *That's my girl.*

My probe started off slow. This was different, and I almost jumped back. This wasn't searching for a wereanimal; there wasn't a wereanimal to be found. I backed up, slowed down, and tried for something gentler, leading with the wolf, not the panther.

Piper's eyes got huge, and I was afraid she might collapse. She quaked and I could feel her muscles weakening. Her breathing became ragged.

Mom and Dad slipped in behind her. Mom placed a hand on her shoulder to lend support.

I focused only on Piper, and not everyone around us.

My first discovery was that she had a headache; that was interesting. *Stop. This is about the seed of a wereanimal.* I let the wolf lead. She sniffed around. We didn't find anything until we were deep in the core and she—we—found the seed. It was hard to detect, but it was there. Piper had the seed but it was years away from becoming active.

I froze, and Piper's eyes grew wider. I relaxed, and she did as well. Okay, slowly, I had to move slowly. I backed away and released her. Once my wolf was no longer in Piper, she slumped. My parents grabbed her and settled her on a chair. Everyone stared at me.

"Well, first of all, she has a headache." They all gave me weird stares. "That was the first thing I figured out. I could, well, I could tell things about her. She has a healed broken arm, too."

Everyone turned to Piper.

She looked like she wanted to run, she was so freaked out. Her scent was spicy and a little sweet, like prey. "When I was seven, my bike slipped off the curb and I tumbled down a hill. I tried to stop myself and only managed to break my arm. How did you know that?"

I squeezed my hands together as a cascade of emotions fought for dominance within me. "Please don't look at me like I'm a freak." Her condemning gaze hurt. "When I was probing for the seed of a wolf, I could just tell things about you. Anyway, yes, you have the seed of a wolf deep down. I don't know if that means you will become a werewolf or that you just have the potential. I believe it means that if you do become one naturally, the change is several years off."

Now everyone gaped at me like I had grown a second head. Ducking, I felt more freakish than normal. I fisted my hands to stop them from shaking and took a step back. My shoulders rose as I hugged myself.

"Jade, you are the coolest sister a guy could ever ask for," Owen said, pulling me into a hug. When his mouth was near my ear, he added softly enough so that no one else could hear, "Don't worry, sis, you are not a freak. Don't let anyone make you feel less than you are. Your abilities are seriously amazing. Remember that."

He backed up, looked me in the eyes and gave me a wink. "Freak," he said for everyone to hear. His lopsided smile said it all.

Everyone laughed, though Piper still looked a bit green.

Dad walked over and wrapped his arm around me. "Jade, we may need to open this discussion up to the full pack. You need to do more explaining and testing so that we can all figure out what's going on."

Sighing at the implication of 'pack meeting', I gave him a half-smile. I'd figured this was going to happen next.

Mom turned to my brother and my best friend. "Owen, if you really want to try for the panther, we can try it in a controlled situation later today, if Sarah would be up to it. She may not have known exactly what she needed to do to infect someone fully, especially since you're already a werewolf. We're treading on new territory here."

Sarah rubbed the back of her neck, but nodded.

"Then we have a plan," continued Mom. "Let's clean up and take a break from all this. We can meet up at three for the Sarah and Owen show."

She grabbed her plate then turned to me and Piper. "Piper, I know you're a bit confused, and you really shouldn't be here for Owen's next animal attempt; it will be ugly. Maybe you and Jade should talk a bit? Jade can walk you home." She turned back to Sarah. "Sarah, I think you should call your parents and discuss this with them. This is a big decision you're making, and they should be involved."

After giving everyone their marching orders, she nodded and took her leave. *I'm not sure she has any better idea of what's going on than the rest of us.*

Piper followed me to my room for our talk. I wasn't sure she wanted to, but Mom made it sound more like a command than a suggestion. "You ok?" I asked.

"I don't know. You were right about the headache. A

lot has happened today. I'm glad I saw you transform; it was weird. Your mom was right, it was ugly. At the same time, there was a beauty to it. If you're right, that will be me someday. That makes me extra glad to have seen it."

We got to the room and she grabbed her stuff before we headed to the front door. When we were outside, she continued, "But the probing. I could feel you in my head. It was like a warm calming pressure flowing through me. It isn't that it was unpleasant, it was just unexpected, and, Jade, how can my girlfriend do such unnatural things?"

Unnatural. The word made me wince, but I knew she was reeling. "Are they too weird for you?" I asked carefully.

We walked for a bit in silence. Finally, her gaze met mine, a tear forming in the corner of one eye. She looked down at her hands. "I don't know. I think I have to go home and think about this. I'm going to discuss everything that happened today with my mom. My guess is she'll be over to be 'probed' before the day is done. Being a nurse, she'll find your ability too interesting to pass up. I just need time to think."

I'm turning into more of an oddity than even she could handle. On the walk over I fought tears. I didn't want to be a freak. When we arrived at her door, I leaned in to hug her, but she flinched.

Tensing, my eyes widened. Seeing my hurt reflected in her eyes, I spun on my heel and bolted back home.

From behind, her voice followed me. "Jade, wait!"

I wasn't about to stop. It was all too much.

When I got home, I shook with pent up emotions needing release. Tears gathered at the sides of my eyes and my heart beat fast in my chest. I needed to find Sarah; she would help me figure out what was going on. Where in this beast of a pack house was my best friend? Gods above, I had so much in me to release. I wanted to vent to my pack mate, my best friend. Finally, I found her.

She and Owen were making out on one of the basement couches. *What the hell?*

That was it, my head was going to explode. This day had turned from bad to awful. Whirling, I charged up the stairs to my room, locked the door, and collapsed face down on my bed.

CHAPTER 8

Someone knocked on my door. A quick sniff told me it was Sarah. I rolled over and checked the clock: just after one. I wasn't needed until three. I ignored her.

"Jade? You okay? I mean, you aren't, I can feel that, but do you want to talk?"

I buried my head in my pillow.

After a few minutes, I heard her walk away.

My phone beeped. I ignored that, too. I stayed in bed.

I heard Mom and Dad discussing Owen's afternoon. Dad sounded livid. "I can't believe you gave permission for this, Hazel."

"He was going to continue to try no matter what. This way it's going to happen under our supervision."

"I…"

They moved away and lowered their voices before I heard more.

At just before three, I dragged myself from bed and headed for the backyard. When I got there, I found everyone had arrived before me, including Aunt Allison. I didn't see Sarah, but I sensed her, which meant she was probably behind the privacy screen. Owen stood near the house a bit wild-eyed.

I wonder if anything specific is expected of me. Maybe I should've checked my phone before coming out.

Not only was Aunt Allison an expert on panthers, she was a veterinarian. She claimed she didn't know 'people medicine', but she knew enough to patch up pack members when they got hurt and a werewolf's fast healing ability took care of the rest. Bevin and I were slowly taking over that role where we could.

"Jade, you made it!" Owen sounded pleased. "I wasn't sure if you were coming when you locked yourself in your room."

I managed a wan smile. "I wasn't going to miss this. You may need medical care, and Sarah may need psychological care. I just needed to be alone for a few minutes, that's all."

"Are you okay?" Mom asked.

I hunched my shoulders and glanced aside. "No, not really, but give me more time. It was a rough few hours."

"How was your walk home with Piper?" she asked. She took a step towards me and looked into my face. "You're not okay."

I frowned as I thought about her statement. *She really doesn't know.* Being my alpha, she usually knew my emotions, often before I did. "It wasn't good…"

"Mom, Jade," Owen said, interrupting us. "Now isn't the time. Let's focus on the big, beautiful panther."

As if on cue, Sarah came out from behind the screen. She stood just over waist height, pure black with dark brown eyes. Though she stood tall, I could smell the almond scent of nerves coming from her. Not biting people was the first rule we were all taught.

Closing my eyes, I took a deep breath, inhaling the scents of the backyard, the trees and the grass, wild animals, and of family. I needed to center on the familiar. Slowly letting it out, I tried to release everything from the last few hours. When I opened my eyes, my focus shifted to what needed to happen now.

Mom nodded, walked over to Sarah, and knelt in front of her. She placed a hand on her head in a calming gesture. "Okay, Sarah, just like I explained. A simple bite can do it for a normal person, but the deeper the wound the better."

Rising, Mom walked back over to me and Owen, placing her hand on his shoulder. As she spoke her voice shook. "You will heal fast, which, I believe, means you will need to have a lot more damage inflicted. I know that this won't be easy." She looked back and forth between Owen and Sarah. "But if this is something you both want, this is how it has to be done." Shaking her head, she went back over to Sarah.

A chill ran down my spine. *She really doesn't like this idea, but he's an adult and doing it with pack is better than doing it alone.*

Putting a hand on Sarah's haunches, Mom said, "I suggest biting both thighs and his midsection a few times. The big thing to remember is, try not to eat any of the meat. Human meat can be addictive and can turn you rogue, which would be really bad."

Positive Mom and Sarah had gone over all this already, I knew Sarah hearing it again in panther form was crucial. It was easy to forget things when the animal side took over, and this was too important to mess up.

Mom stood and came over to us, exchanging a worried look with Aunt Allison. "Owen, to make this a bit less painful, because you know this is going to hurt…a lot, why don't you lie down on the stretcher. My guess is Sarah will have to bite you at least a half dozen times to infect you. Anything less and your wolf will heal you too quickly for you to be turned. Jade was probably changed by Candice because she was almost killed."

Owen blanched. No doubt, reality hit him, but he got down on the stretcher. He wore a pair of running shorts and a tank top. He took off the tank top and threw it towards the house.

I stood on one side of Sarah, Aunt Allison on the other. I was the best person to stop Sarah if she got out of control. Aunt Allison and I together were the ones who could help heal Owen once he was bitten. My parents stayed close in case we needed extra muscle, or if Owen needed to be dragged away while Aunt Allison and I held Sarah back.

Sarah looked up at me sadly. I wasn't sure if she was sad for me, sad for herself, or sad for Owen. *Maybe all three.*

I bent down and gave her a hug, briefly resting my cheek against her soft fur. "He wants this. It's safer with the pack around than what you two were doing before. It'll be okay."

She huffed, and then attacked. I flinched, despite knowing she needed to do this quickly and efficiently. If she went slowly, it would mean more suffering for her and Owen. She did a double bite on each thigh. She hit the femoral artery on the left leg and blood gushed everywhere. Owen's eyes bugged out. He didn't want to scream and cause Sarah to stop, but after seeing the blood, he whimpered and passed out.

Mom lost color in her face. Clamping her jaw tighter, she braced herself from leaping at Sarah. A quick glance at Dad was enough to see him standing like a statue, jaws clenched, hands fisted. I could smell his minty scent of frustration at the situation. He didn't like this idea, but he knew this was the safest resolution.

When I turned back to Owen and Sarah, she had

moved up to his torso. She chomped on his middle. A bit of blood from his leg hit her eye and she flinched while doing her first bite on his abs. Sarah bit once more, and then backed off, shaking her head, eyes wide.

"Go to the stream and rinse out your mouth." Dad slapped Sarah on her back. "Then come back."

While he dealt with Sarah, Aunt Allison and I started in on Owen. His wounds were bad, the bites deep. On a couple, Sarah must have dragged her teeth because there were long slices that would require stitching. Damn, we hadn't counted on that. Wereanimals healed fast but this much damage needed a helping hand.

We staunched the bleeding quickly and carried him into the medical room. The room was such a contrast to the rest of the house. It held a bed jutting out at an angle, cutting the room in half. A counter and cupboards with all the medical supplies and equipment we would need lined the far wall. A chair sat next to the bed.

A TV hung on the wall, rarely utilized since werewolves healed fast. I had a feeling that the people who sat with Owen tonight might be watching movies to pass the time.

Aunt Allison and I got everything figured out. Once we identified the worst injuries, I paused and took a calming breath.

Aunt Allison rubbed my back. "You can do this, Jade. I know this is one of the worst cases you've seen, and you normally have Bevin with you, but you can do this."

"It's Owen."

Her voice calmed me. "And he has a wolf helping. Just take it step by step."

I glanced at my aunt and gave her a smile. "Thanks."

I started in on Owen's thigh first; that gash was the worst. Once bandaged up, I moved to one of the abdomen bites which needed a few stitches. Though bites were rarely stitched, his skin was torn, and it would heal more cleanly held together.

By the time I finished, it was late. The aroma of pizza wafted in from the kitchen. *Yum...cheese and meat.* My mouth watered as I cleaned up before going for food.

Sarah's parents joined us for dinner. The three of them sat at the kitchen table with a plate of pizza. They had missed the afternoon show but knew what their daughter had done. Though supportive, they also seemed unnerved. Her mom's hands shook as she lifted her pizza. Her dad, however, acted like the rock for the family. A calmness radiated from him as he rubbed Cindy's arm and gave reassuring smiles to both of them.

"Will he be ok?" Sarah asked. She looked a bit green and wrung her hands. Though it had been a few hours, she still breathed erratically.

"He's stable." I sat down at the kitchen island and grabbed some food. I took a bite before answering further, swallowing my pizza down with a swig of soda. "I stitched one of the wounds, more for my peace of mind than anything else. You remember your attack in Florida; the wereanimal in you heals wounds quickly enough. He will probably be up by tomorrow evening." I shook my head. "I'm not really an expert."

Tom, Sarah's dad, gave me an admiring look. "You should think about double majoring in medicine and veterinary sciences. You're more of an expert than you give yourself credit for."

I simply looked at him, too tired to respond in any intelligent way.

Sarah gave me a half-smile and said, with a bit of her sass coming back, "Jade found out she can mentally probe a person to diagnose them."

My head dropped down to my arms and I groaned. *Too much. I need a week off. How can today still be today?* I lifted my head and reached for more pizza. Food was more important than being overwhelmed.

Both of Sarah's parents stared at me quizzically.

"That's really cool," said Cindy, her mom. "That will come in handy as the pack's healer. Having to deal with so many issues without a team of medical experts to help you, any advantage you have is amazing."

She gave Sarah a one-armed hug. Cindy had come a long way to accepting me, Sarah, and the werewolves. When Sarah and I were first attacked in Florida by a werepanther, Cindy saw me as the enemy. All her fears for her daughter got piled on me. For a short time, they asked me to stay away from her and the family. It was both shocking and refreshing how accepting they now were. As if she read my thoughts, Cindy smiled and said, "Jade, you're more and more of a wonder to me. I'm so grateful you were with us in Florida. I know that it's made your life harder, but it has made our life much more understandable. I have no idea what we would have done if you hadn't been there."

"Thank you," I said, and I meant it. A weight lifted off me. Her angle on my weirdness was refreshing. She didn't see me as a freak; she saw me as an asset.

"Could you tell if it worked? Will he have two animals?" Sarah asked. Her scent changed to spicy with her emotions, nervous but hopeful.

I averted my gaze for a moment. *I'd hate for her to have gone through all that for nothing. So much trauma, hers psychological, Owen's physical, only for nothing to come of it.*

"I didn't check to see if it worked. Owen was pretty torn up and out of it. I don't even know if I can probe when someone's passed out."

"Wouldn't it be a good idea to try?" Dad asked, always in training mode.

I sagged, tired. Today had been long and rough. Turning around, I searched everyone's expressions. Their faces all held such wonder and hope, I knew I couldn't disappoint them.

Sighing, I took another bite of pizza. "Let me finish my dinner and then I'll try. I need energy."

Everyone seemed to take that as good reasoning, so I

focused on pizza. Yum.

Owen was still passed out when I returned a half-hour later with Aunt Allison. Still pale, with bandages on his legs and around his waist, Owen slept like the dead, his breathing shallow yet steady. I could hear his heart rate and it sounded strong. I placed a hand on his forehead; his temperature seemed to be within normal parameters.

As I checked him over, I realized I wasn't sure how to do what they were asking. The directions Mom had given Sarah were to put your hands on the weaker member's shoulders, look into their eyes to show dominance, and bam. Instant information. Well, I could do the shoulders bit, but that would be awkward. Then there was the fact that Owen's eyes were closed. Someone could hold them open, but that would be weird, and probably gross.

I sat there, staring at him.

"You're thinking about this too hard," said Aunt Allison.

My voice came out almost as a wail. "I don't know what I'm doing, Aunt Allison."

"I would say follow your instincts, but this is so strange, I don't know which instincts you would be following. Why don't you just hold his hand and go from here?"

"Instincts. Hand. Right."

I fisted my hands, opened them, and then shook them out, trying to release my pent-up nerves. *Okay, hold his hand. I can do this.* I sat in the chair next to his bed and gently took his hand. I closed my eyes to block out everything but Owen.

What the hell am I doing?

I sat by my half-gnawed brother, holding his hand. Well, at least that much made sense—until you added in the part that he had asked to be chewed on and my best friend had been the one to use him as a chew-toy. *How did my life get so weird?*

No wonder Piper had run out. Biting back the hysterical laughter threatening to bubble from me, I tried to focus on Owen. I had to focus on Owen, not the horror of the afternoon; that would only bring heartache.

"Anything?" Aunt Allison asked.

Opening one of my eyes, I glanced at her. "Umm, not really. I don't really know what I'm supposed to be doing here." I opened my other eye and my mouth scrunched in disappointment.

Aunt Allison rubbed my shoulders encouragingly. "Maybe think about Owen, his body, his possible panther, and his injuries. Try to send yourself into him, like you did before. Just, this time, do it mentally, not with your sight."

"Mentally, right. You make it sound so reasonable. Actually, nope, still sounds crazy. Even when you say it in your calm doctor voice."

Her laugh brought a smile to my face and my shoulders dropped. Okay, time to try again.

I closed my eyes, and this time, I focused on Owen and his emotions. My panther helped me. It was like she asked permission to search, so I gave it. She flowed out through my hands, and I went with her. And then, we were in Owen. Ouch. I nearly recoiled. He was messed up and his wolf was busy making the fixes. His wolf stared at me, ears back, and snarled, then turned away to get back to the repairs that required his attention.

As I sought the seed of his panther, I noticed more about his injuries. The internal ones were being healed—the wolf had been working from the inside out. Then I noticed the wolf wasn't working alone; there, deep down, was a shy panther.

Whoa, it had worked. My panther went and nosed Owen's panther and he came out. It nosed me back. It wasn't a black panther like mine, but a dark brown one.

Hi, beautiful, I said.

It bowed its head shyly, then looked up at me with shining brown eyes. Eyes that matched Owen's.

The wolf trotted over and butted my hand away.

I turned and surveyed the injuries. *Can we help?*

It shook its head in dismissal.

Trying to respect Owen's wolf, I slowly backed out until I could let go and look up at Aunt Allison.

Before I could say anything, my stomach growled, and my head swam with a wave of dizziness.

Aunt Allison grabbed me before I fell. "Let's get you back to the kitchen."

I finished a full piece of pizza before talking. "His internal organs are being healed. The wolf started on the inside and is working outward." Everyone looked at me, shocked. They hadn't expected that. "Oh, and his panther is dark brown colored, not black."

And at that, the room erupted with noisy chatter.

CHAPTER 9

Owen woke up the following afternoon.

He had never been alone during his recovery. Even when I'd been eating dinner, Mom went to sit with him. Usually, either me or Aunt Allison monitored him but everyone had taken a turn.

That afternoon, I was in my room, reading the backlog of texts on my phone from the day before. First, there were texts from Sarah and Owen—which was how I knew he'd woken up. They'd wondered why I'd been avoiding them. They didn't realize I'd seen them making out. *I'll have to deal with that later.*

Then there were the texts from Mom and Aunt Allison letting me know what to expect and asking me to join them in the backyard. Over the next several hours, other texts came in from José and Bevin, asking me for updates on life. I wasn't ready for any of it.

Nothing from Piper.

Sarah came to my door. "He's up!"

Yes, it's time. I jumped up and ran. I got to the infirmary before I realized I'd actually left my room. Whoa.

Owen sat up with a goofy smile as I approached the bed. "Hiya, sis. How long have I been out? I woke up with only Dad here, but he said I had to wait for you or Aunt Allison." His eyes shone and he sounded hopeful. "I feel good. Different, maybe?"

Smiling back at him mysteriously, I poked around at his belly and leg. I gave him a quick once over. Everything looked great. The room filled as Sarah, Mom, Dad, and Aunt Allison entered, but I didn't look up.

His happy-go-lucky smile turned into a glower. "Jade, talk to me!" he snarled.

"Okay, you look fine. All healed up. You took on a lot of injuries. I actually stitched you up a bit but pulled the stitches out this morning."

Owen gaped at me. "Stitches?"

I lightly punched his shoulder and gave him a big grin. "Yes, needles and everything. Your biggest enemy and you survived. Anyway, Sarah bit you just after three yesterday afternoon, it's currently four in the afternoon. Twenty-five hours. So, up in time for dinner. How very like you." I smiled evilly. "I, um, looked into you when you went under."

His mouth fell open, his eyes widened, and a small, "What?" escaped him.

My deep breathing calmed me. "But you were healing fine. Apparently our werebeasts heal us from the inside out, and by the time I did the probe, your internals were well on the way to healing. Your externals—" I bopped him on the shoulder again. "—were finished late this morning, and your body was ready to admit you were healed…well, now." I finished up my summary of his healing.

He just looked at me, his wide eyes brimming with so many questions.

"Jade," Mom said sternly.

"Right, okay, yeah. Your panther isn't black like mine or Sarah's."

I had to hold him down before he leapt from the bed. His smile so big I thought his head might explode in pure joy.

"Oh, my gods. It worked? It really worked? Oh, my gods, I can't believe it. I have two animals. I can become a panther? I can run with you and Sarah? I can't believe it, is this real? Are you messing with me? Holy wow, really, Jade? I'm a crazy freak like you?"

He finally took a breath, and his eyes wildly searched the room for Mom. "I have a panther in me now, really? Sarah is one of my alphas? I can't believe it."

He swung his legs over the side of the bed but didn't try to stand up. His gaze shifted from Dad to Mom to Sarah to me. "When can I try to become the panther? What happens next? Oh, my gods. Will I need Sarah to pull out the panther? Can you do it? Can Jade do it? Will I be able to do it on my own? How does this work? Mom, what do we do next?" He spoke so fast the words tumbled over each other. But his excitement infected everyone in the room. When I turned, there were matching smiles on everyone's faces.

Grabbing his shoulders, I gave him a shake to get him to hush up.

"Excited much?" I asked him with a grin.

He grinned back, his enthusiasm infusing the room.

Mom came over and gave Owen a quick hug. "Let's eat first, then we can discuss our next steps."

We brought him out to the living room. Dad had to give Owen some extra support, putting his arm under Owen's and helping him out to a couch. Although Owen was completely healed, he was still a bit weak. His body had burned through a lot of energy without fuel. He needed food.

Mom ordered Chinese food. With all the excitement, no one wanted to make dinner.

While waiting for the food, Mom got a call from Piper's mom. She walked into the dining room but I could hear her end of the conversation. There was some person in the morgue that she wanted Mom to check out. She would be the lead nurse tomorrow and could sneak Mom in. Mom didn't state why she was going in, just that she would go.

After the call, Mom left to pick up the food. I figured during dinner wouldn't be the right time to ask about the call.

Mom pointed at Owen with a chopstick. "I know you're excited, but we're going to wait until after the next full moon to have Sarah bring out your panther if you can't do it yourself. On Wednesday, we have our next training session. If you can't do it yourself then, you can wait."

Owen wilted under Mom's gaze, but he smelled of a mixture of excitement and determination, like a pine forest with a citrus overtone.

After dinner, my parents left me, Sarah, and Owen alone in the living room.

Sarah asked, "What happened between you and Piper? I feel like we haven't talked in days."

I got up and paced the living room. I studied my fingernails. After a few minutes, tears burned my eyes. I held them back. I had to let my best friend know. "Probing her, flowing into her, figuring out about her werewolf, it was one weirdness too many. After I walked her home, she froze me out. I haven't heard from her since. She's been a norm too long to be with me."

I tried to say this simply, but my voice broke and I knew they both heard it. Owen looked like he wanted to get up and hug me. At the end, I dropped onto the couch next to Sarah.

She cuddled against me. "I'm sorry, hon. She'll come around. Her life has been completely turned upside down. Give her time, she'll figure it out. I was a norm, too."

I bit my lip. *Sarah definitely knows what it's like, having your life turned upside down because of this pack.*

"I wish she had other friends to talk to. She said she would talk to her mom. Do you think her mom will understand this weirdness, or do you think she'll also see me as the ultimate freak?" I asked, continuing to study my hands.

Sarah gave me a big hug. "You aren't a freak, love." She looked me up and down. "Well, maybe a bit of a freak. But only in the best way. My parents came around and they love you *because* you're a rarity." She gave me a huge smile.

"Hear, hear," said Owen, who had been silently listening in the reclining chair across the room.

I scrunched up my nose and looked up at Sarah. "Is this a bad time to say when I got back from walking Piper home, I saw you two making out?"

They both blushed and looked away.

I turned to Owen. "What about Brooke?" There may have been some snark in my voice. I didn't like Brooke. Head of the cheerleaders and the top mean girl in Owen's class. She was nasty and had it out for me once they started dating.

"We broke up before graduation," Owen said. "She was getting frustrated that I kept going over to all of you during lunch. She said I had to choose her or you. It wasn't a hard choice."

Sarah muttered, "Brooke is such a piece of work!"

I wanted to be dumbfounded but nothing about her surprised me. Certainly, her ultimatum didn't.

Staring at him, I tried not to laugh. When I got my mirth under control, I continued, trying to be a supportive sister. "She did *not* make you choose between her and me! That doesn't even make sense. I'm your sister. Did you tell her we're family and what she said made no sense?"

"No, I just said if she really felt that way, I chose family. And I walked away. It didn't hurt as much as I thought it would." He looked up at me and smiled sadly. "I realized she didn't mean as much to me as she used to. I think with my shift from norm to werewolf, a lot of internal bits shifted, too. My need for pack and family increased. Brooke was against anything family, and that just rubbed me wrong."

I went over to him and gave him a hug. I really did like this newer version of my brother.

"So, how did this morph into you two being together?" I asked, gesturing between Sarah and Owen. "And why hide it?"

"Well," said Owen, wriggling in his seat, "you know how cool she is, and just look at her. You like girls, you should get it. Sarah's down to earth, smart, and gorgeous.

How could I go wrong?"

I just looked at him, shaking my head.

"Yeah, I get that." I turned to Sarah, who blushed, and raised my eyebrow. "It's you I'm confused about!" I smirked.

Sarah shrugged. "Can't help it. I'm young, he's cute, I'm exploring." She just laughed.

Rolling my eyes, I plopped down next to her. "Okay, fine, but why are you hiding it?" I asked again, grabbing a pillow to hold in my lap. "You're my best friend; you're supposed to tell me *everything*."

Sarah slipped her arm around me. "Well, we weren't really sure you would be okay with it. We've always been best friends and I didn't want this to be weird."

"Of course it's weird, Owen is my gross big brother." I stuck my tongue out at him, and he returned the gesture. "But that doesn't mean you shouldn't tell me what's going on in your life. We're besties. It's weird, but I'll adjust."

I rested my head on her shoulder.

Leaning his elbows on his knees, Owen's eyes narrowed. "Does this mean you're okay with us going out on dates? Because I really want to take Sarah on a nice date; no more sneaking around."

I pulled back from my friend. I wasn't sure she was breathing. "Of course!" Giving Sarah a kiss on the cheek, I smiled. "And you'll tell me all about it later."

One to two times a week in the afternoons, Sarah, Owen, and I went to the woods behind the zoo to train with Aunt Allison and other pack members. The sessions with her mainly focused on fighting in animal form. Dad scheduled them later and later in the evening so that various other pack members could join us. This week training was held on Wednesday evening, so Dad had fewer wolves to play with…er, run his fight-training simulation.

Usually, it was either one-on-one, panther versus wolf, or two-on-one fighting. We did some maneuvers two-on-two, really letting Sarah and I learn how to fight together. Panthers were normally independent, but Dad wanted us to know how to work jointly. He was very comprehensive in his methodology.

Despite his aversion to studying, Owen had jumped in on learning about panthers and how they fought. He had done almost as much studying as I had. Therefore, he ended up helping Dad figure out the best way to set up the training program for me and Sarah.

That week, Sarah, Owen, and I arrived early and moved to the private woods situated in the back. Several of the pack would be coming out for the group training, but we were there early to see if Owen could shift to his panther.

Sarah's mom stayed back at the house with Pebble so she wouldn't be alone.

Owen stripped down, got on his hands and knees, and looked up at me. "Okay, sis, what's a good panther thought?

Maybe mice? Catnip?"

I glared at him. "I don't know, just try to shift, dork!" For this first shift, I wanted to see what he could do on his own. Tips would come later.

Though he dipped his head down, I could tell he was smiling. After a few minutes, he grunted in pain and the familiar crunch and pop of bones moving filled the silence. He bowed his back in agony and his face elongated. Fur grew along his limbs. It didn't look right for a panther. Several minutes later, his grey wolf stood there yipping at us.

Dad knelt. "No worries, son, you'll figure it out. Jade did."

A few minutes later, two other pack members showed up. Luke and Tyler came over to stand near us. I could hear others coming down the path behind them.

Luke said, "I tell you, Tyler, my neighbor was pissed. She had just bought that bookbag for her daughter and it was destroyed. They were at a park playing. She'd run her daughter to the bathroom, and when they got back, shreds. She's convinced it was a wild animal."

Dad's voice rang out. "Suit up! Or...down, really. Training time."

Sarah and I moved away from where the wolves were shifting. We stripped and got down. Breathing to calm myself, I let my panther out. Knowing what would come next, I felt determined to be successful this time. Sarah and I ran into the woods. We circled the area to lay some false trails and then selected some trees to perch in.

A tree branch poked into my stomach, but I held my position. I gazed over at the next tree and saw Sarah, frozen on her branch like a black statue hidden in the leaves. I couldn't understand her ability to hold her position so steadily.

Down on the ground, three wolves approached. I gently rubbed the branch, making a sound like a leaf in the wind. Sarah's eyes snapped up to mine. I deliberately nodded three times slowly, then angled my nuzzle down to the wolves. I continued to watch her to see if she would spot them, too.

She did. Her muscles tightened but she stayed where she was.

I, too, got into a fighting position, deliberately. I needed to be careful. I couldn't make any mistakes this time. My back paw slipped and a small branch broke. The sound reverberated through the field like a gunshot.

Everyone froze.

Owen trotted out from behind a tree and stood under me, tongue lolling out, laughing at me.

I pounced at him; he darted away.

The other three wolves came at me in attack formation. Just as they got near me, Sarah dropped down on their leader, pinning him to the ground. She clamped her jaws around the head of a second wolf and I leapt forward towards the third.

Before I got there, Dad's voice rang out. "Stop!"

We all stopped and took three steps back. That was the

rule. Spinning, we headed back to the starting point.

Dad paced. "So, what went wrong?"

We're all in animal form; who's he expecting to answer?

Owen ran over and headbutted my shoulder.

I turned and swiped at his snout. I was irritated but not enough to extend my claws.

He backed off quickly.

Dad, still pacing, nodded. "Yes, Jade. You need to control yourself up in the tree. Your greatest defense is your surprise pounce. If they hear you coming, you have nothing."

I rolled my eyes. Plopping down onto my stomach, I crossed my forelegs and put my head on my paws. I wanted to be a healer, not a fighter.

Next to me, Sarah lay down to show her support.

Owen stood on her other side.

Dad shook his head. "I understand you want to support her, but she has to be able to balance up in any tree and not make a sound. She slipped. It could have been a life-or-death slip. She needs to practice that. Allison!"

Aunt Allison came from behind him with a clipboard. "Yes?"

"Please make sure you have them both practicing in branches more. I don't want a slip like that happening again."

I whined but saw Sarah nodding. Great, I was outnumbered.

CHAPTER 10

The following Saturday, I sat out in the backyard watching Pebble play. Mom came and settled beside me on the bench. She held a plate with crackers, cheese, and sausage for us to share.

I selected a few slices of cheese and sausage and made a sandwich. Pebble ran over and grabbed some cheese before running back into the yard. We had gotten her a kiddy pool and bubbles. She was having a blast.

I leaned back, tracking the sun slowly making its way up over the lilac bushes that lined the back of the yard. Their scent perfumed the air. I relaxed and picked more ingredients to make another bite-sized sandwich.

Once the plate was empty and the sun reached the clouds, I turned to Mom. "What did Piper's mom want the other day?"

"You heard that?"

I tapped my ear. "Yep. Two animals, wicked sharp hearing."

She nodded. "You know, you're fifteen. It's adult business."

My head rolled, hitting the back of the bench. I shut my eyes and tried to think calm thoughts. "I know. Tell me anyway."

"Jade. This really isn't anything you need to worry about."

I sighed. "You went to the morgue. That means there's a dead person. She wanted you to go, but that isn't quite kosher, so she had to sneak you in. That's why it mattered she was lead nurse that day. The only reason she would call you in is if the dead guy looked like he was killed by a wild animal…or a rogue wolf. Stop me if I'm wrong…"

The bench creaked. I wasn't ready to open my eyes yet. Mom placed her hand on mine. "You know, I sometimes wish you weren't so smart."

She stayed silent for several minutes. We sat, her hand on mine, with the sounds of Pebble's laughter as a background song. Finally, she squeezed my hand as she let out a gust of breath. "I think it was a wolf." I opened my eyes and gazed up at her. "There were so many scents in the room and on him from the examination, it was impossible to pull any smells from him. But his wounds were similar to other attacks I've seen."

"Should we be worried?"

"I don't think so. The body was found outside of town, not that close."

"Do they know who the person was?"

"No, it was a homeless man. I guess he disappeared while panhandling for money a couple days ago. Besides that, we don't really know."

Pebble let out a squeal that made me flinch. I sat up as she ran and leapt into the pool, splashing water everywhere. I turned to Mom to ask a question, but seeing her face soften, I dropped the subject. She needed this time as much as Pebble did.

The next day, we had the pack meeting.

The meeting was going to be long, boring, and long. I didn't want to attend but I had no choice. I doubly didn't have a choice; I was pack and the meeting was partially about me…again.

Piper would probably be coming. If she came, she'd be in the basement with the kiddos. If I saw her, it would be the first time in a week.

I took Pebble to the meeting room early so we could stake out a place and observe the incoming pack members. *That's my reason: to find a good seat early—definitely not to hide.*

We sat in the front across from the door. That way we

weren't near any walkways and no one would have a reason to pass near us or look too closely. No one had been told about Pebble. The story was too long to explain individually, and we'd only been back from Illinois for a week.

As people entered, I told Pebble who they were and why she didn't have to worry about them. These were the pack members and they would all become important people in her life.

The first to arrive was Tanner. "Hey, Jade, how's summer treating you? Who's this?"

"Summer has been great. Dad's training program, you know." That brought a sympathetic smirk. "This is Pebble."

He opened his mouth to say more, but Aunt Allison walked in, saw me, saw Pebble, and came over to sit near us. Jackson, her husband, came in and sat behind us as well. Uncle Jackson was Mom's brother.

"Hi, Uncle Jackson, Aunt Allison."

Pebble's eyes got big, digesting this information. She whispered the word 'uncle' as if she were getting a feel for how it felt and tasted in her mouth. She had met Aunt Allison the day Owen had been bitten, but not Uncle Jackson.

"Hey, squirt," Uncle Jackson said, "I hear you're getting into all sorts of trouble again."

I smiled. *Here are two of my biggest supporters. I couldn't get into trouble that they wouldn't help me out of.*

"Well, you know me, trying to keep all you old fogies on your toes," I teased.

He ruffled my hair, chuckling. "Good for you."

Pebble looked up at me, face contorted in confusion. Her brows had come together above her eyes. I smiled back at her encouragingly.

Aunt Allison looked at her and then to her husband. "This is Pebble. I met her the other day; she's lovely."

"Hi, Pebble, remember me from the other day? I'm your Aunt Allison."

"The best aunt you could ever want," I added helpfully.

Pebble offered Aunt Allison a small smile and wave before hiding her face in my side.

Slowly, the rest of the room filled. Some people looked over at us quizzically, but most ignored our corner of the room. Everyone was more curious about the sudden need for a meeting than about us.

"Hi, everyone," Mom began. She explained about Owen and Sarah trying to get dual animals. I shot Owen a glance and he ducked his head as the pack made sounds of exasperation and incredulity at their actions.

Mom quieted the group with an alpha glare. "It was determined Owen had the potential for a panther, so we gave him another chance…"

I tuned Mom out as she continued the story. The pitch of the room rose and fell as she relayed the events. Some vibrated with questions but one eyebrow from Mom kept the room in line as she continued.

"In the end, we have determined Owen has a panther."

There was a collective gasp in the room.

"Yes, Clare," she called. Usually, people didn't raise their hand.

"Has he transformed into a panther?"

Mom tilted her head. "Excellent question; for the next part of the meeting, I would like Jade to come up."

I froze in my seat and stared at her.

"Yes, Jade, this part is your story, not mine."

I squeezed Pebble's hand and slowly stood. As I made my way towards the stage, Aunt Allison and Owen moved to sit with Pebble so she wouldn't be alone.

On stage, I took a calming breath and surveyed the crowd. After a second breath, I answered Clare's question. "Well, no, Owen hasn't transformed into a panther yet."

"Then how was it determined?" Tanner asked, giving me a quizzical look.

In for a penny and all that. I closed my eyes, centered myself, and then opened them. I slowly gazed at everyone in the room. "It seems I can determine a person's wereanimal as well as their potential for one with touch." I went on to explain how we believed I had discovered Owen's healed broken arm in a similar fashion.

"What are you talking about?" Andy asked, looking stunned. "You can heal by the placing of hands?"

"No, not heal, at least not that I've done yet, only diagnose. I guess it's more like I can see inside you, sort of. That isn't quite it, I just don't know the right words." I was losing the crowd.

Their stares were a range of expressions, from scared to intrigued. It felt like Piper all over again.

The meeting kept going. I finished my part as quickly as I could, and let Mom take over to discuss Pebble. Once we got to that part, I didn't pay much attention. I knew the story.

Near the end of the meeting, Dad took over. "I've been monitoring the news. There have been reports of missing pets in the area. I would like everyone to be vigilant and keep me informed of what you hear, both missing animals and found. At the moment, this may be nothing, but I don't like surprises."

Once the pack had their fill about Pebble, Clare asked if I could give a demonstration of my new skill once the meeting was over. I agreed, and things wrapped up quickly.

I immediately went and found José and Bevin and gave them both huge hugs. It had been a while since I'd seen either of them. I also introduced them to Pebble.

"Okay, Jade," Clare said, "I was hoping you could do a demonstration with José."

I looked at her and then at José. "Ummm," I said, intellectually. "Yeah, sure. Let me tell him about what I can do first, though. Don't want to freak him out and lose another friend." That last was said under my breath, but Sarah heard it anyway and gave my arm a squeeze.

Once José understood what he was agreeing to, his smile grew and the scent of citrus came from him with his excitement. "Chica, I can finally know, one way or another. This is fantastic; one less worry before heading off to University."

We sat in chairs facing each other and I took his hands. I decided I didn't need to look into his eyes , so I closed my eyes.

Panther came to the front, ready to do my bidding. She seemed to ask again if I wanted her to go investigate.

Yes, please.

José shivered as I entered him. The first thing I noticed was that he was in great shape. I had done this with Piper and Owen, both of whom had been hurting— only a headache for Piper, but there was still pain.

José didn't have pain. *Okay, focus. Is there a seed of a werewolf?*

I searched. I was getting a bit better at knowing where to look.

Is that why José has no injuries? Is his wolf keeping him this healthy? Or is he just naturally really healthy?

I sniffed around and saw him. It wasn't a seed. I trotted over and nosed a gorgeous red wolf who backed away, not yet ready to interact with us.

Why haven't you come out to play, friend? He bowed his head, and I could almost feel him telling me it wasn't time yet. Two or three more moons.

That shocked me so much my head shot up and I just

looked at him, the human him. José.

"What?" José asked. "It worked right? I mean, I felt you in there. It was like a warm stream flowing through me. Weird. Not bad, just weird."

I just gaped at him for a minute, unable to speak.

Finally, I turned my head and sought my brother. "Um, Owen, I need you for a sec." Owen came over. "Sit, I need to do a test, and you're my best test dummy."

He laughed at me, but José got up and Owen sat.

I grabbed his hand and repeated the process. Once I gave permission and my panther flowed in, I found both animals in him. I was there in the form of the panther, but I nosed the wolf and said *hi*.

The wolf cocked his head and said hi back.

Freezing, I stared at the panther, and asked, *Are you ready to see the world?*

He said, *Soon.*

Shocked, I wasn't sure what to do.

I backed out of Owen a bit more slowly. Once we completely separated, my head spun and I almost passed out.

"Crap. Someone get Jade some water and food."

The next thing I knew, I was lying down on the couch with my head on Owen's lap and he was forcing me to drink something. Then eat something. I finally swatted his hand away and tried to sit up.

"Stop it, sis. The last time you sat up on your own, you passed out. At least let me help you up."

"What happened?" I asked.

"Best guess, whatever it is you're doing takes a ton out of you. Doing it twice in a row was a real idiot move. Was it worth it?"

My brain felt fuzzy. "Yeah," I managed to say, before slumping over onto his shoulder. I drank a protein shake. *Ah, drink and calories in one, brilliant.*

"Okay, Jade," Clare said, "tell us what was worth seeing you turn white as a ghost and faint."

I whipped my head around until I found Dad. "When I'm in there, I can speak to the person's animal."

Dad's eyes got wide.

I continued, "José's wolf—not a seed, a beautiful red wolf—said two or three more months. Owen's wolf said hi, and his panther said he would be ready to come out soon."

At that, the room erupted in animated conversations. I looked up at Owen and smiled at him mischievously. Everyone would be distracted long enough that we could sneak off to the kitchen for real food. He helped me up and we were off.

Owen and I sat in the kitchen eating cookies when Helen, Piper's mom, joined us. "Jade, before we head home, do you have a few minutes?" She glanced at Owen and cleared her throat.

"Sure." I gave my brother a look.

"I can take a hint." Owen grabbed a few cookies and left the kitchen.

Helen sat on one of the island stools. "I just wanted you to know that I think all these skills you're developing are wonderful." She chose a cookie from a plate on the counter. "I know Piper has been acting odd. She's never had friends." She smiled at me warmly. "Or a girlfriend. But I think if you give her a few more days, she'll get her head on straight…or gayly correct, as you girls would say." Her smile brightened.

She took a bite of the cookie and looked at it appreciatively as she chewed and swallowed. "Practice this skill. See how far you can go with it. Remember, you aren't a freak, you're an amazing young lady with new abilities. Piper knows this, too."

She took a few more cookies, gave me a one-armed hug, and left.

I stared at the crumbs on the empty plate as I ate the last cookie. Although they were gone, Helen's words gave me hope.

CHAPTER 11

The morning after the big pack meeting Owen was up before me. Padding into the kitchen for coffee, I found him eating cereal. I grabbed a bowl and sat down next to him. We sat in silence eating, and drinking coffee.

Finally, I squinted at him, checked my watch, and gave him a quizzical look.

He shrugged. "Cat?"

I nodded, my hopes for a quiet, uneventful day slipping away. Mom came in from the living room where she had been reading a book.

Owen's head snapped up. "I want to try again."

We both stared at him. As I finished my bowl of cereal, Mom poured herself some coffee. She leaned against the counter, mug in hand and stared at him, eyebrow raised.

Placing my mug down, I grumbled. "I don't think Sarah is coming over today."

"I know; I just want to try," he persisted.

He's been patient for over a week. I'm surprised he waited this long. Apparently it's been harder on him than we all knew.

I shrugged and went back to breakfast.

Mom looked at him, frowning slightly as if considering the matter.

Dad's voice came from his bedroom down the back hallway. "If it doesn't work today…" He joined us in the kitchen and added, "…I think you should wait to try again when we're all at Aunt Allison's. You'll need to have Sarah there to help you."

Owen nodded, looking a bit stricken. After breakfast, we went outside and Owen got into position on his hands and knees. He stared at me. "What should I do?"

He was so nervous—serious, but nervous. It filled the backyard like the sweet scent at a carnival.

Last time, I didn't give him any tips, letting him get the feel of the challenge for himself. Knowing how hard the struggle was, I had to do more this time. "I focus on my hand, what it feels like to be a wolf…but you've never been a panther, so that may not help. I also send my panther to sleep, but you don't feel your animals the way I do, so I'm not really sure."

I paced the yard, thinking, moving my hands in time with my thoughts. "I guess, imagine the panther inside you. Picture your hand as a dark brown panther paw." I grimaced. *That's such lame advice.* "Breathe and relax…you know, mindful meditation?"

Owen nodded as he took it all in and then glared when I mentioned the last bit. Shrugging, I offered him a sheepish smile.

He sighed. "Okay." Dropping his head, he began to breathe slowly.

"Jade," Mom said, "move away. I want to see if he can do this by himself. No helping him."

My pacing had brought me close. I backed away to where Mom and Dad stood watching. Owen was alone, on his hands and knees, trying to relax, and stressed at the same time. He smelled of both animals. Realizing my nails pressed into my palms, I shook out my hands. I was getting anxious for him.

Dad came over and slid his arm around me. "Jade, you can't help him, and your stress won't help either. If you can't be objective, you will have to go inside."

Pursing my lips, I closed my eyes and found my center. *Calm.* I opened my eyes; Owen hadn't moved. He panted heavily and the wolf scent saturated the backyard, overwhelming the scent of his panther. I made a face. *Not good.* A tension in the air signaled the start of his change.

It flowed over him quickly and soon a gray wolf hunkered in the grass, tail between his legs. He whined, discouraged.

"I'm sorry, Owen," Mom said, "I think we should start with bringing your panther out forcibly so that you get the feel. Then we can work on you doing it alone. Remember, it took Jade a few months to get her wolf form out on her own, and we still aren't sure how stable that process is. Go off and run for a bit. I'll make some pancakes for you."

Eyes downcast and sad, but releasing the woody scent of determination, he ran. Watching him, I felt bad for him. I wanted him to learn to find his panther, but part of me felt vindicated in how hard it had been for me to find my wolf.

On Wednesday, we all met at Aunt Allison's for panther training. Sarah knew about the failed attempt. After discussing what we were going to do, Sarah pulled the panther out of Owen. The process went slowly since it was new for both of them. It looked painful, but once it was done, he was beautiful, and dark brown in color.

Sarah knelt next to him, petting him. "I know that was painful, but being able to do that was really cool."

He nuzzled her, licking her face.

I laughed at her enthusiasm, then shook my head. "Gods above, get a room. No one wants to see you two flirt."

Owen chuffed and trotted off. Sarah and I transformed.

The three of us ran for a few hours. For Owen's first transformation into a panther, there wasn't going to be any training, just running and playing; today was about Owen learning his new form. He climbed trees and practiced some mock-fighting, trying to pounce on us. We showed him how to leap, and he managed a good eleven feet. Swimming was a new adventure. We found some small game as we ran around, so we did ingest some calories.

We took the back way through the woods between the zoo and home, having agreed to take the time to run home. Aunt Allison would bring our clothes by the house. We only needed to cross one road; recalling Owen's accident last year, this time we were extremely careful.

When we arrived, I found a quiet spot apart from Sarah and Owen. They changed to human and then got dressed, laughing together about all the fun we'd had as panthers.

Suddenly, I felt their eyes on me. They probably wondered why I hadn't transformed, but I ignored them. I stared at my paw and pictured my wolf. I shut my eyes and imagined my wolf's paw and how it felt to have those tiny paws with the long claws churning up the dirt as I ran. I wasn't sure if this would work, or if I really wanted it to work, but today was the day for new things.

Pain lanced through me like I had never experienced before. It felt like my animals were at war and my body was the battlefield. They were tearing me apart from the inside out. I let out a yowl.

Agony was all I knew. My muscles ripped apart and reformed. My bones reshaped. I wondered if my body had found its way into a garbage disposal, over, and over again. My vision darkened.

No! Passing out is not *an option. I must stay awake.* However, it was almost too much for my mind to comprehend.

"Jade!"

Was that Sarah's voice? But there was too much pain. Wolf, I had to focus on wolf.

It was too late to stop what I had started. My body shifted.

The scent of my alphas settled around me. They must have come from the house, but no one came close. They couldn't help me; no one could help me. I'd done this to myself. The pressure of their eyes on me was one more thing I experienced…one more pain.

Did I smell cayenne? Was that disgust?

Or was it the deeper spice of horrified?

Did I smell a sweeter scent of vanilla? Was that fascination?

I closed my eyes to focus on me and what I had done to myself.

No, don't think about your audience, Jade.

Disassociate from the soul-crushing agony. If you're distracted, only the gods know what will happen. Focus on that damn wolf's paw!

My bones cracked, the sound sickening in my ears. My body parts moved, grinding in unnatural patterns. My fur receded and grew in some places at the same time. When the movement was over, I lay there panting. So. Much. Pain. The echo of it remained afterwards.

I had no idea what I had done to myself.

"Holy hell, Jade, what have you done?" Sarah asked.

What had I done? Did it work? Am I a creature from nightmares?

Owen whooped in the background.

Mom's voice sounded stern, but I felt the concern under her anger. "Jade, I don't know if I should ground you, help you, or commend you."

I was too numb to understand what she was talking about. I couldn't even think anymore.

"I don't know if you want me to train this or not. She's too out of it to be of any use," Dad said, his voice shaky. *Was he worried about me?*

"If this is going to be useful, it'll have to be trained," Mom declared.

I trembled. I was lying on the ground. I got up slowly, panting.

Mom grabbed a bucket of water and brought it to me. *She must be really concerned; normally she sends animals to the lake.* I lapped up some water, then moved over to the doors to check myself out in the reflection. Green eyes in a black wolf face stared back at me.

I was a wolf.

I had gotten to wolf on my own. I lifted my ears and panted, quivering with joy. Yes! I leaped up and yipped—a wolf laugh.

Wait, I've done that before. No, I've managed to get to wolf from panther.

I trotted over to Owen. I reared up, and he gave me a form of a high-five. Everyone else just grumbled at us.

Mom rolled her eyes. "When you can, become girl-Jade again so we can eat and talk." She turned and walked away. I heard her mumble, "Teenagers," under her breath.

"That was cool," Owen said. "It looked freaky as hell, though; a panther turning into a wolf. Holy hell, that was freaky. Did it hurt as much as it seemed like it did?"

"Warn a girl next time, and yes, she was in a *lot* of pain. As her alpha, I can tell you: it was intense," Sarah said, kneeling beside me to give me a wolf-hug. "Don't you ever scare me like that again, you hear?"

I gave a small yip to let her know I heard her.

Unable to turn back to human yet—it was too soon—I ran into the woods, ate a rabbit, and then ran to the lake for a swim. It was late by the time I returned home. Mom was the only one up. She looked tired sitting at the table drinking her glass of wine. "Is it viable?"

"I don't know. It hurt, like, more than anything I've ever felt hurt."

"Well, we can see if practice helps. If it's that painful every time, then it won't be useful to us. The transformation was really slow, too. I don't know if you realize it, but that was the slowest change you've had to date."

I gaped. *I guess that makes sense. It was also the most painful transformation I've ever had.*

Two days later, Piper sent me a text.

Hey. Can we talk?

I read it a few times. Both before and after exercise drills.

It took a day to sort through my thoughts. Was this a good thing or a bad thing? Did she want to break up with me? *'Can we talk' is never a good sign, right?* After another day of psyching myself out, I finally picked up my phone.

Yeah, I'd like that.

The reply came back quickly. Good.

Look, I'm sorry. I was dumb. Can we go for a walk on the path by the pack house?

Dumbfounded, I gaped at the phone for a few seconds but then we arranged to meet. Thirty minutes later, we were walking south on the bike path on opposite sides with a couple of feet between us. Almost like strangers. It hurt, but I needed the space to protect myself, just in case.

After a few minutes of silence, Piper sighed. "I'm sorry. I shouldn't have freaked out. I don't know why I did. It's just..." She waved her hands.

Watching my feet, I continued to walk. I wouldn't help her with this.

She stopped, forcing me to halt as well. "Will you look at me? This is hard."

I froze. Clenching and releasing my hands, I tried to get a hold of myself. I had no calm, not for either of us. I spoke slowly and quietly. "You weren't made out to be a freak by your girlfriend. A person who should be there for you."

I shook my hands out, finally facing her.

Piper's eyes misted but she stood tall. In this, she was not backing down. "I know. As soon as you turned away, I wanted to race after you, but it was too late. Then I thought you probably hated me for how I acted. I didn't know what to do. The only friends I have are your friends. I tried talking to my mom, but parents are not the best for this." She sighed and looked up at the sky. "I am so sorry for messing this up so badly, Jade. Everything in my world has changed so much, but you're the best part of it. Please."

Closing my eyes, I took in her words along with her scent. A honeydew lost scent wafted from her, blending with the earthy scent of loneliness. *Could it be—has she missed me as much as I've missed her?* I bit my lower lip. Opening my eyes, I saw a tear trailing down her cheek. Suddenly, I wanted to take her in my arms and soothe away her loneliness. "Piper." I shook my head and she took a step back. Lifting my hand to her, I quirked half a smile. "No, I mean, don't cry. I've missed you. Every day, I've missed you."

Her eyes widened. "Really?"

I nodded. Slowly, I approached her and took her hands.

"Yes, really." I leaned down and our lips met. My hands rubbed up her arms as hers gripped my hips. Something in me which had been misaligned clicked back into place. After what seemed like forever or no time at all, we broke apart and I smiled at her.

Gently, I held her right hand in my left and we continued our walk, catching up on things we'd missed over the last few weeks.

CHAPTER 12

Pebble's reluctance to shift at her first full moon weighed heavy on me. I knelt in front of her. "What's up, hon? You did it for us once already."

She crossed her arms over her chest. "It hurts."

She had an earthy, sweet scent; she was sad and scared. I knew she hid her real reason for not wanting to shift, but she had a closed-off expression and I didn't want to push her. I rubbed my hands up and down her arms. "I know it hurts. But it's important to not fight the change. If you do fight it, sweety, you'll change anyway---—and then it could happen when you're alone. And it will hurt more."

Her chin hit her chest and she sniffled. "But, Jade, I don't want to be a werewolf. I want to stay here with the other kids." Her breathing roughened.

"I know, love, but this is really important." I lifted her chin so that she stared me in the eyes. I tapped her nose. Her nerves were still raw. Taking a deep breath, I released my epsilon calm. Her eyes widened and her breathing evened out.

A tear made its way down Pebble's cheek. She sighed and then nodded at me. "Okay, Jade, I'll do it. Will you stay with me?"

"Of course."

I led her out to the backyard, where Mom and I stayed with her behind the privacy wall. Her transformation was as slow and painful as the last time. Once she was furry, she seemed to calm completely and her mood improved. It was cute how much her wolf matched Owen's wolf.

She pranced around the backyard while Owen and I transformed into our wolves. Owen immediately ran up to her to sniff her butt. With a yipping wolf laugh, she chased him and returned the favor. We played together for about an hour. Afterwards, we climbed up into the treehouse to wait for the rest of the pack. Pebble didn't like watching others change, so she hid under the blankets and I curled up around her, big spoon to her little spoon.

During the run, I stayed with her. Her scent turned sour; she was overwhelmed.

The pack didn't bring down anything big, only rabbits and small rodents. Pebble didn't seem interested in eating. She tucked her tail between her back legs and she kept backing away from the others. Her sweet fear-scent and reluctance distracted the rest of the pack. All the wolves seemed on edge during the run.

I need to take her home. I ran to Mom and signaled I was taking Pebble back. Once home, we climbed up into the treehouse and curled up together. Within a few minutes, she was asleep, safe with me. I sat with her as the night went by, listening and watching for the others to return.

Though the pull to transform was almost overwhelming the first night of the full moon, there wasn't an absolute need to run and hunt. Running simply felt good on muscles and bones newly transformed.

The next morning, I woke early, separated myself from Pebble and Owen, who had joined us after he'd finished his run, grabbed my robe, and headed in. The heavenly scent of coffee filled the empty kitchen and I poured myself a mug. Grabbing a muffin, I sat. A couple minutes later, Pebble came in, opened the fridge, grabbed a juice box, and came over to sit by me. Stretching, she grabbed a banana.

After taking a sip of coffee, I placed it down on the table and slid an arm around her shoulders. "Can you tell me what made you sad last night?"

She tensed and shook her head.

Tearing off a piece of blueberry muffin, I popped it into

my mouth and considered her. The earthy, sad scent was back. "When we ran that first time, you weren't sad, but last night you were."

She pulled the straw off the juice box and maneuvered it into the box. After taking a sip, she turned her sad eyes up to me. "Why do wolves have to be so mean?"

Heart breaking, I tightened my arm around her. "Oh, sweety, they don't."

Her brow furrowed. "But they do. All those other animals…they didn't deserve it."

Licking my lips, I made a decision I hoped my parents agreed with. "If you want, I'm sure you could run earlier, and stay home during the pack run."

Her eyes shifted down to her hands as if she were in trouble, then she nodded quickly. Leaning over, I gave her a hug. "I bet the kiddos will hang out with you all night."

Gazing up at me, her scent shifted to a citrusy hope. "You really think so?"

Smiling wide, I nodded back. "I do."

The alphas officially decided that, for future runs, it would be easier on Pebble to transform earlier in the day, have a quick run, and then sleep in the treehouse while the rest of us ran as a pack. She was a werewolf, but she was also a five-year-old girl.

One day, she would be older and ready for the full run and hunt, but for now she didn't have to hunt cute animals. While she was awake, the older kiddos would take turns sitting with her until she fell asleep.

Over the next month, Owen learned to control which wereanimal he transformed into. His control was faster than mine. He had several people helping him figure out how to do it. For him, the wolf was much easier, but he did learn to get to panther as well.

Sarah and I watched as Owen shifted. "So, Sarah, when are you getting a wolf?"

She snorted. "Well…"

We both winced as Owen grunted at a painful spot in the slower shift of his panther transformation. Forcing my focus to Sarah, I said, "Still on the fence?"

She shrugged, "Yeah. I'm happy with what I have. I don't know if the thrill of having two animals is just Owen's excitement when the two of us talk, or something I want."

That made sense. Owen's enthusiasm could be infectious.

As for the rest of the pack, so far everyone else was happy being a single wereanimal: a werewolf. One animal was more than enough to deal with. I didn't disagree with them.

The next few weeks flew by. Pebble acclimated to life at the pack house, and the pack got used to seeing her running around. Dad included her in the training, focusing on controlling her wolf and learning who she could and couldn't tell about werewolves and the pack.

Mom and Dad decided on homeschooling. Most of the pack members could take a day or two a month off, which allowed for us to set up a schedule for her learning.

Late in August, Owen and José left for college to move into the dorms. Classes wouldn't start until after Labor Day, so they both came home for Labor Day weekend. My family decided to have a small barbecue with immediate family and friends. Other pack members could come, but most decided to do their own thing.

Sarah came through the door holding a bowl covered in Saran wrap. "My parents are taking the day to themselves. Are Piper and her family coming?"

I looked over. "What's in the bowl? And no. They have some tradition with travel and Labor Day. Bevin and his family, José and his family, and Owen are coming. So, not that small of a get-together. Half the pack?"

"Yeah, you guys don't really do 'small'. And potato salad."

My belly rumbled and my mouth watered. Sarah's dad made great potato salad.

José came in a few minutes behind Sarah. "My mom is heading around back. She said Dad is tired of spending time with Owen."

"I bet," I agreed. Alejandro and Owen had been driving back and forth together as Owen moved his stuff down to campus.

"I heard that!" Owen bellowed from his room.

We all grabbed the side dishes from the kitchen and headed to the backyard.

Bevin showed up a few minutes later. "My mom and sisters went to my aunt's, so it's just me and Dad. How are the dorms?"

Owen just shook his head. "Having two animals means my nose is more sensitive. The dorms stink, literally."

I laughed. "Finally, I'm not the only one complaining."

Dad came out wearing an apron that read, 'Have fire, will burn!' He waggled his brows at us. "Food's ready."

Bevin jumped up. "Great, I'm starved." Bevin was in the process of transitioning from female to male. Because of the testosterone injections, he tended to have a huge appetite.

I followed, as did the rest of the table. After we ate, we played some games. I went to get some water, and José followed me. "Jade, I'm feeling sick. I may head back to the dorms soon." I touched his forehead. He was burning up.

"Hold up, can I check something?"

He backed up a step. "You want to do that thing again? Do you think it's time?"

I shook my head and waved my hands. "I don't know, that's why I was going to check. Maybe."

He doubled over, obviously in pain. "Jade, I'm going to be sick."

"Mom!" I yelled.

Mom ran over and sniffed the air. I didn't know what she smelled, but I leaned in and, taking in a breath, José smelled wild. Her eyes glowed as her alpha side came forward, and her face grew very serious. "Go get your dad."

"Mama," José groaned. "I want my mama."

I ran. When I found Dad, I told him Mom needed him

right away. I ran to get Clare, José's mom, to let her know he needed her. I followed her back to José.

When I got there, he'd already begun the shift. After a few minutes, a huge red wolf stood amongst us. He looked angry and lunged at Dad. Dad grabbed his snout. José snarled low in his throat. Suddenly, he shook his head and his vision seemed to clear. He tucked his tail and backed up with a whine.

Clare dropped down in front of him and gave him a big hug. He whimpered and licked her face, his tail wagging.

Mom grabbed his muzzle and stared him in the eyes. It took a couple minutes, but José finally lowered his eyes. He was now part of the pack and Mom was his alpha. Mom nodded. "Go, run, then return."

And he was off.

I was thrilled José's entrance into the world of werewolves happened when he was with family and not in the dorms. He had been terrified that it would happen right at the start of such a big new chapter of his life, perhaps when he was all alone.

At least his first shift happened in a safe place.

When he returned, he shifted to human and got dressed. I found him sitting at a table with a plate of food. His head rested in his hands.

"You okay?"

"Not really. This isn't how I wanted to start college."

I sat next to him, close enough for our shoulders to

touch. "I know. You could live at home and commute for the first few weeks."

"No, that would be even weirder."

"Then call. I know how hard this all is. You helped me; let me—and the rest of us—help you."

He smiled down at his plate. "Bevin said the same thing. We have a standing date to talk every night or two."

Grinning, I bumped shoulders with him. "Good. Take him up on it. I may be epsilon, but he's always been my rock. Let him be yours, too."

CHAPTER 13

After Labor Day weekend, school started for the rest of us.

Sarah and I approached the door slowly. It felt like it did the first day after spring break. The first day at school as werepanthers. Then, I had been Sarah's helper; today she was mine.

"It will be okay, Jade, you survived the end of sophomore year."

A group of four boys walked by. My eyes watered. Spending the summer with the pack, I forgot what it was like being in a crowd. Not only did I have to remember how to block all the scents coming in, but also the emotions.

I gulped. "I don't know, Sarah. I think it's gotten worse."

"Boxes, or whatever…" She had compassion in her voice, but her eyes danced.

Mom taught all the kiddos basic meditation techniques. Her favorite was to separate emotions, and I guess scents, into boxes to deal with later.

I took a deep breath—and instantly regretted it. Why did meditation always start with breathing? Coughing, I tried to slow myself down. I inhaled through my mouth and closed my eyes. I squished all the horrid boy-smells into one box. I smashed the fake, flowery perfumes floating nearby into another. Finding an incinerator in the back of my mind, *bam, fire, done. I don't need any of that for later. I opened my eyes.*

Narrowing her eyes, Sarah watched me. "Better?"

Ready to head to the lockers, I nodded.

Sarah wore an evil grin. "You know, being your alpha, that was an interesting roller-coaster you just took me on." She swung her arm around my waist and ushered me inside, where we found Bevin waiting by our lockers. A senior this year, he was a year ahead of Sarah and me.

After hugs of greeting and putting things away, we all headed to our first period classes. Last semester, Sarah and I shared first period. This semester, she and I went different directions. However, Bevin was in first period AP biology with me.

"Hi, Jade!" Tiffany all but yelled to be heard over the noise in the hallway. She was a popular girl everyone knew. I was pretty sure she was friends with Brooke, so I hadn't expected her to be talking to me. Her perfume was so thick my eyes watered, and I sneezed. *Okay, maybe I'm not as prepared as I'd hoped. Work in progress.*

"Hi, Tiffany. Have a good summer?"

"I'm running for class president and wanted to give you my platform." She handed me a piece of perfumed paper and walked off. *Great.* I was gone from her notice as quickly as that.

Quickly, I read the paper. I snorted. *Nothing special.*

Bevin grabbed it from me. Scanning it, he wrinkled his nose. "Wow, she put in a lot of effort to basically say nothing." He dropped it in the recycling bin as we made our way into AP bio.

First and second periods were okay, but three kids in third period had body spray on so thick, my head pounded with a migraine. I kept sneezing and finally asked if I could move. How had I gotten acclimated to this last year?

Things evened out as the day continued. In history, the last class of the day, the teacher wanted everyone to get to know each other. Recently graduated from college, she was new and had energy to spare; she didn't seem to care that everyone in the room already knew each other. Digging through my bag for my notebook, I let the class sort themselves out. I didn't care who I ended up with. I knew everyone anyway.

"Hi, we're the last two left. I guess that means we're partnered up."

Not recognizing the voice, and tearing up in response to the over abundance of cologne, I stared into the brown eyes of a short, nondescript boy with mousy brown hair. He was about Piper's height and must have been new because I had no idea who he was.

"Ah, yeah, sure, hi." I dabbed my eyes with a tissue. "Sorry, allergies. I'm Jade, and you are?"

He ducked his head as if embarrassed. "I'm Cody. I'm new here."

Smiling, I waved to the desk next to mine. "Welcome to our fine establishment. I hope you're better at history than I am. I can't wait to see what we're supposed to do in this very exciting assignment." He snorted at my deadpan voice.

We spent the next thirty minutes answering a few personal questions: do you have a pet, what is your favorite class, color, place to visit. Each pair presented to the class. Then we finally started learning about history.

The next day at lunch, Cody approached my group. "Hi, Jade, I don't really know anyone here, and you seemed cool in history class yesterday. I know this seems weird, but I wondered if you minded if I joined you."

Speak of the devil; I'd only just told them about history class and the new kid. *We may be weird, but we're mostly friendly. Having him join us will cut down on what we can discuss, but we all understand feeling left out.*

"Everyone, this is Cody. We have history together, and his favorite color is orange." Searching the faces of my friends, I frowned when they all gave noncommittal shrugs. We all shared an unspoken conversation. Cody slouched, waiting. His hair threatened to fall over his eyes like a shield. Like Piper, it seemed as if he could blend in anywhere. He also wore too much body spray. Then again, I thought everyone did. I was still fighting the third period perfume migraine. I sneezed and shook my head with the force of it.

He took a steadying breath and continued. "I know approaching an established group of friends is strange." Flipping his hair from his eyes, he turned to me. "But I was hoping, since we seemed to get along yesterday in class..." He gave a wan smile. "You seemed like the least weird person around here."

My brow furrowed in confusion. Then I raised an eyebrow; I had learned this action well from Mom. "Least weird. Now I know you're just making things up."

He laughed. "Fair, but we did have fun yesterday."

I nodded. "True, and you saved me from having to 'meet' someone I've known for most of my life." I narrowed my eyes, pretending as if we hadn't already decided.

"Sure," said Sarah, the most outgoing of us, before I could torture him more. "Always room for another weirdo." She smiled welcomingly.

"There's a first for everything," Bevin mumbled low

enough that only Sarah and I could hear him.

After a brief hesitation, Cody slipped in next to Bevin and smiled hopefully.

Bevin nodded in greeting. "Nice to meet you, Cody. I'm Bevin, that's Sarah, and Piper, the really quiet one next to Jade. If it's going to freak you out, Jade and Piper are a couple."

Piper blushed and I laughed loud enough to be heard over the clatter of the lunchroom. It was just so unexpected, having to explain to a stranger. Piper and I sat together and often held hands and kissed so if it was going to freak him out, better to find out now.

That's one way to welcome someone into our group. Bevin, for his part, was not wearing his normal plaid button-down shirt that he loved so much. Today he sported a black long-sleeved shirt. On the front, in rainbow letters, were G.S.A. It stood for Gay/Straight Alliance, one of the clubs he went to. Freshman year, when he was learning his way around the school, José introduced him to the club. They attended together until José graduated.

Cody chuckled as well. He gazed off into space for a minute as if making a decision, and then said, "Since I tend to like guys, I think it would be pretty hypocritical of me to be against two ladies dating."

I smiled in approval. *Okay, this might work.*

His scent changed. It was mixed, a combination of caution and hope. I could only catch it because the emotion was strong enough to emote over the scents he wore, otherwise he tended to be a dead space for my nose.

I returned my attention to my lunch.

"Put you in your place quickly," Sarah said to Bevin.

Oh, this is going to be fun.

"So, Cody, where are you from?" Bevin asked while staring intently at his food.

"I'm from Illinois. My dad and I just moved up for his job." Cody gave us all small smiles between bites of his pizza and sips of his chocolate milk.

"What does he do?" Bevin asked, turning slightly towards him.

"He's an attorney at a law firm. His firm's opening up a new branch in the greater Madison area, and we were one of the families who got to relocate up here. Hooray. Every kid's dream to move from the greater Chicagoland area to farmland, no?" His sarcasm was not lost on any of us. But he followed his statement up with a warm smile.

"I don't know," said Bevin, sounding a bit defensive. "This area isn't that bad. You could've done worse. At least the people around here are nice. Not to mention, having fresh air, trees, and nature can be a benefit." There was an edge to that last bit.

"We'll see," Cody said, turning his smile to Bevin. "I have my hopes."

That startled a small smile from Bevin. *Interesting.* Watching the two of them go back and forth, I was getting chills; could this be the start of something for Bevin?

"Do you have any brothers or sisters, Cody?" Sarah asked.

He paused before saying, "Nope, I'm an only child. It's just me and my dad."

His eyes kept sliding to Bevin between bites of his lunch. He no longer checked out any of the rest of us.

"Has it always been that way?" I asked.

"Yeah, well, no, my mom passed away a few years ago. It's hard to think about." He sounded sad but detached. I opened my mouth, about to ask another question.

"Jade, enough of the twenty questions," Bevin said, giving me a *stop it* look.

I could smell the concern he felt towards the new kid. *Interestinger and interestinger.*

Cody turned to Bevin and gave him a shy smile. "It's okay, I get it." His eyes met mine, dancing. "I know about you from history." He turned to Sarah. "How about you? Siblings?"

We spent the rest of lunch discussing families, siblings, and the school. He and Piper compared war stories about being the new kid in town. By the end, we were all laughing.

CHAPTER 14

"Happy Birthday, Jade!" Pebble's tiny voice sang as I put on my shoes.

I gave her a quick hug. "Thanks, squirt, but I've gotta run. See you after school."

Mom's voice came from the kitchen. "Before you go." She came up behind me carrying a cupcake with the number sixteen in hard sugar. "Happy birthday." She hugged me. "Now scoot, you're late."

Squeezing Pebble in another hug, I gave her a kiss on the cheek. Grinning, I thought about how well she was doing with her home-schooling. This arrangement let her meet all the pack members and their families. It was a win-win. Today Aunt Allison planned on taking her to the zoo on a field trip. *I hope she loves the animals as much as I do.*

Not wanting to be late, I dashed out the door and caught up with Sarah two blocks from school. She smirked. "I thought you were skipping school as a birthday gift to yourself."

Shivering at the idea, I rolled my eyes. "Would I gift myself all that stress?"

She laughed. "Are we still meeting up with José tonight for dinner on campus?"

Face hard, I gave her a suspicious glance. "Aren't you arranging that…or Bevin? Please tell me I didn't have to do the planning."

She laughed as we continued on our way to school. "No, it's been arranged. Bevin will drive us downtown. We'll have sushi. It'll be great."

We picked up the pace to get to our lockers before the bell rang. When we arrived, Bevin was missing.

Piper shut her locker and then hugged me. "Happy birthday. Bevin came and left. He said he had something to tell Cody and he'd see you in class."

Frowning, I went to open my locker. "I hope he doesn't bail on tonight; he's our ride."

Piper seemed to fold in on herself. "I'm sorry, I forgot to ask."

Sarah rolled her eyes. We all liked Piper but her meekness could be a bit much. I was trying to help her be more secure in herself, but it was an ongoing process.

I gave her an encouraging smile and then packed my bag. "No worries. I'll ask him during class. I'm running late, so if you don't mind, I'll head there now."

"He's really cool." Bevin's eyes sparkled as he gushed about Cody—as he had been for the past ten minutes. I wanted to ask about the ride but didn't have the heart to interrupt. I hadn't seen Bevin this excited in a while.

Cody was a senior like Bevin and they shared several classes. Cody was smart. Cody was cute. Cody lived close enough to Bevin that they could walk home together on the days Sarah and I went to Aunt Allison's place. In a Cody-haze, Bevin continued, "He likes the same books and movies as I do. And he's cool with me being a science nerd."

I tilted my head. "I don't want to sound ignorant—and I really don't know how to ask this—but does he know about *you*, yet?"

I don't want Bevin to be hurt if Cody is uncomfortable around trans people. "I would think that would be an important piece of information," I added quietly.

Rolling his pencil between his fingers and avoiding my eyes, he took a deep breath. "He doesn't, but right now we're just friends. If things go further than friends, I'll tell him. I just don't know if this will become more."

I stared at him then slowly raised an eyebrow. *The*

attraction between the two of them was pretty obvious from the start. I took a long breath and let it out slowly. "You really like him, though."

"I do," he said. Bevin's sapphire eyes sparkled when he spoke about Cody.

"Oh, honey." I grabbed his hand. "I know this is hard, just so very hard. I don't even know what advice to give you. Keep talking with him; if things seem to be going well, tell him." I gave his hand a squeeze. "Actually, that's bad advice. You spilled the beans about me and Piper. I think you should rip off the band-aid and tell him your story, and soon. That way, if this thing builds, you'll know it's building on something real. Yeah, that."

I wasn't sure if my mixed message made any sense at all. Sometimes I had to talk out my thoughts to know what I was thinking.

He squinted at me. "I think I can wade through all of that." He gave me a quick hug as he laughed. "But class is starting. Let's discuss this later. Like after school, or this weekend."

I could hear his unspoken *or never.*

I bumped his shoulder with mine. "Or tonight? When you drive us all to dinner?"

He blushed. "Oh, gods, I forgot. Happy birthday. I'm a horrible friend. Yes. I am driving everyone tonight."

We had been in school long enough that the scents of all the people became a background nuisance. But, every now and then, when someone walked too close wearing too much cologne, I sneezed.

Bevin laughed; he knew why this was happening to me.

During lunch, we sat outside since the weather was still nice. *Clean air, yeah.* There weren't many people near us. Cody joined us, as had become his custom.

"Have you seen this new book?" Sarah asked, holding it up. "The main character is trans. I can't believe it was one of the books our English teacher put on the reading list for the quarter. How cool is that?"

I smiled. *Okay, Sarah is good. Really good. She saved me from bringing up the topic.*

Bevin glared at both of us. His anger prickled against me. I wrapped an arm around him in support. Sarah wasn't outing him, just bringing up the subject.

Piper glanced between us, confused. "Is that book at all accurate? Have you read it?" she asked Bevin.

Cody watched the conversation then looked at Bevin with raised eyebrows. "Why would you know if it's accurate?"

Bevin and I both froze at the same instant. My mouth dropped open in shock. *Gods! Piper's never had a group of friends and isn't used to filtering her thoughts.* We turned to her. I could feel Bevin trembling.

Piper's eyes widened in horror. "Oh, my gods. Bevin, I am so sorry; it didn't even occur to me that Cody didn't know you were trans." She slapped her hands over her mouth, looking ready to cry. "I'm really sorry. I have to learn how to be around other people."

Bevin jerked away from me and crossed his arms. "You two happy with yourselves? What happened to giving me time?"

Sarah sighed. "Not happy, not sad. I just wanted the topic to come up."

Bevin drooped, shoulders hunching in, and then looked at Cody. In a soft, neutral voice, he said, "I was assigned female at birth." He waved his hand at his body. "I'm…trans."

Bevin withdrew further into himself, his attention all for his diminished pile of fries. His earthy scent told me he was sad and defeated. He thought it was over. Thinking back to AP bio and how much Bev gushed over Cody, I hoped that person stepped up, as much as the gushing made me cringe. Bevin deserved him.

I inhaled sharply. Cody smelled confused and…something more. It was hard to read his scent over his cologne. I watched him with bated breath. He hesitated, then moved over to Bevin and put his arm around Bevin's waist.

Bringing his face close to Bevin's, he said, "I've never met someone who was transgender and transitioning. And I don't know what this means to me or us. But I really am gay, and I really like guys. To me, you're just a hot guy. You hit all of my buttons and I haven't been trying to hide my attraction to you since the school year began."

Throughout this, I could smell the hope on Bevin, but he hadn't moved. Cody was about to take his arm back when Bevin reached over and seized his hand.

Bevin's heart rate increased, and his smell grew citrusy with shock. He opened his eyes and stared at Cody, his expression guarded. "What are you saying?"

Cody blew out a breath and looked around the table at all of us transfixed by his words. He got a determined spark in his eyes. "I don't know if it will end up being too much for me, but I kind of want to see where this all goes. If you're willing to take a chance with me?"

Piper's jaw dropped. I couldn't help but smile. She was cute in her obliviousness. I knew when we weren't needed or wanted. This conversation needed to be private.

Sarah, Piper, and I quietly got up and left. We found a new table far enough away to give the guys some privacy. They leaned in close to each other and talked.

"Any news on your apprenticeship?" I asked Piper.

She watched Bevin and Cody, transfixed, but finally shook herself away from the drama. Her eyes lit up as she spoke. "Luke said I could start coming to his shop once a week and learn about glass blowing. I'm really excited."

Sarah wrenched her eyes from the boys. "Glass blowing?"

Piper blushed, but nodded emphatically. "I saw some of his work and it was amazing. He does it as a hobby and said he would teach me. He sells his pieces at the farmer's market over the summer. If I do well, I could start making money doing art." She bounced and her sassy red hair bounced with her.

I smiled and wrapped my arm around her. Dropping my head onto her shoulder, I gave her a squeeze. "That's amazing. I love seeing how excited you are about this."

Piper quivered in her seat. "It will be perfect." She suddenly got very still. "I just remembered…did your mom tell you about the second person attacked?"

I sat up and rotated to face her directly. "Yeah. We talked about it." Suddenly my mind caught up with what she'd said. "Wait, a second person?" Dread washed through me. "In town?"

Piper licked her lips as she gazed at me, then nodded. "Could it be the lone wolf that attacked Pebble's family?"

"Why would the lone wolf be up here?" mused Sarah, staring up at the clouds in thought. "Could it be following Pebble?"

"Gods, I hope not. That poor girl has already been through enough. He had a chance with her and let her go; it would make no sense. At least she's being home-schooled and there are always wolves around her."

"Not always wolves," Piper said. "My mom is on the teaching schedule and so are some of the other non-wolf parents."

"Huh," I said. "That's true. But what I meant is, there are always adults around. She isn't alone."

Sarah continued to watch the boys as she spoke to us.

"How is her therapy going? Is she sleeping through the night?"

Rubbing my face, I imagined Pebble's small body when she woke me with her whimpers. It didn't happen often, but she still had nightmares. "Mom and Dad have been going with her twice a week. I think it helps. She's been coming out of her shell, really opening up to the rest of the pack."

The bell rang. I had English with Sarah right before lunch but no classes at all with Piper. That was the worst part of my day—not having classes with my girlfriend. At least I had both AP bio and Anatomy with Bevin. I ended the day in history with Cody. Now that he'd opened up more, we were quickly becoming friends.

At five, I was dressed and ready for my birthday dinner when Sarah showed up. She looked me up and down and shook her head. "That won't do."

"Why not?" I wore a pair of jeans and a t-shirt. It was my birthday. I should be able to wear whatever I wanted to wear. Pebble was sitting on my bed, giggling and eyes shining with glee.

Sarah turned to the girl. "What do you think, does Jade look ready for a birthday dinner out?"

Pebble smiled widely and shook her head.

I groaned. *Why am I always outnumbered?*

Wrinkling my nose at her, I growled softly. "Then what,

little girl, should I wear?"

Beaming, she jumped off my bed and ran to the closet. She rummaged for a bit and came back with a short red skirt and a black tank top.

I grumbled while Sarah applauded. "That's more like it. She has an eye."

"Where did she even find that in my closet?"

"Oh, those were Candice's clothes. I threw them in there when we cleared out Pebble's room. She wore your size and had better fashion sense than you. I knew they would come in handy. Now, be a good girl and put them on." Sarah went to my closet and found a grey jacket to go over the skimpy clothes. "Now for your hair and make-up."

Pebble cheered over my groan.

An hour later, Bevin pulled up in a Subaru Outback. Sarah and I skipped out to meet him and he stepped out of the car. His eyebrows rose and he let out a low whistle. "Damn, Jade, what are you wearing?"

Shrugging, I dropped my gaze to my outfit. "Never trust Sarah and Pebble alone together...ever." I hopped in the car, taking shotgun. Sarah climbed in the back, and then we were off.

We stopped by Piper's and she sat in the back next to Sarah. The drive to the parking lot was quick—even with Bevin's granny-style driving. When I got out and Piper saw what I was wearing, her breath caught. I heard her heart rate increase as well.

Sarah slipped past me and whispered, "Told ya so."

I circled the car, grabbed Piper's hand, and we entered the restaurant. The smells of fish and salty soy hit me, along with the chatter of people. José, sitting in the back corner, waved and we headed over to him. I sat between Sarah and Piper. Bevin sat next to José.

"Happy birthday, chica. Have fun at school today?"

Bevin groaned. I chuckled. It was so nice to not be the one in the hot seat. José looked over at him with narrowed eyes. "What happened?"

Piper blushed. "It was all my fault."

Bevin glared at Sarah. "It was *not* your fault, it was hers." He pointed with his chin. "She decided it was time Cody found out about me. Piper just took the ball and ran with it, so to speak."

José scowled, but I could smell his citrusy amusement. He stared daggers at me and Sarah. Being epsilon, his dominance display didn't work on me. Sarah being an alpha, it wasn't going to work on her either.

Bevin sighed and then chuckled. "Enough. It worked out in the end. Cody is now my boyfriend." His breathing hitched and his hands trembled. José turned to him sharply, then his posture loosened up and he smiled in encouragement. Bevin smiled back. "I know. He just rolled with it. Must be because he's from Chicago. He's never known anyone like me, but he said he wants to try."

José took Bevin's hand and squeezed it. The contact seemed to calm Bevin. Ironically, José seemed more agitated. I wasn't sure why. I tilted my head and frowned at him. He shook his head and we all got down to reading the menu.

CHAPTER 15

"Piper brought up the second attack at lunch this week," I said to Mom on Friday night during dinner. "She, Sarah, and I wondered if the same rogue could have attacked these guys and Pebble's parents."

Owen, who'd come home for the weekend, frowned. "What? Man, I am so behind living in Whitewater." He faced me, an accusation in his eyes. "You know, you could text."

I made a face at him. "I don't remember a 'Happy Birthday' text from you."

Mom took a few bites of asparagus. She wore her "teacher look," as if pondering how to present the information. "The person was attacked by a werewolf, but I don't know if it was the same one who attacked Pebble's parents. We shouldn't assume." She sighed and swiveled to Dad, giving him a grim shake of her head. "We have a rogue in town."

Coughing, I grabbed my O.J. Once I could breathe again, I said, "I thought you said the first attack was out of town. I thought we didn't have to worry."

Her face dropped. "I was wrong." Looking back up, she said, "Tanner is setting up a rotation to watch the area, and Dad is putting together a regular schedule to watch the house and Pebble. She'll never be unprotected."

Well, at least there's one thing I don't have to worry about.

I slid my focus to Pebble, then back to my parents. "I was wondering about that; do you think the lone wolf could have followed her?"

I wasn't happy we were discussing this in front of Pebble but we were a family that didn't hide problems. If she was being followed, she should know so she wouldn't wander off alone. She'd run from me once, the first time she'd shifted. I wanted her to be extra careful going forward.

Pebble stared down at her plate and poked at her vegetables. *Is she even following the conversation?*

Dad put down his fork and gazed at the young girl. "I don't know, but we aren't taking any chances. What's the official word on the deaths?"

"They are calling them wild animal attacks, breed

unknown," Mom answered.

Pebble still looked at her plate. She sucked in a breath. "Can I go watch TV…with an ice cream treat?"

"Yes, honey," Mom said, rubbing Pebble's head. "That sounds like a wonderful idea."

Pebble cleared her dishes, grabbed a treat, and scampered off to the basement. We heard the TV turn on to a cartoon, loud enough to drown out our conversation.

"That's it, she's better trained than Owen," I teased.

Owen rolled his eyes and snorted a brief laugh at the truth of it.

"How much of the victims were eaten?" Owen asked. "Is this lone wolf a real danger to the public?" Eagerly, he asked, "Do you need me to stay to help find him and fight?"

"Too much was eaten," Mom answered, looking worried. "And it escalated on the second death. I wonder if these were the wolf's first real taste of human meat. If they were, we may not be able to find all of their victims."

"Did you get a good smell of the wolf on the second man?" I asked.

"No, and it was a woman. The hospital had already cleaned out all the wounds by the time I got there. No scents but disinfectant smells. The pattern of the wounds is what tells me a werewolf made them. I have seen too many werewolf attacks to not know what they look like."

I gazed in the direction Pebble had gone. "Why would this wolf be coming after her, if he left her alive in the first place? He had the opportunity to take her already. Do you think he thought his original attack was fatal?"

Dad looked at me, face tight. "Jade, don't assume this creature is male. We don't know anything about this werewolf. We don't know that it's the same one. We don't know that this rogue is after Pebble. We really don't know anything. You need to stop making assumptions. We need to follow the patterns we see and the clues we find. If you make assumptions, more people can and will be harmed."

Swallowing noisily, I had a feeling Dad spoke from experience.

With a glance at Owen, Dad continued, "As for you, kiddo, I want you at school. It's safer, and I want you to do well in your classes. School should be your first priority, just like it is for Jade. Tanner has military training, as does Greg. Other pack members have police and military training as well. We have fighters and trackers to help keep the pack safe from any number of rogues."

Owen sighed, but didn't argue with Dad. This was the alpha speaking, and you didn't fight the alpha. Not if you were smart. And Owen was smart, past fiascos notwithstanding.

Owen's eyes danced, a spark of excitement in his voice. "On a totally different subject, in which form are Jade and I running tomorrow?"

Mom's gaze shifted back and forth between us. "I've been thinking about that. I think Jade should go as a wolf to help José. This will be his first pack run. Owen, you should go in your panther form, so Sarah isn't alone."

Owen's grin informed us of his opinion on that. Though the two of them had kept their relationship private for a while, they hadn't been sneaky enough, and everyone knew. Owen loved his panther form; I could smell how thrilled he was.

I smiled wryly. *If he had to choose one and only one wereanimal, I think it would be his panther.*

The next morning, people showed up early for the full moon run. There was, thankfully, no pack meeting. For once.

José was nervous. He walked in before Owen was even out of bed and found me doing my morning jog. I could smell the almond scent of his nerves and when I looked over, he was wiping his hands on his pants. He clenched his fists a few times, shaking out his hands and pacing in a tight circle before stopping. Finally, he joined me on the track.

Was he trying to run the wolf out of his system? He had never wanted to be a werewolf. His dream had been to stay a norm, with a husband, cats, and kids. His scent kept shifting from nervous to scared, and I wasn't sure how to help him.

After running, we moved to squats, pushups, chin-ups, and other torturous "fun."

When we switched to stretching, he asked a question.

"So, how is Estrella doing now that she's in high school?"

I frowned thoughtfully. José's younger sister, Estrella, was one of those popular types. Like Owen, she was athletic and had a huge group of friends.

Chuckling, I said, "You know how she's doing. She rules the school. Everyone loves her, including the teachers. She's beautiful, smart, and popular. If I didn't know how nice she was, I would absolutely hate her."

"Jade, I don't know if I'm ready for this."

He was so stressed I could taste almonds.

"You are." I grabbed his hands and gave them a squeeze. "How's college?"

Smiling weakly, he replied, "Classes are hard, but good. Lots of cute boys. Some of them even like boys." His eyes got distant and after a moment he sighed, weariness creeping into his voice. "Living in the dorms would be better if I couldn't smell, well, everything. I can smell the stench of everyone on my floor. Cute as they are, teenage boys living on their own for the first time are gross." Shaking his head, he stopped stretching and sat cross-legged. "My roommate is the worst. Jade, I can smell other student's emotions; lust, fear, if they are cheating. It's the worst. How can you handle it?"

I mirrored his sitting position. "Do you remember how bad I was after spring break? You and Bevin had to help me a lot. What I want to know is how Sarah handled it so well."

"I'm a great actress, silly," Sarah said as she strode in. "Have you already run?"

At my nod she sighed and then took off on her own.

"So, back to you, José. You'll be running with us today." José froze for a second before I continued, "Mom decided I should run as a wolf so that you'll have a friend to run with."

"I could smell you relax from a half-mile away!" yelled Sarah.

Laughing, I squeezed his hands. "Were you really that stressed?"

José just gave me a look.

I took a steadying breath and tried to spread my calmness to him. "I know you never wanted this, but you know everyone in the pack. They're family. Have they figured out how dominant you are as a wolf?"

At my touch, his shoulders dropped. He gave me a grateful smile. "No, my wolf hasn't been formally introduced into the pack. Today is going to be fun all around. I don't know what to expect, or what I hope for. I just want to go back to campus and take a huge pop exam that will determine my position in college for the next year. You know, something relaxing."

I laughed and scooted next to him. I wrapped my arm around him and kissed his cheek, then rested my head on his shoulder. "You'll do great. Your wolf will be amazing and you'll have a wonderful run. Just wait and see."

Once we were done working out and had showered, we headed over to the house for food and liquid.

"José!" Owen yelled from across the house. He ran up,

wrapped his arms around José and pounded him on the back.

"How's *your* college? Classes? Good roommate? Professors? Any hints you can give me?"

José laughed, squeezing Owen and pounding his back. "Dude. College is good. But my roommate stinks. I don't know how you all have gotten used to the *smell* and smell of such tight quarters. Classes, hard; professors, confusing. Some are good. Hints, yeah, we can talk after I survive this run."

"It'll be great." Owen's eyes shone, almost manic. "I don't know why you're so nervous. We'll go out, run, find a rabbit, and Bob's your uncle, home for dinner."

José just shook his head in disbelief. "One day you'll gain weight from your constant focus on food, and then you won't only think with your stomach."

We all looked over at Dad, who was munching on breakfast, still lean despite eating every time he passed through the kitchen.

"Or maybe not." José laughed.

We spent the day catching up on school and the goings-on for the last month. Before we knew it, evening had fallen.

Gradually, everyone else had shown up. Piper, Dillan, and Bevin were now the oldest kids in the basement. As a high schooler, Estrella had been enlisted to help. The four of them were setting up the movie and making sure there was enough food, games, and distractions for everyone for the night.

I headed down.

"Hi." I hugged Bevin and Piper. Then, after a beat, I

gave Estella a hug. "How are you adjusting to high school? I never see you around."

Estrella shrugged, smiling. "It's cool. It's a lot like middle school, just with more friends."

Of course it was. She was always so positive, it made my teeth hurt.

I surveyed the basement. "Where's Dillan?"

"He's out with wolfy Pebble. We're all taking turns until she falls asleep. None of us like for her to be alone," explained Estrella. She gazed at me wide eyed, as if I were slow. New to leadership; I'd give her time to adjust.

My face broke out in a big smile. "Cool." Turning back to Bevin and Piper, I decided to not respond in any other way. *I can be the bigger person.* "See you two in the morning. Have fun with all the kiddos."

They smiled and waved, already busy with the games.

I headed back up. Everyone was making their way outside and I knew José would be nervous.

I found him outside near the treehouse. "Do you want to go wolfy first or last?"

He sighed and, gazing up at the moon, shuddered a bit. "I don't want to go wolfy at all, but I guess I want to get it over with."

He turned his back, stripped down, got down on his hands and knees, dropped his head, and waited. For new wolves, changing always took longer. He panted a bit. Bones shifted, popped, and changed. His body morphed, growing fur, and then he transformed into a beautiful red wolf. He shook himself out and snarled. He turned towards me, ready to attack.

I tilted my head peacefully, watching him. Running just encouraged the attack more. The wolf would see me as prey. I tried to be unthreatening, hoping his human mind would recognize me before he attacked. He growled, and I think he would have pounced if Mom hadn't grabbed his snout in time.

"Thanks," I said weakly.

"No worries. I was watching for it."

José's eyes cleared and got wide, then he shook again, and tucked his tail.

Mom let go as he whined. "Now, don't do that," she scolded him. "Everyone starts off attacking; it's when you don't attack that we get worried. The fact that you were willing to attack Jade is the most impressive part. Her calm usually beats the fight out of all of us. Tanner," she yelled. "Come here."

Another big red wolf trotted over. Tanner's wolf had more gray streaks in his fur than José and was an inch taller. He looked at José and then bowed his head in submission.

"Well, I'll be damned." Mom said. "Jade, on your knees."

Getting down, I looked José in the eyes. He stared back. His eyes glowed amber and beautiful. We just looked at each other. His tongue lolled in a wolfish laugh, and I joined him in a human giggle.

After a minute, I looked up at Mom.

She nodded. "Okay, okay, into wolf form. It's time to run."

I moved towards the treehouse to strip and fold my clothes in a neat pile, and then I got into position.

I told my panther to sleep, and my wolf to come out and play. Focusing on my hands, I imagined them as wolf paws. I was getting better at this and the change happened faster. Pretty quickly, I was a big, bad, black wolf.

Trotting over to José, I rubbed noses with him.

I took him around to sniff the pack. Most of the pack bowed down to José, showing he was dominant to them. Being epsilon, I was outside of the hierarchy. Owen rolled over and showed his belly. He was in panther form and just being a dork. Sarah rumbled disapproval at his antics and he quickly showed proper panther pride behavior. I snorted in amusement.

Once everyone exchanged smells, we were off.

We ran for a few miles and then Mom led us on a chase, having caught the scent of game. I lifted my nose to the air and scented a herd of deer.

Despite his fears, José howled at the moon, singing to Mondara, and ran with abandon. His love of the hunt swirled around me in an aroma of joy. Others joined in with his song. It was a good thing our woods were so remote and no one would be able to hear our glee.

Mom directed us into teams to chase the herd down. One deer tripped, and that was the one we focused on. She had us split up and take turns running the deer down, tiring it out. Once the deer was tired and slowed enough, Mom leapt in for a killing blow to the neck while Dad hit the gut. Then Sarah leapt from about thirteen feet to land on top of the deer, toppling it. The triple play was more than the deer could withstand.

The rule of the pack was that the alphas got their fill first, all three of them. Once they had eaten, the rest of us were allowed to have whatever remained. Fortunately, the deer was big enough so that no one would go hungry. We were far enough in the woods that anyone finding the carcass would believe natural predators had killed this beast.

After our meal, we ran for a few more miles until we found a stream. We all drank and then splashed in to clean off. On the way back, we found some rodents to eat, crunching them up like tasty snacks. The run took a lot of energy, so no matter how much we ate, when we woke up in the morning a big breakfast would be welcome.

We returned to the house early in the morning just before the sun came up. I leapt up into the treehouse along with Sarah. We usually separated ourselves since we were the panthers, and even though I was a wolf, I still felt connected to her. This time, José and Owen joined us. We found blankets and pillows and fell asleep curled around Pebble.

When I woke in the morning, I climbed down, found my clothes, got dressed, and went in to start a feast for the pack.

Being an early riser meant I usually helped cook breakfast. As other people woke up, they would join in.

Helen was already in the kitchen, preparing the meal. She, too, tended to wake up early and was a great cook to boot. She handed me a cup of coffee. She was also amazing. "Did you have a good run?"

I yawned and took a sip. She made the best coffee. I don't know how she took our beans and our machine and made it better, but she did. "How is this better?" I mumbled.

She chuckled.

I tried to clear my head with some coffee and answer her original question. "Yes, the run was good. We brought down a deer."

She blanched but didn't comment. Apparently, she was growing accustomed to the ways of werewolves. After shaking herself, she said, "I add a cinnamon stick to the grounds before it brews."

I squinted and tilted my head, confused. "Huh?"

She smiled warmly. "The coffee. It gives it a bit of a cinnamon flavor. You like cinnamon; that's why my coffee tastes different."

I stared at her for a minute before my brain clicked on. I clearly needed more caffeine. I took another drink. "Oh... that's really good."

She smiled and continued to prepare food for an army of wereanimals.

CHAPTER 16

The run seemed to calm most of José's fears. He was dominant. Very dominant. Most likely, he would be an alpha one day.

My place in the pack was to become the pack's healer. It looked like José's place was going to be leading. He was cut out for the role, if he wanted it. Being the healer suited me better; I liked the idea of healing, not making decisions.

Would it be weird if the alpha couple was gay? I chuckled at the thought.

He sat down next to me while I ate my breakfast.

I bumped shoulders with him. "So, you survived."

He sipped his coffee then studied it. "Apparently."

"Did you have fun?"

"Hmmm."

I slid a glance over to him and smirked.

"What?" he snarled.

"You had fun…I could tell."

He huffed. "It wasn't as bad as I feared."

I rested my head on his shoulder. "I'm glad you enjoyed yourself."

He slipped his arm around me and kissed my forehead. "Thanks for sticking with me, chica. It helped."

On Monday, after school, Sarah and I sat outside the building.

I leaned my head against the building. "If we go to my place, we have the basement."

Sarah shook her head. "And Pebble and whoever is teaching her. Look, we have a huge paper due and we can get a chunk done together, but only if we focus. I know we can do it at your place, but my place is empty."

Scrunching up my face, I thought about the number of people probably at pack house. "Okay, but—"

Estrella came running up to me, breathing hard. Her normally perfect ponytail was disheveled. She tugged on my arm. Her eyes glittered wildly and mascara ran down her cheek. Her voice rose in strident tones. "Jade, I need your help. Please, come with me. It's an emergency!"

"What's wrong? What happened?"

Her voice was nearly a wail. "Just come!"

We followed Estrella around the corner to the front of the school. A group of freshmen gathered at the side of the road. Two girls and a boy stood over a second boy sprawled on the ground surrounded by a flurry of paper. It looked like he had been tossed there like a rag doll, arms and legs splayed out, and his school bag had exploded along the way. Glinting in the sunlight, his broken phone lay off to the side on the sidewalk. *It's strange what you notice during a crisis.*

Estrella's eyes were pleading. "Jade, you have to help him, he was hit by a car."

I looked from the three strangers to Estrella. "Estrella, I'm only a junior in high school. I'll do what I can. Have you called 911 yet?"

They all nodded.

I did a quick survey of the area from the boy on the ground, to the three kids watching us, and back to Estrella. I hoped she would get the hint about how much I could help. The kid didn't look good; a gash on his head trickled blood. When I searched the area, I saw the car that hit him still parked by the curb with a crowd near it. The driver was bent over the steering wheel, shaking, head in their arms.

A few kids looked our way, but whenever people moved in our direction a few of Estrella's friends blocked them. Apparently, she had set up a no-fly zone.

My focus returned to the few friends who were by the

downed kid.

Estrella yanked my arm. "Don't worry about them, they won't tell."

My entire body tensed. I glared at Estrella and then looked over at Sarah.

Sarah huffed. I smelled her frustration.

I shook my head. This was a bad idea, but what could I say? "Okay, I'll see what I can do."

Kneeling by the boy, he didn't look too broken up. He had some scrapes, but no other huge gashes. It didn't look like there were any broken bones. I checked for a pulse. Panther asked permission to check him out.

Yes.

Closing my eyes, I followed Panther in to see what was wrong with the kid.

Her assessment told me the boy's heartbeat was too weak, but I was more worried about his head. Too much blood. His skull was fractured and there appeared to be a cut in his brain from a bone fragment, and bruising. The landing hadn't been light.

Can we help? I asked.

We can help, panther replied.

The other boy snapped, "Estrella, what the hell? She isn't even doing anything! She's just sitting there with her eyes closed! Shouldn't she, like, bandage his head or something?" I almost lost the connection. His scent, a mixture of disgust and something spicy, overwhelmed me with its thickness. He wore almost as much cologne and body scent as Piper had worn when I first met her.

Focus, Jade. Focus on Panther!

"Hush, Clinton, let her work," Estrella whispered.

"But..."

I stopped listening.

The head wound was the worst. Panther and I cleared some of the foreign debris from the cut and started to close it up. Before that was finished, I became lightheaded and began to tip over.

Sarah's hands on my shoulders kept me up. Suddenly, I had a bit more energy to work with. I took a deep breath as my head cleared. I decided to move on and see where else I could help. A broken rib. I lined it up and started to mend it.

Sirens sounded in the distance.

I slowly backed out of the injured boy. When I opened my eyes, I knew I had done too much. I swayed and put my hand on the ground to steady myself. Sarah was behind me, supporting me.

When the EMT workers jogged up, I said quickly, "He has a broken rib, and his heart is barely beating. If you perform CPR, the rib will probably pierce his lung and he won't survive."

They stared at me for a second before shaking their heads and starting their own triage. They put him on a stretcher, loaded him into the ambulance, and then the vehicle sped off with siren wailing and beacons flashing.

Sarah looked at me quizzically. "Was all of that true? Because those EMTs didn't look like they took you seriously."

I dragged my eyes up to her, trying to stay kneeling and upright. My entire body trembled. "Yeah. He also has a concussion, but they'll figure that out from the blood." I huffed out a laugh. "I don't know if I could have done more with time. If you hadn't touched me, I probably would have passed out. Did you feel the drain when I took some of your energy?"

I spoke low; no one could hear me over the police sirens still blaring.

She nodded slowly. Her hands rested on my shoulders to help keep me up. "I was curious if that was what it was. I'm really tired and hungry. I think we should call for a ride."

She took her hands away and I almost fell over again. I leaned on her legs as she pulled out her phone. She found the number before I could argue. The cops and the quantity of people surrounding the car overwhelmed me. I lost focus.

When I reoriented, Estrella's friends watched me closely. *Grrrr. I need to keep track of my surroundings.*

"Was that for real?" the boy asked skeptically, his scent a cinnamon-cumin mix. Snide little brat. I really didn't like this kid.

Crap. I need to look strong. I narrowed my eyes at him. "That depends on what you're talking about."

"Did you just touch Thompson on the wrist for, like,

a few minutes and figure out all of that stuff you told the EMT?"

I stared at him, then at Estrella. My head pounded. Fatigue took over and everything grew muddled.

Estrella's voice became bossy. "Clinton, Jade just checked for blood pressure. She obviously felt a slow heart rate."

"What about what she told the man about Thompson's rib?" one of the girls asked.

"Star, I'm sure it had to do with hearing the rasping in his breathing, duh."

Star? Estrella—"star" in Spanish—has a friend named Star. That's funny. I almost laughed but had no energy.

Estrella was really good at making this stuff up. I wondered if her parents knew how good she was at spinning a story. She should become the pack's spokesperson. Despite her fast talking, her friends didn't seem that convinced. Sarah slowly helped me up so those kids didn't have a position of power.

I stared them down, each in turn. "Look, I've been studying medicine since I was six years old. Does it make more sense that I used the clues I could see, hear, and feel, or that I'm magical?" I said those last words in a ghostly voice to add mockery to them, waving my fingers around.

The three of them just rolled their eyes at me and finally Star said, "Yeah, what Estrella said makes more sense."

"You've been studying medicine since you were six?" asked the second girl, sounding awed. She, like the boy, wore enough perfume to drown a boat; it made me sneeze. *Gods, my head aches. What is wrong with their bodies that they feel the need to cover their scents so thoroughly?*

"Yep," I replied brightly. Anything to avoid what we had been discussing.

Estrella offered me a bright smile then shifted it to her friends. "She knows what she's talking about, January, just trust her."

Clinton's lip twisted up in a sneer. "Wow, you really are a nerd. I mean, I've always heard that about you. You're notorious around here for being, like, the smartest person ever, but six?" *Snide little brat, indeed.* Clinton's words cut, but I simply raised an eyebrow at him. Hadn't I just saved his friend? But he wasn't going to reserve his forked tongue for just me. He directed a hateful question at Estrella. "How do you even know her?"

She looked lost for a second, but I had this one. "I'm best friends with her older brother. I've known her for years. Sometimes, it's good to know the nerds—and to know how to be nice and not a jerk. It just may save your life. Or the life of one of your friends."

Estrella looked embarrassed, but Sarah and I decided at that point to turn and walk away. This kid was so not worth it. Sarah put her arm around me for support, but she let me give the impression that I was leaving on my own power.

We hadn't gotten far when Bevin and Cody joined us. "I thought you two were long gone," I said, a bit confused.

Bevin stared at the freshmen behind us. "We were halfway home when I realized I had forgotten one of my books in my locker. We returned just in time to see you talk to the EMT and face off with that bratty freshman. Who was that kid anyway?"

"Clinton someone…I don't know," I answered.

"How do you even know them?" asked Cody, frowning.

"You see the pretty girl, long dark hair?" He nodded. "That's Estrella. She's the younger sister of one of our best friends. A guy who hung out with us last year, who then had the audacity to graduate and start college this year. Jerk! Anyway, she's popular, but really nice. Some of her friends seemed okay. That Clinton guy, not so much." We headed for the parking lot. "When her friend was hit by a car, she asked if I could help out."

Cody peered at me more closely. A slightly minty scent of confusion broke through over the scents he covered his body in.

Head throbbing, I explained, "I've been studying medicine for a long time. I went over to help. Clinton lashed out. Probably because he was scared for his friend," I ended, trying to avoid another explanation.

Sarah shook her head as we walked. "He probably lashed out because that's the kind of person he is. I've seen him around, he's just a jerk."

Cody nodded. "He should've been more appreciative. You did a kind thing." His words warmed me. "Well, Bev, shall we go?"

The two of them headed off. Sarah and I just watched them go. The happiness they both felt in each other's presence was amazing to see.

Our heads turned as a horn honked. A black car with tinted windows pulled up. I recognized the vehicle.

"Our ride awaits," I said with a half-smile.

Sarah practically carried me over, but she made it look like I walked, in case any of the bratty freshmen still watched. We climbed into the back seat. Once the door was shut, I slumped down, barely able to hold myself upright. "Hi, Tanner."

Tanner looked back, shocked. "What the hell?" he demanded.

Sarah did the talking for me. "A boy got hurt, Estrella asked for Jade's help. She did her probing thing, and went too far, I guess. She even took some of my energy; don't ask, I really have no idea. Anyway, I'm surprised she stayed on her feet long enough for you to get here. I think it was purely to not have to explain things to more people."

Tanner nodded and drove us away from school. The next thing I knew, I was on the couch with a wet towel on my head and someone forcing me to drink water. I scented the air. Sarah, Tanner, and Pebble were in the living room with me. Slowly, I sat up and the water turned into toast, which eventually turned into more substantial food.

Tanner, Pebble's tutor for the day, continued her lesson

on different types of animals. Because Sarah was there, they played a game, competing to see who could identify an animal first. Sarah gave each identification one beat, but not more time than that. The score was close. By the time they finished, I'd made it through the toast, a piece of cheese, and a beef stick, and my parents had gotten home from work.

"Okay, what happened this time?" Dad asked, little sympathy in his voice.

I wasn't sure exactly what happened, but I told the tale. Everyone stared at me in shock.

Sarah explained her part, ending with, "She kept swaying. I immediately called the house and told Tanner we needed a ride. She kept up a solid face until we got in the car, then she all but passed out."

"She *did* pass out," Tanner growled. "It just took her a minute to realize she was in a safe enough place to drop her guard and let it happen."

"Well, damn," said Mom, "this new skill comes with pros and cons. I wonder how much healing you can do with it—and how much the healing takes away from you. If healing a person harms you, is it worth it?" She raised her eyebrows. "Did you say Estrella's three friends saw all this go down?"

"Yeah, but she is an amazing fast talker," Sarah replied. "I almost believed the story she spun. I don't think we need to worry about those three telling any tales of the amazing healer Jade. They probably think she's a big dork who's been studying medicine her whole life and knows more than the doctors. If anything, knowing us has hurt Estrella's street cred." She ended with a laugh. Sarah could be as popular as Estrella, but she enjoyed hanging out with me and Bevin. I smiled. *Sarah always went with people over popularity.*

Mom closed her eyes, looking pained. "Still, I'm going to have to call in Clare and Alejandro and talk with them. Then I'll have a talk with them and Estrella all together. She should know better than to ask you to do anything pack-related in front of norms, no matter how much she thinks she can trust them."

Dad knelt beside the couch and squeezed my hand. "From the sounds of it, Jade saved the boy's life."

Mom gave me a loving smile, but her words were anything but loving. "Possibly, but that isn't her job. Saving one person's life at the risk of all of ours isn't a trade I'm willing to make."

CHAPTER 17

Bark bit into the pads of my paws as I leapt from branch to branch. In panther form, I could fly through the trees almost as fast as I could run on the paths with two legs. The wind ruffled the fur on my face as I bunched my back legs to…

An insistent beeping sound invaded my dream. I rolled over into my warm covers, trying to recapture my escaping dream.

My phone continued to beep. It hit me that it was the ringtone for Aunt Allison. *Oh, no! An emergency.* Snapping awake, I saw it was two a.m. I answered the phone. "Mmm."

Aunt Allison's voice, sounding as tired as I felt, was clipped, each word short and precise. It woke me further, like cold water splashing in my face. "Five minutes, front door. Emergency pick up. Call Bev."

"Mmm." Hanging up, I rolled out of bed. I put the phone on speaker and found Bevin's number on my favorites list. As the dial tone purred, I grabbed jeans and a shirt to wear off the floor. They smelled mostly clean.

The call went to voicemail. I tried again. While I waited for him to answer, I found a pair of clean socks and pulled them on.

"Eh?"

"Mornin', Bev. I'm getting picked up by Aunt Allison in—" I checked the clock, "—oh, hell, two minutes. We'll swing by your place next. Love ya!"

I hung up, found a coat and my wallet, and ran to the kitchen to write a quick note to my family. *Aunt Allison called at 2am for emergency. ~Jade.*

Rummaging in the fridge, I grabbed three sodas and some energy bars, threw them in a bag, and headed for the door. When I got outside, my aunt was waiting. I jumped in and handed her a soda. She looked as tired as I felt and smiled gratefully for the caffeine.

"Did you reach Bev?"

Grunting an affirmative, I took a drink. She navigated the dark streets to his house. We found him waiting for us on the stoop, similarly attired in jeans, shirt, coat, and holding a bag of goodies from the kitchen. He jumped in the back seat.

He checked out what I had and snorted. "Great minds think alike…and so do ours."

I laughed.

Aunt Allison drove about ten minutes before I had enough caffeine in me to form a complete sentence. "Okay, details on this pickup? It's been a while since we've had a pickup this early."

In the back, Bevin grunted as I heard him handling his can of soda. "Gods, it's early."

She shook her head as if to clear it of cobwebs. "Oh, sorry! I'm half-asleep myself. Zack, a lone wolf who lives in Sun Prairie, was doing a midnight hike near Devil's Lake and tumbled off a rock face. He thinks he may have broken his leg. It's healing wrong. All in all, he needs medical help and I'm just the driver this time. It's your first solo…or duo run."

I let my head fall back on the headrest and sighed. "So, he took a midnight hike, probably without any light source. From what you said, he fell pretty far, messed up his leg. Now we get to rebreak it. And you won't help."

"Nope."

"But I'm tired."

Bevin chuckled behind me.

I glared at the roof of the car. "You're not helping."

"I will be helpful later…unless you don't stop complaining. Then I'll just sit back with Allison and watch…amused."

I growled. It would have been more impressive if halfway through it hadn't turned into a big yawn.

"I'm so scared." His deadpan voice was not convincing.

Another fifteen minutes and we arrived. We took out flashlights and followed the trail Zack said he had taken. It was a ten-mile loop and rated difficult. *Great.*

The first part of the path wasn't bad, but soon enough it got steep and rocky. Bevin walked behind me and had to catch me so I didn't fall…repeatedly.

"So, how many times have you landed on your butt in gym this year?"

I wanted to snap at him, but since he'd just caught me for the umpteenth time, I didn't have much, if any, ground to stand on. Once I had my footing again, I turned and glared at him.

"You know, that would have been much more impressive if it hadn't taken you five minutes to manage it."

Snorting as I navigated a tricky turn, I tried not to break my own leg on our rescue mission. "You know, I don't fall that often in gym. I don't know why everyone thinks I do. And I have the new gym teacher this year. She's fresh from college and *so very excited* for everyone to learn. *It's so much fun.*" I said that last in a bit of a manic gym teacher voice.

Bevin laughed, as he was meant to. "So, only once a week."

I whipped around to punch his arm, slipped on some loose rocks, and landed on my butt. Bevin laughed so hard he grabbed a tree to stay standing. I just tucked my head between my knees and sighed. Once he had himself under control, he helped me up.

Three miles into the hike, we found the point where Zack had gone over. It looked like someone had swept all the dirt and pebbles off the side of the path. We got onto our hands and knees and squinted down. I estimated the drop to be about fifteen feet. Well within the limits of a leaping werewolf if they were prepared for the jump. Zack had obviously been taken by surprise.

Bevin gently knocked into me. "See anything?"

It was dark. He obviously could only see for a few feet. The light from the flashlight didn't reach the bottom. *Norms, am I right?* "Yeah. He's down there."

At the bottom of the cliff, lay a man in jeans and a jacket on his back, resting with his head on his pack. It looked like he was doing something on his phone. I searched with my flashlight and found a path to our right.

I was about to stand when I heard, "Path's that way."

Zack pointed over his head in the direction I had seen a path.

"Thanks, saw that. We'll be down in a few."

We stood and pointed our flashlights towards the almost non-existent track. It was more of a game-trail than a path. Bevin put one hand on my shoulder. I wasn't sure if it was for my stability or his sight.

Immediately, I started to slip and jerk to maintain my

balance. Bevin squeezed my shoulder in support. I paused and closed my eyes, focusing on wolf. I needed help. Wolf came forward, infusing my sight and muscles just a bit. Suddenly, I could see even better, and my footing was fantastic. I skipped ahead, slipping out of Bevin's hold.

I heard him mumble, "What the hell?" right as I reached the bottom.

When we got to Zack, he was lying where I had seen him from the top, playing on his phone. "Hi, guys. Ready to fix me up?" He pulled his attention from his phone and looked up at us. "Well, hell, you're only kids. What? I don't rate the adult team?"

We just stood there staring at him. It was just after three in the morning. We were tired. We had school soon. And he was going to be picky about who helped him?

My voice came out flat. "Can I check out your leg?"

"Sure, toots, have at it." He gave me a mocking half-smile.

My face fell into a hard stare before I dropped down next to him. I rubbed him from thigh to ankle. Panther asked to help. I agreed. I repeated the action more slowly. I heard a crack, much like the time Owen had gotten hurt. The drain caused my arms to shake. I panted. One more time, I repeated the action, getting lightheaded. This time when I got to the area of the break, I stopped, shut my eyes, and focused. I could feel the bone knitting together.

I pulled back, breathing hard. I looked at Zack. It felt like I was under water.

He stared at me, shocked. "What the hell did you do to me, girly?" He bent his knee and moved his leg around.

The world tilted. Zack's face changed from elation to shock as he reached out to catch me. He stared down at me and then up. "What's wrong with her?"

Bevin's voice came from far away. "Healing like this is new to her, she doesn't know when to stop."

"I'll carry her back to the car. Can you grab my bag?"

I didn't hear Bevin's answer. The next thing I knew, I was in the back of Aunt Allison's car, its motor rumbling. My head rested in Bevin's lap.

His eyes slid to me, and his voice was flat. "Good, you're awake. Can you eat or drink anything?"

At my nod, Bevin helped me sit up and he handed me food and a beverage. I drank the soda before starting on the energy bar. "I have got to stop doing that. Half the time I don't even know if I'm controlling the fix or if it's just my animals. How's Zack?"

Aunt Allison shot me a glance full of concern in the rearview mirror. "He said you fixed something in his leg that's been bothering him for a few months. He said thanks, and he'll take the 'kid team' any day."

"So, after what we did, he still calls us the kids, huh?"

Bevin laughed, his neutral expression transforming to a stunning smile. "Yep."

Aunt Allison looked at me again. It was like she needed to see into me but couldn't while driving. "Are you sure you're okay, dear? I really didn't like seeing you passed out in a stranger's arms."

"Yeah, I don't like being passed out much better. I'm good. I'm glad that his leg is good to go, though, especially being a lone wolf. How long has he been in the area?"

Up front, the turn signal clicked. "Oh, about two years. He knows he could join the pack, but doesn't want to join a pack in the Midwest. He thinks he may move out west."

I nodded in understanding. Though, I didn't know how hard it would be to join a pack and then move on. *There's so much I don't know…*

We stopped at Bevin's house just before four. Aunt Allison turned back to smile at us with pride in her eyes. "You two did great for your first solo mission. It was harder, being in the middle of the night. Do you want me to talk to your parents about missing school today?"

Bevin looked at me with a smirk. "Nah, we have a big exam in bio today."

Clutching my throbbing head, I groaned.

CHAPTER 18

The next morning, well later the same morning, I was eating breakfast when Dad turned on the news.

The anchorwoman was in the middle of a sentence. "…dead by the park. His parents were concerned when he hadn't returned home by his ten o'clock curfew and went out looking for him. Authorities found him early this morning, apparently attacked by the same type of wild animals that attacked two other victims. We go to Tracy at the hospital for more information…"

A different voice spoke. "Thanks, Karen. Doctors here are reluctant to name the kind of animal that would leave a boy in the state he was found. He went out with his friends last night, but at nine p.m., everyone was heading home. The park he was found in is about six miles from where he separated from his friends, and seven miles from his home. No one's certain how he ended up there."

We all stared at the TV in disbelief. *Another victim.*

"Who?" I whispered. "Who is it?"

"It doesn't look like the body was dragged here," the news lady continued, "which leads authorities to think that perhaps the boy, Clinton Johnson, got into a car with a friend or stranger, and somehow ended up here. How that drive ended up with him mauled by a wild animal is the real question. We hope to have interviews…"

I dropped my mug and coffee splashed all over the table. Mom and Dad looked at me in shock.

"What?" Dad asked.

My hands shook. "Clinton Johnson, that's the name of the jerk boy yesterday. Maybe I shouldn't describe him like that, but Estrella's friend who was being mean to me, that was him. Yesterday he was being a jerk, and today he's—oh, gods!"

I ran to the bathroom and threw up. *Oh, gods! How could that happen to someone I knew? I was just talking to him yesterday. He was mean, but then we were mean back. Gods!*

After my stomach calmed down, I brushed my teeth and then called Sarah. She hadn't heard the news, so I told her. We talked on the phone right up until we met up a block from the school. In between talking about the news,

I filled her in on Zach and the adventure Bevin and I had taken the previous night.

"My parents tried to convince me not to come today, but sitting at home wouldn't have helped at all. I need the distraction of a normal day at school; though, it probably won't be normal. I wonder how Estrella is doing."

Sarah's head tilted. "Well, at least you know the rogue isn't that lone wolf, Zach. He couldn't have offed Clinton and made it out to Devil's Lake for his hike, right?"

Thinking about it, the timing seemed off. I would mention him to Dad, but it did seem like Zach had been too calm to have just eaten a human when we'd met him.

I didn't have to wait long to find out about Estrella. The pretty freshman found me by the lockers and cried into my shoulder almost the moment I arrived. I did what I could to calm her using every bit of epsilon essence I had. It seemed to help.

Estrella sniffed, face wet with tears, and still looked beautiful. "Star, January, Clinton, and I hung out last night after visiting Thompson in the hospital. He's doing better." She hiccupped and blew her nose into a tissue. "It was late, and we all headed home. I called José to tell him about the day and then I went to bed. I didn't think to check in with my friends. Does that make me awful?" She sobbed out that last bit.

I hugged her harder, shaking my head and whispering the word, "No."

She continued, "I didn't even know until this morning. Why would he be all the way across town? There's no way he could have walked there. They think he was attacked at like ten-thirty or eleven. That's only an hour or so after he left us, and he was walking towards home. Sonnara help us, that's in the opposite direction! What do you think happened, Jade?"

I'm not sure why Estrella thinks I have the answers. I rocked her in my arms. "I know my mom and dad will do everything they can to figure this out. They aren't going to just ignore some wild animal attack."

It's probably something more than a wild animal but we can't discuss that here.

She pulled away and stared at me with her large brown eyes. "Thanks for listening to me. I know we aren't as close as you and José, but it's nice to know that you're here. You're like a big sister to me."

After one more hug, she ran off to be with her friends.

Bevin watched her go. "She'll be okay. She's strong like her brother, and he's going to be the first gay..." He stopped and looked over at Cody.

Cody squinted and twisted his head. "First gay what?"

Piper, who sat on the floor reading a magazine, quietly said, "First gay engineer in their family."

Sarah started to howl with laughter. I couldn't help it, I joined in.

Bevin just smiled and shook his head.

Cody watched us like we'd all lost it, shrugged and moved to sit. His locker was on a lower floor and until he got it moved, he had to get to this area prepared for the day.

The administration held a school-wide assembly to discuss the death and let us know that there were counselors available if anyone needed to talk, cry, or just sit with someone. I just wanted the normalcy of a regular day. After the assembly, they held shortened classes, so we had some distractions. Because most of the juniors and seniors didn't know Clinton, our teachers tried to run classes as close to schedule as possible. Our big AP exam was moved back a day. We got a quiz in its place.

At lunch, Cody remarked, "At least it happened to a snake."

"Cody!" I blurted in shock. Then more quietly, "I mean, he wasn't the nicest kid, but did you even know him? He was worried about his friend. I wouldn't wish death on anyone."

"No one?" he asked, looking surprised.

I looked at him, confused. "No. No one."

"What about a killer? Would you wish death on a killer?" he challenged.

What the hell? I shook my head. "What the hell? This is a weird topic, what has gotten into you?"

Cody gave off a weird scent, challenging and dangerous. "I'm just curious. I'm not glad, exactly. The kid got eaten by some animal." He spoke in a rush, almost tripping over his words. "But at least it wasn't that nice friend of yours, or you, or Sarah, or Bevin. I mean, it could've been worse, right? And historically, the death sentence is one of the most discussed and controversial topics. Right?" He spread his hands and raised his eyebrows.

I glanced aside at Bevin; he seemed shocked by this conversation, too. *It sounds as if Cody's trying to figure something out. See what our boundaries are about people around us dying.*

"You say you wouldn't wish death on anyone; I was just trying to see if that was true."

I frowned. "What I would hope is that the wild animal would eat other animals and not people," I said. "And I've always been against the death penalty."

Cody blurted out, "What about that homeless person? Who else was hurt there?"

My jaw dropped. I blinked at him. "Besides the homeless guy? His family; I'm sure he had one. And the community. People are scared. Do you really not see that people getting mauled by a wild animal is bad?"

"No, I do see it as bad, I just wanted to get you out of your depression and feeling something different." He smiled at me. He smelled…smug.

This is really messed up. Does he think we're playing a game? "What the hell. Are you kidding me?" Piper moved closer to me and took my hand. I stared at Cody, blinking in confusion. From his scent, I could tell he was concerned about me, but this conversation was becoming too weird.

Bevin and Sarah laughed. It sounded forced and out of sympathy. "I don't know, Cody," Bevin said. "That was pretty harsh. So, where do you really stand on all this?" His eyes were intent, almost pleading.

Cody gave Bevin a sheepish smile full of emotion. His tone became apologetic. "I was just messing with Jade; she needed it to break her out of her funk. I think what happened to this Clinton kid—and those other people—is awful. A travesty."

Cody's scent changed again. He was completely focused on Bevin, now. He leaned over and gave Bevin a kiss on the cheek. Bevin blushed.

Oh. Okay. That happened.

On Friday, the five of us went to see a movie. Owen, who was home for the weekend, came along. We parked at the far end of the huge lot so we could talk while walking to the entrance.

A guy with a red hat spat out, "Two girls, two guys, and a mixed couple. God, what is this country coming to?"

The girl with him just laughed, an ugly sound.

I recognized them. *Billy and Joanie Jinx, the most horribly ignorant and racist couple in Stolzburg.* They had graduated my freshman year. I'd heard they married after she got pregnant during their junior year. Even though she had a miscarriage, they'd stayed married.

I kept walking, as did Sarah and Bevin. Owen turned around, walking backwards. He spoke in a jovial tone. "Well, if it isn't Billy Jinx, as I live and breathe. I never thought you would make it this long out of jail. And Joanie, not pregnant? I'm surprised he's letting you out of bed in such a state." He tipped his non-existent hat, as we kept working our way to the theater.

Joanie let out an indignant squeal. "Who said I ain't pregnant?"

"Snowflake." I heard Billy running at us, but we kept moving.

Suddenly, Sarah whirled and punched him in the nose. I saw a tooth fly. Billy scudded on his butt down the length of the aisle.

Never underestimate the strength of a werepanther.

His words were slurred through his squished and bloody nose. "I'll sue you…you black monkey." Joanie hovered over him, gaping at Sarah.

"I have five witnesses saying I did nothing to you, you racist imbecile!" she flung over her shoulder as we walked away. After that, we made it inside the theater and to our seats unbothered. Everyone was still pretty riled up, so I tried to lay down the calm. Cody's head swung around like he was trying to find the chamomile tea. Everyone else smiled at me with a thankful nod. The benefits of being epsilon.

CHAPTER 19

I sat in front of the lockers with the gang before school when Thompson approached me. He side-stepped up to us. "Jade? Right?"

Lifting my head, I met his gaze, smiling. "That's me."

He hunched his shoulders by his ears and scuffed his feet, sizing up a group of upper-class students. "So, yeah. Estrella and Star said you told the EMTs about my ribs. Maybe saved my life. That was cool." He nodded.

My smile froze on my face. I shifted my eyes over to Sarah, brows racing to my hair line.

Her lips thinned; she tried not to smile.

Looking back at him, I shrugged. "I didn't do much. But yeah, no prob." I tried not to sound flippant. Really.

He huffed. "Sorry, this is weird. I don't remember anything about that day. And I've lost one of my friends. I mean, he was kind of mean, but he was in my group. So, yeah. Thanks for helping out."

He turned.

Closing my eyes, I tried to remember I was better than this. "Thompson." He turned back to me. "You're welcome." This time I actually sounded and felt sincere.

He smiled and nodded before striding away.

Cody mumbled, "Damn straight, you should be grateful Jade was there to help you." Louder, apparently unaware Sarah and I could hear his mumbling he asked, "Do you believe him?"

I thought about it for a minute. "Yeah, I think I do."

Homecoming was coming up, and though it was something I had never cared for, we decided to go to the dance as a group.

Piper had always wanted to dress up, and Sarah wanted the three of us to go all out with dresses and make-up. Since I didn't own anything really fancy or understand them, she was going to have to take the lead on this one.

When we went to the shop to look at dresses, Cody asked if he and Bevin could join. Bevin looked like he would rather do anything than go shopping, but Cody was the type of gay who liked helping ladies with fashion…I guess.

Any help is a bonus, and Bevin can be my partner in hating everything shopping related. Why should I be the only miserable one?

"Aren't you excited to try on dresses?" Cody asked me.

I suppressed an urge to roll my eyes. Could anyone really like shopping this much?

"Not really, I've never been that into shopping," I replied.

"But playing dress-up can be fun." His big smile made it sound like he was talking to a child. "Don't you ever do that with your sister?"

I laughed. "No, she's new to my family, and dress-up hasn't been one of our games."

Cat and mouse, more likely, I thought.

"I bet she would have loved coming out shopping today. I'm surprised you didn't bring her." He actually smelled relieved…which seemed weird. His words sounded like he wanted her here.

I squinted at him. "You want me to bring a five-year-old shopping? Do you even know any five-year-olds?"

He mumbled under his breath, "Probably better than you." I didn't think he knew I heard him. His smile became sincere. "I have girl cousins I've taken care of, especially when I was younger. It's an age I've had a lot of experience with."

The truth in his statement was surprising.

The first store had, well, dresses. Sarah and Cody said they were exquisite. It was welcoming to see Cody interested in something besides Bevin and history class. They were also expensive. The store was sparse, with a few highlighted dresses on the wall and on center displays. Most of the dresses were black or navy with sequins highlighting areas where the fashion industry assumed women had curves.

I tried on a few that Sarah or Cody selected, and they did look good, according to Sarah and Cody. Bevin always gave a tired thumbs-up at the appropriate time, and Piper always thought I looked great. She wasn't a good judge.

Eventually, Piper and I found two that looked like a matching set. They were both one shoulder, A-line dresses with a split up to the front to our upper thighs. The beading flowed from the chest and circled our waists. They were in matching sassy red with an attached flowing cape. My cape was off-white and Piper's was a light pink.

Meanwhile, Sarah found this deep indigo number—a low-cut, V-neck dress with criss-crossing straps in the back. Beading strung across the chest and dove down the center to the hem. It was breathtaking on her.

The sales lady came and looked us over. She gushed over them all, but exclaimed that if we all went together, Piper and I would look too similar, like we were together as a couple.

Cody crossed his arms and lowered his brows. "That would be the point," he said, a little sharply.

She blanched.

"But they're both girls," the lady protested.

Cody grinned, a challenge in his eyes; he'd come a long way from the shy boy I'd met the first day of school. "Yep, they are. Well, young women, if you want to be exact. Once you develop a chest, I don't think 'girls' is still appropriate. But yes, they are a couple. Two lovely ladies who love to go out together. Don't they make a stunning pair?" He waved his arms as if presenting the two queens of the ball. As fierce as I was becoming and as I was trying to get Piper to be, we both wilted at the attention. *This isn't the type of positive attention Piper needs.*

Why wouldn't she stop? "But I don't get it. Shouldn't they find young men to take them to the dance?"

Enough of this. "I'm going to change," I said to Sarah. "Thank you for your time," I told the older woman. The three of us took off the gorgeous dresses and put our own clothes back on.

We went to other stores. We found other dresses. They weren't as stunning—or as expensive. I found a new red dress and Piper found an off-white dress. Though they didn't match in color, they were both the same style and the hem ended just above the knee, flaring a bit. They wrapped around the waist and left one shoulder bare. Mine had a burst of rays coming from my left hip in off-white, and hers had the same design in red. Piper and I stood looking in the mirrors. She grinned. "We're a matched set."

The sales lady came over and looked at us. Her name tag read: Kelly. She was all smiles. "I don't want to assume anything, but if you two are going as a couple, those dresses would be perfect."

And sold!

We all smiled at her.

She had us turn and gave us a calculating stare. "I have some simple but understated jewelry that goes with the style of those dresses. If you both wore the same necklaces and earrings, I think you'll make quite a statement at your dance."

She went off to grab the jewelry. When she got back, Cody looked at everything together with a trained eye. "This will work out perfectly."

Bevin sat in a window seat, staring at his phone. I think he was reading a book. He gazed up with a positive word when called, then zoned back out every time. His turn was coming soon; he needed something to wear; too.

Sarah came out in a dark blue dress with sparkles all down one shoulder and around her waist. She would look stunning in a garbage bag, but when she tried, it was just unfair.

Sarah should be walking down a fashion runway.

"Oh, now that is lovely," the sales lady said.

After making Sarah turn, she gazed at the ceiling. "I may have a better dress."

I was dumbfounded. This was probably the most expensive dress in the store, and Sarah looked fantastic in it.

Kelly returned with a turquoise number, more understated than the dark blue one. Shrugging, Sarah tried it on. The color shone against her dark skin, and the modest cut accented her curves.

My eyes popped. Wow! I would have never picked that dress out. It looked plain on the hanger but paired with Sarah's natural beauty, she would stop traffic. Even Bevin had put down his phone and gaped. Owen would be a puddle of goo in her hands.

"You're good at your job," Cody said with raised eyebrows. Coming from him, that was high praise.

"I can't believe how much I love this dress," Sarah gushed, turning to see herself from every angle in the mirror. She looked down at the tag. "And it's, like, half the price of the other one."

"It is also on sale," said the salesperson. "I know I should have sold you the expensive one, but I knew this one would be even more breathtaking on you. If you don't mind my suggestion, no standard jewelry. It would take away from the image. I have this star tiara that would be exquisite. Light make-up, all natural. That's all you need to steal the show. You are lovely." She went over to a wall and pulled down a tiara. It had several inch to inch-and-a-half stars across it and two bands to hold them in place. Sarah really would be the belle of the ball.

I never liked buying dresses, but if I ever had to again, I knew the store I would go to. We all thanked her as we checked out.

"I can't believe how smoothly that last store went," I said, still in shock.

"The right store and the right dress can make the night," said Cody.

That must be some weird kind of gay logic.

I raised an eyebrow at him and he laughed in delight, a vanilla scent surrounding us all. I had to admit it, he had made the day go much better than if he had not joined us. Bevin was all smiles at our enjoyment of the day, though I could smell his bergamot scented relief that it was finally over. Despite our focus on dresses, Cody had found a couple of suits for the two of them to wear as well, with matching button-down shirts in contrasting colors, and ties. They looked good together.

The night of the dance, Sarah and Piper came over to get ready. Pebble sat on my bed while Sarah did everyone's hair and make-up. Long ago, she determined I couldn't apply complicated cosmetics on my own. Just because she was correct was no reason she had to point this out. Once she and Pebble decided the three of us were ready, we made our grand entrance into the living room.

Owen, wearing one of dad's black suits with a shirt that matched Sarah's dress underneath, nearly fell over when he saw Sarah. I wasn't sure when he'd gotten the shirt, but together they could be on the cover of any magazine. "Whoa! I don't know who looks best. Kidding." He got up and wrapped Sarah in a hug. "You look phenomenal!"

Personally, I thought Piper and I made a charming, matched set.

We piled into Owen's car and he drove to the dance. The school gym was decked out in gray and purple streamers and balloons. To the left of the door stood a table with snacks and a punch bowl, as well as bottled water. Several teachers monitored the table to make sure no student spiked the punch.

We made our way in amid the murmurs of several students. Sarah made as much of a splash as I had expected. Immediately, Tiffany and Amber, two of her friends from basketball, ran up to her and Owen and dragged them off, gushing at how wonderful Sarah looked and how much they missed Owen. Sarah shot a glance over her shoulder and mouthed, "Be back."

I sighed, then grabbed Piper's hand to drag her onto the dance floor. Surprisingly, I didn't need to drag her. Vibrating with excitement, she dragged me. We got to the floor, and my embarrassed, shy girlfriend came to life. Her body moved and glided in ways I couldn't hope to emulate. I tried. At one point, I felt Bevin's hand on my back stopping me from falling.

He leaned in close to my ear. "Did you know she could dance like that? She may take the spotlight from Sarah!"

I laughed and brought Bevin and Cody into our circle.

Eventually, I tapped Piper on the shoulder and pantomimed raising a cup to my lips. She waved me on but stayed on the dance floor. I made my way to the refreshment table, where I found Sarah and Owen.

My brother handed me a water bottle. "You never told me Piper could move like that."

Glancing over my shoulder, I shrugged. "I didn't know. This is our first dance. If we put her and Sarah together, heads will explode."

Owen and Sarah laughed.

Once hydrated, the three of us rejoined Piper. A space opened up for Sarah and Piper, and—as I expected—they got a lot of attention. I decided to ignore the rest of the students and enjoy the night.

On Sunday morning, I woke up and headed to the kitchen. The sliding door to the backyard was open and I could hear whimpering in the backyard. Following the sound, I found Pebble in the treehouse in wolf form, curled in a ball, shaking. I couldn't ask her why she was upset while she was a wolf. I climbed up to calm her. Sitting beside her, I petted her and cuddled with her. She continued to whimper. I decided to try something new. Putting my hand on her paw, I closed my eyes. My wolf asked for permission to go inside.

Yes.

We entered Pebble. She was physically fine. Instead of finding her wolf, I found her.

Hi, Pebble.

She looked up sharply. *How are you here?*

I don't know, this is one of my abilities. I'm in your mind, not really in you. Are you ok?

I had a bad dream. I dreamt of him. A face, an image of a man floated past me. The image morphed into a wolf with red eyes and a snarling snout. It attacked before turning into smoke. She screamed. I hugged her, or tried to.

Do you dream of him often?

No. A simple answer for a scared girl.

Did you know him before this all happened?

Yes, he was my dad's partner at the bookstore.

Why hadn't we asked this before? Had we asked her anything about her attacker?

Do you know his name?

John Fortune floated in her mind, but she said *No.* The little wolf in my lap squirmed.

Okay, I'm going to go back to the wolf side, I'm getting a bit dizzy. When Mom and Dad wake up, can we tell them all of this?

No! she said. But *'yes'* echoed in her brain.

Well, hell!

When I backed out, I took one look at the small, gray wolf in my lap and knew something had gone wrong. My vision went blank and something hard slammed into my head.

A howling wolf was the last thing I heard.

I woke up in bed. Hadn't I gotten out of bed already? I tried to sit up but was so dizzy I almost passed out.

I groaned and heard footsteps running to my room.

"You're up," said Owen. "What did you do this time?"

"Ummm, nothing?" I had no idea what I had done. I didn't even really know what day it was. My head pounded. "Day? Time? Year? Coffee?"

Chuckling, he left and came back with the nectar of the gods. He sat, wedging himself behind me so that I could sit without passing out before handing me the coffee. As I drank, he caught me up. Last night was the dance. This morning, Mom found me passed out under a howling Pebble in the treehouse in the backyard. While he explained this to me, my parents arrived.

Right, Pebble.

Mom stood in the middle of the room, face flat. Dad leaned against the doorframe looking disheveled, holding his own mug of coffee as if it were a lifeline. They all stared at me.

"I found her in the treehouse upset. I couldn't talk to her as a wolf. I thought I would try something else."

"Try what?" asked Owen.

"Try having my wolf talk to her," I said weakly.

Eyes wide, he asked, "And it worked?"

"Had you even eaten anything?" Mom asked, exasperated, her arms dropping to her sides.

"Well, no, but she was so sad, I had to help her."

Mom leaned against my desk, hands on her hips. "So, you did something that completely drains you at the best of times, with no resources? We nearly called in Allison to give you an IV. I almost wish we had. River, go grab her another coffee, with extra cream." I shivered at the threat. Her eyes narrowed. "And a protein shake. She needs to refuel, or she'll pass out before she's done with this story."

After I had the shake and more coffee, I told them about my conversation with Pebble.

"Wait, you can *talk* to us, as people, when we're in animal form?" Owen asked.

"I don't know. We have to do a lot more testing to figure out what the hell I can do. I'm just sort of winging it and passing out a lot. And ouch, I have a headache. Just sitting up and telling you this is taking just about everything I have."

"She knew the guy, and said his name was John Fortune?" Dad asked. My story must have woken him up completely. At my nod he said, "On it," and disappeared.

I had been thinking about it. I said, "I don't think the current problems we're having are with the same werewolf. I think that guy was after her parents."

Mom nodded. "Pebble's memories seem to indicate that."

We talked a bit more, but agreed I would spend the rest of the day in bed. *Food in bed, great.*

The next attack by a rogue werewolf occured while I was passed out on Sunday.

CHAPTER 20

Monday morning, I woke up early and headed to the barn for a quick run. Afterwards, I showered and went back to the house for breakfast.

Mom and Dad sat glued to the TV.

My face contorted in confusion. The TV was rarely on in the morning. As I poured a mug of coffee, I asked, "Why the TV? Everything okay?"

Mom shook her head and moved to pour cups of coffee for herself and me as I headed to make a bagel. She said, "A retail worker was found dead behind the movie theater. Another animal attack. They've narrowed it down to a wolf or rabid dog."

Dad, eyes still on the TV, muted the talking heads, but I watched the images as they flashed on the screen. The news covered the retail worker found half-eaten. When they showed her ID, I gasped. It was the sales woman from the first store we had gone to before the dance—the woman who couldn't imagine Piper and I going to a dance together in matching red dresses.

The information streamed across the bottom of the screen as Dad said, "The police are setting up a curfew for all people under the age of eighteen until the attacking wildlife can be found."

I searched for the youngest member of the family as my heart pounded in my chest, but I didn't see her. "Where's Pebble?" Then, holding my bagel prepared with cream cheese and jelly, and coffee in my other hand, Dad's words penetrated. Curfew. Restriction on movements. Grumbling, I sat down to dig in.

He turned off the TV and finally faced me. "They warn that all others should go out in groups and be vigilant. We already have the patrols. I'm not sure what more we need to do. I'm debating sending you to school with a driver."

Rubbing my eyes as I saw my freedoms slipping away, I took another sip of coffee to ground myself. "Please, no. I think I'll be safe. I don't think we'll be attacked on the way to school."

Mom sat down next to me. "With a rogue werewolf in

town, and you the daughter of the alphas, I just want you to be extra careful."

I looked down at my coffee, searching for inspiration against having a full-time bodyguard. Finding none, I tried drinking more. "How about more training? Sarah and I walk together. There's only a block and a half I'm alone. After school we'll come here or go to the zoo. If I get better at fighting, both as a human and in animal form, I'll be safer."

Dad considered me. "I don't know if that's enough. There's a rogue out there, and until he or she is found and taken care of, no one is safe. However, you're right about the training. I think we need to go up north for a training weekend and the full moon."

I perked up at that, with a huge smile. "Up north?"

Dad smiled back tenderly. "What would be more suspicious than a couple of panthers running around, or a pack of wolves? Our land is private, but with all this tension, I worry people may poke around. If someone sees our pack out running, it could cause quite a scare or spur a witch hunt. We'll go out of town for the next full moon run."

He was right; a pack of werewolves didn't normally attract much attention. Having our own pack lands was usually enough, but this month there were too many people on alert and out searching for wild animals.

At the next full moon, the pack rented a bus. *Pack road*

trip! I hadn't been so giddy in a long time. Several of the pack families, including Piper's and Bevin's, stayed home to watch over Pebble, who was too young for fight training. She would be safer at home.

Owen came up from university as well. "This is going to be epic. I remember hearing about these getaways, but we never went." He practically vibrated in his seat.

I sat next to José, who had the window seat. He had a couple of big assignments and exams coming up and was attempting to study.

I cocked my head at Owen. "Don't you have studying to do? I have homework, José is studying, how come *you* don't?"

He turned to watch the scenery. "Sister of mine, you just don't understand college life."

We finally arrived at the cabins. The pack owned twenty-acres of forest in the Campbellsport area. An old cabin with basic rooms, electricity, and plumbing had been built with fifteen rooms. Each room had beds for four people. The cabin was nestled on the edge of a one-acre clearing, where we all gathered to listen to Dad detailing the weekend's torture regimen.

Once we reached the cabins, we all shifted, except for Monica, Tanner's wife; she wasn't a werewolf. She had been my sixth grade English and seventh grade social studies teacher. She was tough as nails. Physically, she stood a foot shorter than Tanner, but I had known her from a young age, and she had always been larger than life. She came up to run the drills. We would spend most of the weekend in animal form, all of us, including Dad and Aunt Allison. Dad, Aunt Allison, and Owen had collaborated and come up with the drills.

Monica consulted the clipboard. "Jade, Owen, Sarah, panther form. Into the trees. You have thirty minutes to shift and cover your trail. Then the pack is coming to find you. This is a game of hide and seek. Don't forget they have noses."

Shooting a look over at Owen and Sarah, I saw matching smiles.

We grabbed our stuff and brought it to the cabin. We threw our clothes on our bags, shifted as quickly as we could, and were off.

When we got to the edge of the woods, we ran around about a hundred square feet, scratching a few trees, and scent-marking them. Before we climbed the ones we chose, I approached Sarah. I put my paw on hers and using my epsilon ability, said, "Hi."

Her eyes grew huge, but I heard an answering 'hi'.

I quickly stepped back before I used up too much energy.

She stared after me as I bounded to my selected beech tree. I found a sturdy limb and waited for the wolves.

Watching her climb, I could see the forest and the limb Sarah perched on. It was about twenty feet from me. Owen found a tree further away, tall and strong. Owen had found a maple tree whose leaves had turned brown, to match his fur.

Squinting, I searched to find the wolves. *Nothing.*

Closing my eyes, I listened. *Nothing*.

I stayed frozen…until my paw started to slip. Panicking, my breath huffed. I heard howls.

I got my paws under me, but it was too late. A red wolf ran under my tree, tongue lolling out in laughter. He was teamed up with Aunt Allison and Chris. I met José's grin with a sigh. After they noted me, they moved on. I tried to get into a better position so the others couldn't find me as easily.

Dad approached with his team: Clare and Fred.

I hunched down silently and watched. This time, I didn't make a sound. Clare sniffed the ground and the air while Dad and Fred sniffed the ground. They passed my tree. Phew!

A minute later, Clare trotted back and reared up to place paws on my tree. She spotted me, pant-laughing. I plopped my head on my paws.

The next few groups passed without noticing me, but Tanner wasn't fooled for a second. His job was finding people, and he was good at it.

The day was fun.

The beginning involved training the wolves' noses. Once the wolves found us, they went back to base camp and we were given time to hide again. And again, the wolves searched for us. Most smiled silently up at us when we were found, though some yipped in excitement.

Despite the focus on training the wolves' tracking skills, I benefited from extra practice sitting motionless in trees. I ended up slipping and making noise about a quarter of the time. Bad, but I was improving.

Eventually, Owen and I had a chance to try to find Sarah. We had no problem, she was our alpha.

As for the others, José, Tanner, and Clare were the most successful at finding us.

After lunch, Dad asked if I could try going from panther to wolf. The afternoon training was of a more tactical nature—or so Dad told me.

After I transformed into my black wolf from panther, the pack smelled like vanilla sweet tea, amazed and a bit freaked out. I seemed to freak them out on a regular basis. After that, I wasn't up to doing much until after I ate the raw steaks Monica threw to me.

Because we were in animal form all day, the nighttime run wasn't a big draw for anyone. We played after dinner, but then we slept. It had been a long, tiring day for everyone in the pack.

For the hunting run the next morning, I partnered up with Clare, Violet, Tyler, Greg, Andy, and Luke. Dad expected us to go out in mixed-animal groups consisting of one panther, at least one dominant wolf, and one submissive wolf. Monica assigned the groups and set the rules. We were supposed to search for big game, such as deer, black bear, or elk. If, by early afternoon, we didn't bring down anything large, we would return for a late lunch. Our training excursion ended at three.

With me in panther form, the seven of us followed Clare, our leader, across the field toward the wooded area. I ran just behind her on her left flank and Greg ran opposite me. Andy was right on our heels, running in the center of our group with Luke and Violet on either side and Tyler taking up the rear. A pack always protected the submissive, its heart.

Entering the woods, we split off from the other two groups, Clare choosing her own direction. We slunk through the trees with our senses on high alert. I took in air through both my nose and mouth, letting scents bathe my tongue. Clare found a game-path but the scents were old.

After about an hour of searching, the hairs on the back of my neck rose. I froze and let out a tiny sound. The pack froze around me. Closing my eyes and pulling in all the information I could, I found what had tickled my nerves. I gave a quick jerk with my nose to the left.

All the wolves lifted their noses in what almost looked like a choreographed dance as they sniffed in the direction I indicated. Clare was the first to catch the scent, but one by one, they each caught it: deer.

Pantomiming, using head-directions we all knew, Clare guided us and we circled our prey. My job was to pounce on the deer's back and the others would come in and tear out its neck and gut for a quick kill. I had a long pounce, but I hoped to get in close, within ten feet.

There it is!

I bunched up my back leg muscles and took two calming breaths. Then I sprang. I flew through the air like black death. A crack sounded through the woods like a branch breaking under a great weight. I landed on the deer. Birds scattered to the wind in all directions. The deer crumpled under my weight and we hit the ground together. My legs gave out under me. A burning sensation flowed along my shoulder and back. I toppled off the deer. And then, white-hot pain seared through me.

My mind went blank.

"Did you see that? *Did you see that?!* Black death from the sky?" someone shrieked from the trees.

Like gathering mist, my pack appeared from the bush. Two of the larger wolves, Clare and Luke, supported me, as we made our way deep into the brush, back towards the camp. I limped, hurting, but I could move. Blood burned on my back.

The voice came again. "What do you mean I'm imagining things? I shot a devil from the sky!"

The group moved slowly, and then I realized two wolves weren't with us. I tried to look around, but my two supporters didn't let me do anything but continue to move forward.

"A bear? You think it was just a black bear? Well, hell, we'd better be careful. He's going to be spitting mad."

Leaves rustled and twigs crackled as the hunters

moved towards us, towards the deer, so I tried to increase my gimping pace. We made it into some thicker bushes and trees in a direction tangential to the one we wanted so that we wouldn't be easy to follow. Once we found a game-trail, we turned and headed back to camp.

I managed a limping trot, my speed increasing despite the pain and the blood flowing down my back. My breathing was rough and labored. The wolves stayed with me as we slunk back to camp. My vision blurred. I didn't know the direction I ran, but I tried to go faster.

Every now and then, Clare or Luke would bump me gently to adjust my course. I focused only on putting one paw in front of the next, getting back to camp. The pain grew with every minute we traveled, jarring up though my body. But the fear of those hunters was worse, so I ran.

As soon as I saw the tents and smelled the other pack members, I tried to sprint. My two missing pack members ran up from the side with Aunt Allison in wolf form. I made it only a few more steps before I collapsed, my body giving out in the middle of the field. I felt the warmth of wolves lying next to me. Before I could get up, my vision lost its fight and I blacked out.

A hand on my head stroked gently. "Shhh," José said. I realized my head was in his lap. "You're safe. Allison has patched you up. The bullet burned a furrow through your shoulder and back, but it's healing. You were writhing too much to be worked on; the only thing that pacified you was having me here and Sarah and Owen nearby. If you want, I can move."

A growl bubbled up from deep in my throat.

He continued to pet and scratch my ears, and I purred.

He chuckled. "Okay, got it. Last time we checked, your shoulder was almost healed. The salve Allison put on you, and the sleep has helped. Do you want to bow out of the jumping competition?" My eyes rolled up to him. He smiled as if he knew my thoughts. "Then rest for twenty more minutes, and we'll check your injury. Your dad will make the final decision."

When the time came, my shoulder hurt, but I was determined to compete with Sarah on how far each of us could jump. Most of the distance came from our back legs anyway. There was a field set up with marks every half-foot starting at ten feet.

On my first jump, I managed sixteen and a half feet. The landing jarred my healing injury, and I panted with the exertion. *Come on, Jade, you can do this.* Sarah had an amazing seventeen-foot leap. *Whoa!* On my second leap, I stumbled at takeoff and barely scraped the eleven-foot marker.

José ran over to me. "You sure you can do this?" He stroked my back and legs. His touch soothed my beast. I rubbed up against him in gratitude.

Sarah, leaping as I cleared the path, pounced sixteen feet.

I trotted up to the starting point and turned towards José. I faced my path and focused on my form and target. I took off, and let my panther free. I flew. When I landed, I heard the hooting from the other pack members watching. I looked down and saw I'd managed to reach just past eighteen feet. Pain shot through me, but so did pride, as I limped off the field.

I heard a low growl as I moved out of Sarah's way. I cleared the path and turned in time to see her flying. When she landed, she had come just shy of the eighteen-foot mark.

Suddenly, I was being tackled from the side; as I rolled to the ground, I saw it was Owen and José. Their laughter reached my ears.

Dad's voice rang out. "Bus is leaving in thirty minutes!"

On the bus ride home, we were all exhausted. I sat next to José again, and Sarah was next to Owen. "I could sleep for a week."

José checked me over. "Long enough to get to Halloween candy?"

I smiled and nodded.

"That panther-to-wolf thing was freaky cool. Do that for candy, I bet you get a lot."

Groaning, I knocked my head on the back of the seat while they all laughed.

Halloween was a week after the pack's get-away. Piper and I decided to take Pebble out trick-or-treating. Piper decreed Pebble would dress up as Little Red Riding Hood.

My costume was the Big Bad Wolf, *har har*, and Piper dressed up as Grandma.

When I asked Sarah if she wanted to join us, she said, "No thanks, I'd rather give out candy this year. I love seeing all the neighborhood kids' costumes."

Pebble hadn't gone out very much because of the rogue wolf. She had done our first walking tour and school field trips, but that was pretty much it. She was more excited about walking around the neighborhood than the candy, I think.

The pack house was halfway into the woods, with about a half-mile driveway. We convinced Dad, who wanted to watch over us anyway, to drive us to the closest neighborhood street, where Sarah lived. We headed towards Sarah's house. Groups of ghosts and princesses mobbed the lit-up homes. We shied away from groups larger than four or five kids.

I hadn't told Sarah about our outfits. When she saw what Piper had picked out for us, she almost hit the floor laughing. "Oh, my gods, you're a wolf!" She was loud enough to get her parents' attention.

They came running, but when they got to the door and saw us, they smiled, and gave Pebble a bit more candy.

Cindy smiled down at Pebble. "Pebble, you look lovely dear. That cape is just perfect."

"Jade's costume's a wolf?" Tom snorted, "Piper, I love your sense of humor."

With a grumble, I turned to leave.

I knew what was in store for me. Our plan was to hit all the pack houses so Pebble would know where everyone lived. The other two seemed a lot more chipper as we headed in the direction of Bevin's house. It took a while to get there since we stopped at just about every house along the way.

When we finally arrived at Bevin's house, he opened up and we had a repeat of Sarah's reaction, except Bevin really did hit the floor. His mom, Janet, laughed pretty hard as well. His sisters were out trick-or-treating with their dad, so they missed out on all the fun.

"Man," Bevin said, when he caught his breath, "Cody was here helping me hand out candy before Mom got home; he is missing out. Can I get a picture?"

Secretly, I was happy that at least one person was missing out on this kind of fun. I glared at Piper, but her smile was just too infectious to glare for long.

"No," I said, but Pebble's begging eyes made me change my mind. *Grrrr.* "Fine."

Shortly after that, we headed home. Pebble had enough candy to last her until Christmas—or until Owen got home and found wherever it was hidden.

The very next day, Dia de Los Muertos, Day of the Dead, the police found the two-week-old corpses of Billy and Joanie Jinx. Their remains hadn't been well concealed, hidden under a tarp in the bed of their truck. However, the truck was parked in an area off the beaten track near a park about a mile from the school. They probably wouldn't have been found but for the smell attracting critters.

It made me wonder.

"Mom, Dad, I'm worried," I said while we ate Thai food at dinner.

"What about?" Dad asked, spicy beef speared on his chopsticks.

"I've been going over and over the rogue attacks in my head. Except for the first two people, every victim can be connected to me in some way."

"What are you talking about?" Mom asked.

I put down my chopsticks. "Well, first it was that Clinton kid, who was killed the same day he was a jerk to me. Then there was the lady at the dress shop who didn't think Piper and I could be a couple, and finally, Billy and Joanie Jinx."

I took a drink of my soda and passed the Pad Thai Dad pointed to. I explained our run-in at the movie theater.

I took a calming breath. That type of hatred always hurt. "Billy was about to attack us when Sarah punched him in the nose. They squawked about suing us and such, but we all just slipped into the movies. That's weird, right? I'm not just being paranoid, am I? Everyone can be connected to me. Every. Single. One."

"Except the first two, right?" Mom said.

"Well, probably. I didn't ever see a picture of them. Pebble and I did give a dollar to a homeless guy the day I gave her a tour of the neighborhood. If it was him, then we're four for five. I don't know anything about that other person."

Mom paused to take in my words. She usually didn't take my concerns lightly. "I think you're making connections where there aren't any. From what you told me, Sarah was at all those places, too; so were Bevin, and Cody, and, for the most part, Owen. There were probably others as well. You're just unaware of them."

Mom took a few bites of her food, eyes distant, obviously lost in thought. Then a small smile tugged at the side of her mouth. "My guess is that this is all random. If it is you, it may be your scent, and not you at all. The werewolf may be following another wereanimal scent and not even really understanding why."

Though what she said made sense, it didn't make me feel any better.

CHAPTER 21

On the way to school the following day, I asked Sarah if she had noticed all the connections between me and the people being attacked.

"Thank the gods!" she exclaimed. "I hoped it wasn't just me who saw all these connections. Though, I couldn't find one with the first two. There was the homeless guy and the other one. Hold on." She took out her phone.

After a few minutes of searching, her eyes widened. "Holy hell, I know this woman." She waved the phone in my face and I saw an image of a pretty woman in her twenties. "She was the waitress at the restaurant Owen and

I went to last summer. You know, after you told us you'd figured out we were together."

My brows came down in disbelief. "You remember a waitress?"

Sarah laughed, it was high pitched…a bit hysterical. "Look at her, she's cute, right? I mentioned that to Owen, and he was like, I didn't even notice with you here. It was cute." She gazed off for a moment. "Anyway, if the homeless guy was the one that you and Pebble gave the dollar to, then all the people can be somehow connected to us. That's weird, right?"

Rubbing my temples, I tried to stop the headache. "You know, you aren't helping. How could this rogue know who we interacted with?"

I stopped, thinking about all the pieces. "I mean, Clinton is mean to me, to us, and is eaten. That lady at the store is a real piece of business and is eaten. Billy and Joanie, well, if anyone deserved it…but no, no one is deserving, no matter how nasty. So, they were horrible to us, and the next thing you hear, they were attacked by wild animals and eaten. How could he or she even know?"

Sarah and I looked at each other and froze. "Who has always been there, besides us? Piper, Bevin, and Cody. And who is new to town?" Sarah asked.

"But we would have smelled it on Cody if he were a werewolf," I said, shooting down the thought before it could take hold. "It can't be him. Not to mention, we didn't even know him for the first two victims. That's ridiculous."

"True, but I'd still like to know him better since he and Bevin have gotten so close. I wish we knew more about him. And really, you can't judge by smell. It could be his dad, like Piper and her dad."

That was true. Cody was a smelly, smelly teen, like every other one! "Most of the guys at school wear just as much cologne as he does. I get dizzy half the time I walk down the halls." I shook my head, dismissing the idea.

She shrugged. "We get ourselves invited over to his house, see if we can learn more about him without Bev around. It's what friends do, you know."

She made it sound so obvious and easy. I wasn't sure if it was really either of those things, but my mind started to chug.

We continued to school as I contemplated how to get invited to Cody's house. In the parking lot, Bevin and Cody joined us. Cody gave us a big wave and had a welcoming smile. He smelled all friend. "Hello, ladies."

"Hey," I said, thinking fast, "I was wondering, we have that big exam in history on Friday, and I haven't been able to study because my house is insane. Any chance you'd want to study together?"

Bevin gave me a questioning look then confirmed my story. "She isn't wrong. Her place is loud, so finding a quiet place to study isn't easy. That's why she's always going to Sarah's or Piper's place to study, you know? Maybe your house would be a good spot?"

"Wait, you actually study when you go over to Piper's place?" Cody asked in pure disbelief.

I blushed, and Sarah laughed. "If you knew how important grades were to her, you wouldn't ask."

The heat traveled from my cheeks to my hair line.

Cody laughed. "Sure, we could study at my place. How about Wednesday after school? I need to check in with my dad first, pick up a bit. Two guys living in a house together isn't the cleanest combination."

"Cool, thanks," I said, and we were off to classes.

Sarah gave me a quick half-smile of approval. *The two of us are so devious.*

The rest of the day was uneventful. Afterward, we headed home as a group. We were close to the point where we all would go our separate ways when a large, black, official-looking car drove up and parked near us.

Cody stopped and gaped at the car. "Who's in trouble?"

Tanner rolled down the passenger window and leaned over the seat. He slowly lowered his mirrored glasses. "Get in."

Tilting my head, I raised my eyebrow. "Have any candy?"

Sarah snorted.

Bevin, placing his hands on the window, waggled his brows at Tanner. "Who do you want?"

Tanner sighed. "Why do I always have to deal with teenagers? You and Jade."

I quickly hugged and kissed Piper, promising to give her a call as soon as I got home. Then I jumped into the back seat. Bevin shrugged and followed.

Cody, still in shock, shrieked, "You're just getting in with the scary freak?" His scent turned sour, more disappointed than scared.

Sarah leapt backwards, throwing her hands over her mouth. "Good lord, help us!"

Piper gently laid her hand on Cody's shoulder. "Don't worry, he's Jade's uncle."

Cody whipped around and searched Tanner's face, then looked from me to Sarah, his gaze landing on Piper. "What are you talking about? He looks more like Sarah than Jade. How is he Jade's uncle?"

Sarah mumbled, "Closed-minded much?"

Bevin rolled down his window. "I'll explain later. I'll give you a call, okay? Later!"

With that, Tanner took off.

Trying to suppress my laughter, I asked, "Where are we going?"

"Luke's place. There's been some noise complaints. Allison thinks you two may be needed."

Leaning forward, I watched as the road streaked past. "Luke's? Is this about him and that guy he had to partner up with at work? He complained about it this summer."

Bevin turned to me. "Really? I hadn't heard about this. Luke's always so level-headed. What happened?"

Realizing Tanner wasn't about to talk while driving, I flopped back. "He came over one day, upset about work.

And pizza."

"Pizza? How can you be upset about pizza?" Bevin sounded hurt about this.

"Blue cheese and anchovy." I shivered at the memory.

Bevin made a face. Tanner's gaze jerked to me in the rearview mirror. His deep, velvety voice filled the car, full of disgust. "You're kidding, right?"

"I don't think so. Can you imagine the smell?"

We all just paused, thinking about how badly that pizza would offend our noses.

Before we could continue our discussion of the ruination of pizza, Tanner pulled into Luke's driveway. Luke lived in one half of a duplex, a small two-story painted a bright yellow. As I opened the door, I heard a crash come from inside and flinched.

I dashed up the stairs, but Tanner quickly passed me to get into the apartment first. He stepped through the door slowly. Inside it was dark. I peeked in and a side table flew through the air and hit the wall with a crash.

"Crap!" Tanner bellowed as he ran in and tackled Luke to the ground. Tanner was a tank, but Luke was only a few inches smaller, both in height and girth.

Slowly, I followed. The room was a mess. Pieces of furniture and dishware lay in piles all over. Clothes and papers were in the mix. Luke growled under Tanner, pushing him up almost in a reverse push-up.

"Let me go, man, let me go…let me go…let me go…"

Over and over.

Bevin and I looked around. The tension in the room filled the space thickly. I could swim through it. I got to the kitchen, and though the cupboards were empty of dishes, the room itself was clean. Apparently, Luke had saved all the destruction for the living room.

Tanner's voice cut through the space. "Jade!"

I turned; Luke's eyes glowed, and it seemed like he was about to throw Tanner off him. He let out a primal snarl.

"Jade! Hurry!"

I closed my eyes, found my center, and released my epsilon calm. It cut through the stress, the tension, and the emotions of the others in the room. Everything went silent and still. As I opened my eyes, my focus landed on Luke, who stared at me with wide eyes, his breathing rough. Tanner still had him pinned down.

Deciding they were contained, I continued my search of the kitchen. *What could have upset Luke so badly he lost control?* With dread flowing through me, I found a bottle of pills in the kitchen. It was a supplement from a local pharmacy: L-theanine. My apprehension became a growl. Carrying the bottle out to the living room, I sat on the couch near the two men. Bevin saw me and joined me.

I looked at the bottle then at Luke. "Whose are these?"

He still looked and smelled terrified. "Mine? I mean… mine. Why?"

"Why are you taking them? Who suggested them?"

Hands fisted, I tried to sound as calm as I could, but I could feel my heart rate increase. Tanner gave me a strange look.

"Um, T.J. gave them to me."

It was a punch to the gut and my vision blurred. My body went rigid. "What, now?" The words were low, but in a room of werewolves, they all heard.

Bevin rubbed my back. The look on his face told me he could feel my inner turmoil, especially at the mention of the brother I had to kill.

Luke tried to wet his lips. "Last spring, you know, after he got that new job. It was awful. He was really stressed. He said someone told him they helped relax a person. Knowing I could be stressed at work, he suggested them to me, too."

I tried to take a breath but could hear how rattled I sounded. "Did he give them to his sister, too?"

"Yeah, sure, of course. You know how high-strung Candice was."

The tears burned a line down my cheek as I dropped my head into my shaking hands.

Tanner watched me closely. "Jade, what is it? What's wrong?"

Every muscle in my body tense with emotion, the bottle crashed into the wall as I threw it with every ounce of strength I could. It hit hard enough to shatter the plastic. Pills flew everywhere. I couldn't stop the tears. "Those pills. Those bloody pills. They cause werewolves to be violent.

They cause them to act crazy." I jumped up, pointing at the dent I put in the wall, tears burning tracks down my cheeks. "They could cause a wolf who had been my brother for six years to turn around and try to kill me."

CHAPTER 22

I lay curled in bed, reliving the pain of losing T.J. and Candice. Tanner had dropped me back at home and went to my dad's office to discuss the situation about the herb and Luke. If he'd been taking L-theanine for a while, Luke could be the rogue werewolf we'd been looking for. The idea made me shudder.

Pain lanced through my body again at the memory of Candice clawing and biting into me, her teeth tearing chunks from me. My last hope of survival had been curling into a ball to protect my soft bits. If Sarah hadn't shown up when she did, I wouldn't have survived. I hated coming back to this memory, always afraid it would end differently. It was the reason Dad was so adamant on all the young wolves learning to fight and defend themselves. He wouldn't risk our lives. Hot tears streaked down my face towards my pillow.

A knock at the door brought me out of my memories. Before I could answer, it opened and then silently closed. Sniffing, I smelled Piper approach the bed. She didn't say anything, just curled in behind me, spooning me. I rolled over as she wrapped her arms around me, and I let the floodgates open. She rubbed my back, giving me the comfort I needed.

It didn't take long for my tears to dry up. I took a long pull of air, breathing in Piper's scent. It centered me, made me feel whole. I flopped to my back and draped an arm over my eyes. "Thank you."

"I didn't do anything."

"You were here. That was enough."

"Of course I was here. Bevin called and said you had a rough afternoon. I came over to see if you needed anything. I guess it really was rough."

I filled her in on what happened at Luke's.

Piper furrowed her brow. "Wow, and Tanner thinks he may be the one attacking all the innocent people?"

"Yes…no…maybe. You know Luke better than I do. But the thing is, L-theanine is a nasty herb to take when you're a werewolf."

She shook her head, looking troubled. "But Luke wouldn't harm anyone."

"Did Bev tell you what we found at Luke's place when we got there?"

Piper sighed. "It was really that bad, huh?"

"Yeah, it really was."

It was getting late. We headed to the kitchen to find food I'd smelled cooking. Owen was pulling out dishes for setting the dining room table, so we went to help. Once done setting the table and the food set out, we took our places and dug in.

Mom looked over at me. "You doing any better?"

I nodded. "I think so. We need to make sure to bring this up at the next pack meeting. Maybe send out a pack email, too. I don't want this to come up again in a few months."

Dad reached over and rubbed my arm. "I'll get the word out. Don't worry, pumpkin. And Tanner is going to work with Greg to track Luke's movements over the last few weeks. We'll get this all cleared up. I want you to focus on school. Do you understand me?"

I nodded.

On Wednesday, Cody, Bevin, and I walked home together. Even though it was looking like Luke was the rogue, I still wanted to check out Cody's place and get to know him better. About a block before Cody's apartment, Bevin turned off towards home.

Cody lived on the ground floor of his building and had a private entrance as well as the building's main entrance. He thought it was cool since it meant they didn't have to go through as much security to get in, but it also meant they didn't have as much security. Apparently, he and his dad didn't mind. The ease of coming and going was worth it for them.

We entered a huge box of a room, all white and new-looking. Cody shut the door and my back hit the door. The smell of bleach almost did me in; my eyes watered, and I started to cough.

Cody turned back and looked at me questioningly.

I waved a hand and did a quick head shake. "Dry throat. Sorry. Glass of water? Tour?"

We were at one corner of a large rectangle; he pointed along one of the shorter sides to the other corner where there was a second door, and the kitchen.

He smiled mischievously. "Kitchen. We can get a glass of water there."

Rolling my eyes at his mocking tone, I followed. After I drank some water, I tried to force my coughing to stop.

His smile turned more natural, and he pointed to the cabinets behind him. "Behind this wall is a mud room to go with the main entrance."

Cody's books sat in a stack on the peninsula of the counter. "Why study here versus there?" I pointed to the dining room table. The table and chairs were a warm-colored wood. A nice relief in the sea of white.

Shrugging, Cody grinned. "I like spinning on the stools."

A snort escaped me at the honesty of his response.

He turned to the living room, pointing down the long expanse of room. "Living room and hallway to the bedrooms and bathroom. First room on the left is the bathroom."

I stared at the huge TV mounted on the wall and then shifted my gaze to the hallways just to the right of it. "Good to know."

Turning back towards the door we'd entered through, my eyes landed on a small desk that stood between us and the door. I'd missed it while I was coughing. "That's my dad's home office. If we're smart, we steer clear of anything on the desk," Cody stated.

"He works from home?"

"Nah, just a place to hold his computer and papers."

Confirming the no-fly zone area of the room, I moved towards the peninsula and the spinning stools. The acrid odor of bleach threatened to overwhelm me, and stung my nose.

I sneezed twice. "Wow, Cody, you didn't have to clean this much. I may be female, but I'm also a teenager. Did you guys bleach every square inch of the place?"

"We used lemon-scented bleach," he said proudly, waggling his eyebrows as if the lemon made any difference at all.

"Next time, don't worry about it; this place smells like I

imagine a cleaned-up crime scene would smell." I laughed and sneezed again.

Cody forced a laugh at my joke. *I guess not everyone appreciates my humor.*

We took out our books and went over the info for the test. In the end, we really did have a big exam coming up and I wanted to earn a good grade. It surprised me how good Cody was at the subject; he was better than I thought from class. Time slid by as we studied people and wars of the past.

During a lull in the studying, I turned to him. "So, how are things with you and Bevin going?"

He froze and for a moment I didn't think he would answer. We weren't really that close as friends, and it wasn't any of my business. I just needed a study break. But then he turned wide eyes to me and shrugged. "I figured you would get all of this from Bevin."

"Maybe, but I want to get your perspective on things. That, and I need to give my brain time to absorb what we just studied before we continue. Distraction, man." I must have sounded desperate.

His mouth quirked in a half-smile, he blushed, and his heart rate increased. He wiped his hands on his jeans. His fear of the question wafted off him but I tasted the chocolatey lust as his thoughts shifted from history to Bevin.

I smirked. "You really like him, don't you?"

He stared at me for a couple seconds as if trying to decide what he wanted to tell me about the situation, then said, "It's really between me and Bevin, but yeah, I do."

Truth.

"It's my business because we're friends. We all hang out at school, and you're dating one of my best friends. So spill."

"You don't understand, he kisses better than anyone I've ever kissed." He stared at me in the eyes for this first part, but then his eyes drifted away, and his scent shifted. "After her, everyone else I've ever kissed is like a baby."

Does he know he just misgendered Bevin? This is weird.

I waved a hand in front of his face. "Cody? You okay?" His eyes snapped back to me and his body language shifted again. He started to smell peppery and angry. I frowned and shook my head. "Bevin *isn't* a girl."

His scent changed again, sharper. Frustration poured off of him. He growled, "I know."

His shifts in emotion are going to give me whiplash.

Cody narrowed his eyes. "Do *you* know he's not a girl? You seem awfully invested in his every action."

I raised my eyebrows. "What? I just asked you about your relationship, that's what friends do. What is *wrong* with you?" I sneezed, causing my seat to rotate. I grabbed the counter to stop the turning. "And why so much bleach? What are you trying to cover up?"

"Nothing."

"Really? Do you use this much bleach all the time?"

He glared. "You really want to know?" His voice changed. "Yes!"

"We were trying to cover up…"

The front door opened, and his dad walked in, an older version of Cody, only a few inches taller. I was amazed at how similar they looked. "Hiya, kids."

I checked my watch: six-thirty. *Damn.* I couldn't believe how late it had gotten. Cody leapt up and headed to the bathroom, mumbling he'd be right back.

Like father, like son, apparently—his dad wore more body spray than Cody and reeked of the stuff. I would gag if any more scents entered the building, except that the next smell was food. *I can live with that one.*

"You must be Jade. You can call me Nathan or Mr. Ants," he said, holding out his hand to shake. "It's nice to finally meet one of Cody's new friends. I've heard a lot about all of you, but haven't met any of you, not even the mysterious Bevin. Where did Cody run off to?"

"He said something about the bathroom. We were talking about why the place smelled of bleach and it upset him."

Mr. Ants laughed. "Did he tell you about the fish?"

"Fish?"

He placed the pizza on the dining room table. "I bought a fresh fish for dinner last night; thought I could do what they do on TV. I had no idea how messy descaling it would be. Scales got everywhere. Needless to say, neither of us are very fond of fish, or their scales. The only solution we could find was take-out and bleach…lots and lots of bleach. We may have gone overboard."

Cody came back. He smelled normal again, not angry. He gave a small smile. "Yeah, fish is gross. The smell of bleach is loads better."

Okay, that makes sense. Why all the drama? Cody seems to like shaking me up. I shook my head in confusion. I slid my eyes over to Cody slyly. "Why haven't you brought Bevin over to meet the dad?"

Cody blushed brightly but laughed. "Just haven't, but I'm thinking that will have to happen soon."

Mr. Ants handed Cody plates to bring to the table. "I brought pizza; hope you don't mind meat toppings."

My stomach grumbled. I was hungry enough to eat a horse and pizza sounded divine. "Sounds wonderful." I may have swooned.

We ate, we talked, and I heard all sorts of embarrassing stories about when Cody was young. The two of them had been on their own for a long time. Cody's mom had died when he was in elementary school and these two had been surviving with no other family for most of his life. *Interesting. Didn't Cody say it had only been a year or two since his mom died? They would know, though.*

Sadly, there were no pictures up at the apartment, of her or anyone.

In the end, Mr. Ants offered me a ride home. He seemed like a nice guy, he had good taste in pizza, and Cody and I had gotten a lot of studying done. Despite the chemical attack on my nose, the evening hadn't been a total bust.

CHAPTER 23

Saturday morning, Dad turned to me while eating his yogurt and fruit breakfast. "I want you to be able to do a quick werewolf or wereanimal check with just a touch."

"What?" I was up, I had had coffee; this shouldn't be throwing me.

Beside me, Pebble bounced with excitement.

Narrowing my eyes at her in suspicion, I sipped my coffee. Did she know something I didn't? She was home all day being homeschooled. My guess, she picked up on a lot more than any of us knew. I should spend time with her every night figuring out what was going on. I bet she would tell me. *She could become my little spy—no, my sister spy!*

"I want you to move beyond smell. I want you to be able to ascertain if someone is a wereanimal just by shaking their hand," Dad continued. "I want this determination to happen in under two seconds."

"But why? My nose works so much better," I whined. *This seems like such a waste of time; I don't need more work piled on top of Dad's current training program.*

"Does it?" he asked with raised eyebrows. "When you met Piper, she wore a bunch of perfumes to confuse your nose. My guess is, there may be other werewolves who know that trick."

He grabbed my hand, eyes twinkling with excitement. "What if we could find wereanimals with a brief handshake? What happens if you're in a crowd with too many people? What happens if you have a headache? There are so many reasons why your nose, even if it is one of the best in the pack, can let you down, but a quick touch to check could save your life."

My mind began to catch up. I took a bite of my bagel. "So, now I have to shake the hand of every person in the world? Or do I just go around touching people? That seems a little creepy, no?"

Dad just gave me a level stare, and I knew I had no choice.

This training is going to make my head hurt.

"Fine." Slumping back, resigned, I grumbled. "How is this training going to work?"

"Well, we're going to start off easy. I want you to shake my hand, Pebble's hand, the hand of whoever you meet, and I want you to train your inner beasts to see what they can figure out. So, shake."

With a sigh, I took his hand. Nothing. But the beasts hadn't stirred. Closing my eyes, I found them in my mental landscape. *Who wants to play?*

Panther was usually the more willing to play these games. She sauntered up, purring.

Explaining what I wanted took images more than words. *Is this as weird as it seems?* If no one else experienced their animals as separate, did that mean they couldn't talk to their animals? *That's really sad.*

I opened my eyes and shook his hand again; was that a twinge? Grabbing Pebble's hand, I definitely felt a twinge. *Huh. Cool!*

"Okay, that was fun, are we done?" A smile stretched across my face. I knew we weren't, but wanted to continue the sass. In all honesty, I was hooked.

"Nope, I invited Sarah and her family over, as well as Bevin and his family. You're going to spend the day shaking hands."

As interesting as that sounded, I groaned, pillowing my head on my arms.

It wasn't long before Sarah and her parents arrived. I shook her hand. I felt a twinge again, but it was different. *Was it different?*

"Wait here," I told her.

I dragged Dad over. This was his game; he should have to do what I wanted. I shook his hand, then Sarah's. Then his, then Sarah's. Standing in the hall by the front door, Sarah and her parents stared at me, amused. By then, I supposed they were used to my strange antics.

Once I had my mind around the difference in the feel between Sarah and my dad, I shook Sarah's mom's hand. Nothing. I shook it again. Then I shook her dad's hand. Then I went back to my dad's, and then Sarah's.

"Stop." Sarah laughed. "What in Sonnara's good graces are you doing?" A laugh bubbled up at me as she invoked the werewolf god. She had been studying the twin gods and loved what they stood for. This was the first I'd heard her use one of their names in conversation.

I sighed. "Dad!" I said in pure exasperation. That one word should explain anything weird I was expected to do.

Sarah laughed harder.

"But why?" she demanded.

I rolled my eyes. "Okay, you want more explanation than that, fine. Dad has a theory I can use my new ability to detect a wereanimal in the span of a handshake, but I need to test with different people. But I think different wereanimals feel different. That's why I wanted both you and Dad here."

I prowled the living room. Everyone followed me in. Sarah's parents took the love seat and Sarah flopped on the couch. Dad took one of the recliner chairs.

The scientist in me had taken over. "When Bevin and his family get here, we'll have to set up a sensory deficit with me and see if what I'm sensing is really through my hand, or through my nose and eyes. Hope versus reality."

"That's really cool," Sarah said, head tilting as she seemed to get lost in thought. "We could put a blindfold on you, but how can we keep you from smelling us? Your sniffer is better than most. I mean, I can't imagine how you survived at Cody's place the other day after they bleached the place down."

"It was lemony bleach," I said with an ironic smile. *And the headache I got from that night lasted well into the next day.*

"When are Bevin and his family getting here?" Sarah asked.

Dad looked at his watch, then at his phone to see if he had missed a call or a text. "They should have gotten here before you. Hazel!" he bellowed. "Have you heard from Fred or Janet this morning?"

Mom came running, eyes wild. "Janet is missing!"

I froze. *What?*

"What happened?" demanded Dad, switching to alpha mode.

"Last night, Bevin and his boyfriend got into a fight and Bevin went for a walk. Janet got worried and went after him. Bevin came home just after eleven, but Janet never returned. Fred didn't realize until this morning that she was missing. She usually gets up before him."

She looked between me and Sarah and then back to Dad. "She left a note that she was heading out to find Bevin and to talk to Cody's dad to see what had happened. Fred found the note after getting your text this morning asking for the family to come over. I've called Tanner and Greg. They're heading over to start the search. Fred called the police as well."

Pulling out my phone, I rotated it in my hands. "Do you need Cody's number? Have you tried calling him or his dad? Has anyone called over there to see if she made it?"

Dad's head bobbed. "Send me his contact info, pumpkin. I was going to ask for it; your head is going in the right direction this morning."

After sending him the info, I put my phone back in my pocket. Sitting there, I was unsure what to do next. Our day of games turned into a vigil, waiting to find out what happened to our pack-mate. As the morning went on, pack members showed up. Word had gotten out and no one wanted to be alone. Tanner's wife, Monica, and their son were the first to arrive, then Estrella and her parents. Family by family, they all showed up. I set out food and drinks in the kitchen.

Piper and Dillan herded the kids into the basement to watch a movie or play games. Some of the wolves went out in pairs to search: Clare with my dad, Jackson with Alejandro. No one went out alone.

Eventually, after they made their report to the

police, Bevin and his family came over so they wouldn't be alone, either.

Bevin fell into my arms and wailed. "It's all my fault." He kept saying it over and over.

"No, no, it isn't your fault. You're allowed to be upset and go out walking. If something happened to your mom, it's the fault of that beast, not you."

I tapped into my epsilon side, pulling on a calm reserve within me, and releasing it. It felt like sitting by a bubbling river in the woods.

His face snapped up to mine, eyes red and puffy with his tears, and almost out of control with grief. "No! Don't you dare try to calm me. I don't deserve it!"

I just held on harder as his body shook with his sobs. Sarah came over to add her hug.

When his breathing evened out, we moved him over to a couch, and sat on either side of him.

His dad, Fred, knelt in front of him. "Bevin, this is not your fault. It would hurt your mom if she thought you believed that. It hurts me to hear you say it. You can't think that way."

Fred reached out and took his hands. "Everyone is out looking for her, and no one blames you. You have to stop saying that, or even thinking it. This is about finding your mother, and finding whoever did this. It's not *your* fault." His words were raw and filled with pain.

Bevin nodded, hanging his head as the tears ran down his cheeks. I don't know if he believed the words, but I hoped he would try.

Mom's phone rang, and after she'd taken the call, she marched in, wolf in her voice. "Jade, with me, now!"

She dashed to the kitchen.

Watching her, I hesitated to interrupt. "Can I help?"

She paused in her motion and turned glowing eyes to me. "Just do everything I say." She threw food into a bag. Taking a travel mug, she added what looked like equal parts sugar and coffee, and then she ran to the car. I followed.

She tossed the bag at me. "Eat it, eat it all."

Awkwardly, I caught the bag. My eyes widened when I glanced inside. I couldn't imagine eating everything—a few slices of pizza, a breakfast sandwich, and two energy bars—but when I slowed, she growled at me.

She sped down the road, taking corners sharp enough the food kept hitting my cheek instead of my mouth as I stuffed myself. Coffee sloshed onto my shirt. Just as I finished as much as I could cram in, we arrived at a park. I drank water to help wash the food down and gulped coffee with extra cream. It was too sweet, but mom's ire wasn't worth battling. She wanted me to eat and I ate. She wanted me to drink this coffee and I drank it. My alpha had commanded it.

We got out of the car on the edge of town in one of the wooded areas; less of a park, more of a wildlife preserve. Pine and oak trees provided thick coverage. Up ahead, I saw Jackson and assumed Alejandro was nearby scouting the area. Then I saw Bevin's mom. I almost lost everything in my stomach. Her body lay on the ground, face up, mangled. She didn't appear to be breathing. *Is she dead?* Then her chest moved. *Gods above, she's alive.*

"Has anyone called 911?" I whispered.

Mom stood behind me, hands on my shoulders. "Not yet. We want you to try first. You know how tricky it is with our blood and labs; if you can fix her, it will be better. Do your thing. We have three wolves here. If you falter, we will give you what energy we can."

I approached and knelt on the ground next to her. I barely recognized the wreck of a body. She lay on her back as if she had been fighting. There were scratch marks down her face and side, her shredded clothing exposing her mangled arms and abdomen. It looked like the attacker had taken a few bites from her side and thigh before leaving her. I wasn't sure why they hadn't gone for her neck, though from her position, her neck had been protected. *Where is it safe to place my hands?*

I put my hand on her wrist and both my animals charged in. Panther went for the bigger areas, muscles, bones. Wolf concentrated on the smaller items, pulmonary. I managed it all. Surveying her body, I found where she was in most need and focused the healing there. It was a dance and I was the choreographer.

Taking a deep breath, I got to work. We started on getting her stable; heart, lungs, brain, throat, and her wolf.

There was so much to do; I just found an emergency within her, focused on it, and did what I could to help.

Minutes, hours, possibly days passed. I lost track of time. A straw pressed to my lips, different sets of hands on my shoulders. Time passed.

Eventually I woke up on the couch in the living room dizzy and confused. I wasn't sure if I could move.

"What happened?" I asked. The room spun even though I was just lying there. I couldn't imagine what would happen if I tried to sit up.

"You saved her," Mom said. "You knelt there for four hours, not moving. At times you shook, we tried giving you food, we tried sharing energy. You just wouldn't budge." Mom was near tears, her hands on my forehead. "Then, after four hours, you collapsed next to Janet. We brought you both back here. Allison looked at you and said you needed liquids, so we've been getting you to drink water. Janet is in the medical room, patched up. She's still unconscious. No one knows when she'll wake up. No one knows how you saved her."

She froze, looking off into space. "It's a miracle. You're a miracle. You did it, Jade. You saved her."

She hugged me tightly and then held a cup of something foul smelling up to my mouth.

"Ugh, what *is* that?"

"It's water with electrolytes and calories. You needed something to give you energy."

Mom held me up and I drank it. What choice did I

have? She held it to my mouth. Aunt Allison had made this and my alpha was going to make sure I drank it.

Ugh, it tastes even worse than it smells. "Is everyone still here?" I asked.

"Yes."

"Okay, let's give this a try. Give me your hand." She did. *She's a wolf, heh, cool.* Dad's game was still working.

Okay, I wasn't trying to identify wereanimals, I needed to be able to sit up on my own. I pulled just a little of her energy, just enough to be able to sit up. Mom staggered a little. Her eyes grew wide, but she nodded.

"Can you get up now?" she asked, stunned.

"Yeah, thanks." I got up, took the glass and drank the rest of the evil concoction. "Can I have some real food now?"

She smiled and called out, "Jade wants food."

That brought in a stampede of people bearing edible gifts.

I groaned, and she gave me an evil smile. "Serves you right," she mouthed.

With the food came Sarah, Bevin, Dad, and Fred, the first to hug me while thanking me for saving his wife.

There were questions I couldn't answer and food I could eat. The biggest question was why couldn't I have taken energy from the other wolves there, my mom, Jackson and Alejandro? To that, though, I thought I did have an answer.

"Janet was really bad off when we got there. When my animals realized that not only was she hurt, but her inner werewolf was hurt, they both jumped in to help heal her.

271

She's pack. I don't know if I could have stopped them." Feeling dizzy, I took a sip of water and a bite of cheese. "In the past I've only ever used one animal to look into a person. I think the one I leave behind makes sure I stay healthy. With both of them working on Janet, there was no animal left to watch over me."

I looked over at Dad and saw his face darken. I quickly added. "Yes, I know, we need to discuss and figure out how to not let this happen again."

Everyone in the room chuckled at my preemptive agreement.

"In all honesty, I've blanked out most of what happened. I remember the initial diagnosis, some of the bigger fixes that needed to happen, and someone trying to put a straw in my mouth. Then I woke up on the couch. I definitely lost too much of myself in this save." I dropped my head back on the couch and found my dad. "You're right, Dad, I need to train. I could've saved Janet without endangering myself; that, or we need to find a third wereanimal that I always leave at home." I tapped my head as I said that last part. At the stunned looks I quickly said, "Joke."

Dad grumbled as he came over. "I don't think a third animal is the answer. Training, however, is." He bent down and kissed my forehead before straightening and ruffling my hair.

The touch of pack centered me. "One more thing, I don't know if you picked it up here, but she smelled of wolf—

and it wasn't Luke. Whoever it was probably thought he'd done enough."

Dad's eyes narrowed. "He'd?"

"I don't know, something about it all, it wasn't smell, or…I don't know, there was a feel, it just…I can't explain it." I shrugged helplessly.

A kiss on my forehead. "Pumpkin, you need to rest. We'll discuss this once you've recouped."

Shortly after that, I headed to bed. The food, coffee, and water gave me just enough energy to make it from the couch to my room…with help.

Everyone slept at the pack house that night, and for the most part there was room, but Piper and Sarah stayed in my room with me so I wouldn't be alone.

Once my head hit the pillow, I was out.

CHAPTER 24

The next morning, Tanner and Greg did a security check on all the pack homes to make sure everything was tight.

Janet wasn't abducted from her house; but this werewolf was getting bolder and bolder, and we didn't want to take any chances. Any of the pack members who wanted to stay at the pack house were welcome to stay. However, most wanted to get home.

Janet was still unconscious, so Bevin's family moved in until she woke up. They took over two of the basement bedrooms, one for Heather and Hanna, Bevin's younger sisters, and one for Bevin. Fred would sleep on a cot in the medical room near his wife.

While Bevin and I read in the living room, Aunt Allison and Uncle Jackson prepared to leave. Fred asked for the third time in two days, "Do you have any idea when she'll wake up?"

Aunt Allison's face dropped. "I'm really sorry, Fred. I primarily work with animals, not people. I'm not sure why she won't wake up. I think she needs time. She was hurt badly, both physically and mentally. I don't even know the extent of the injuries she sustained. Or even what repairs Jade managed to make."

She came over and gave me a hug goodbye. "We should think about talking to River and Hazel about you going in again to see what you can figure out." Shocked by this, I almost missed her next words. "It's too soon for that right now. You almost killed herself doing that the first time. You need to rest and rebuild your reserves."

Aunt Allison moved around the room giving everyone a hug as she spoke. She returned to Fred. "Give it a bit more time, for both of them. Janet is stable—which is pretty remarkable at this point. Our only other option is the hospital; but I doubt they can do anything more to help her, and they would have a lot of questions we can't answer."

Fred looked resigned to the news. As werewolves, hospitals were always a risky choice. From our weird blood to our fast healing abilities, avoiding hospitals was best for our safety.

When you took into account that a hurt wolf could lash out, steering clear of norms was best for them, as well.

Sunday was a quiet day. Sarah, Piper, Bevin, and I worked on homework in the basement study room. It was the only quiet room with so many adults in the house. It was usually filled with kids secluded from adult conversation. Today, it was our choice.

"So," I asked, unable to hold it in any longer, "what did you and Cody fight about?"

"It was stupid." Bevin dropped his hands to the table with a long breath. While he spoke, he nervously played with his pencil. "I went over to meet his dad and we had a nice evening. His dad seemed to like me; he even cooked dinner for the three of us. He mentioned you, too. I asked Cody on the way home if he'd told his dad that I was trans."

Bevin paused and a snap filled the silence as his pencil broke in half. He looked down sheepishly and gently laid the pieces down. He balled his hands into fists then shook them out.

Taking a deep breath, he continued, "He said 'no' so fast, I hadn't even gotten the question out fully. I was just so surprised, ya know. I asked him if he was embarrassed by me, and he said 'no' again, but I think he lied. I asked him what the big deal was. He said he just didn't think his dad would understand."

He looked up at us sadly. "From there the fight got ugly. I don't think that Cody, himself, is really okay with it all. Like he said, he likes the look, but not what it's covering up. This is going to be a lifelong issue for me, isn't it? Some gay guys won't like me because I'm not cis." He shrank at those words, like they hurt him. "Straight guys won't like me because I'm a guy. I'm just screwed. Or, more to the point, I'm not screwed."

We chuckled at his joke because we were supposed to, but we knew his pain.

I placed a hand on his arm. "You are totally not dumb to feel this way. Nothing you've said sounded stupid, or wrong, or anything. You'll find someone, Bevin. Someone who loves you because you're amazing. You need to find someone who appreciates you for who you are…which is someone pretty amazing. You'll find a man who can't live without you." My voice was thick with the tears I tried to hold back. I wanted to be strong for my best friend.

He just stared at me. "You make that sound so easy."

Shaking my head, I snorted. "Nothing about dating is easy, haven't you figured that out yet? We're teenagers; we're just exploring at this point. We have time. We're only in high school. College is meant for exploration, right? Then, after college, things can get serious. You have time."

Leaning back and narrowing my eyes, I gave him a calculating stare. "I mean, it isn't like Cody was going to be the one anyway. My theory is you mainly like him because he was the first guy who showed any interest in you—that you've noticed anyway. Your life has been so weird, it would be hard to notice interest at all from any party."

Bevin relaxed a bit and smiled, then placed his hand on mine. "You may be right. I just wanted someone to like me, and he's cute. But I was probably trying too hard."

Sarah chimed in, tilting her head as she thought. "I don't know if you were trying too hard; he was the one who joined our group and seemed to jump through hoops to hook up with you. I think if anyone was trying too hard, it was him."

We all stopped to think about that. *Looking back, it's interesting how he just glommed on to our group and stuck with us this whole time. I've never seen him hang out with anyone else.*

Piper gave her insight. "I've watched him when he walked the halls thinking we were all in or on our way to classes. He's mean to the other students. He can be a real bully."

"Really?" I couldn't picture it. He had said some off the wall stuff, but I just couldn't see him as a bully. "What does he do?"

"It's really sneaky, I don't even think anyone sees that it's him. He'll trip someone or knock off a hat. He does things so that it seems like it's someone else. Then he gets this joyous gleam in his eyes, like he's so happy that he got away with something. Then he just watches as the students he's instigated fight each other."

"Wow, Piper, you sure notice a lot."

She got a far-off look, then focused on us again. She shrugged. "I've always been sort of a fly on the wall, watching and not being seen. I doubt he even notices I'm in our group half the time. He's really focused on the two of you." She pointed at me and Bevin.

I didn't doubt her. Piper had always been good at reading people. "Why haven't you told us this before?" I asked, taking a sip of my coffee and grabbing a cookie off the plate we'd brought down.

"Bevin was happy and I didn't want to stir up trouble. What if I said something, misread things, and it turned out I'd caused a wedge in our friendship? I really didn't want to do that. Be that person." She looked at Bevin. "I'm sorry if I should've said something before."

"Don't worry, Piper, I get it. It's hard to bring up negative things about people, especially without proof. It was fun while it lasted, but I guess I should admit it's time to move on." He sighed as he crossed his arms and laid his head down.

"So," said Sarah, eyes twinkling, "let's blindfold Jade, and see what she can do."

The cookie stopped half-way to my mouth.

Piper's brow furrowed and Bevin chimed in with a confused, "Huh?"

Sarah explained her game. Then, as Bevin gathered stuff, Sarah sought out people. There were still plenty milling about the pack house.

They put a blindfold on me, and then rubbed garlic and lemon juice under my nose. I held some of the garlic under my nose to make sure that was all I smelled. Well, that worked, and it could have been worse. It could have been bleach.

Next, they put noise-canceling earphones on me and turned music on—not so loud that I couldn't hear anything—but enough that I couldn't use audible cues to figure out who was coming up to me. Gah, I felt so out of it like this. Blind, deaf, and nose-blind. This was awful. I hadn't been a wereanimal that long, but I had become dependent on my senses. Lastly, I placed my hand on the table palm up so the "test subject" could come and grab my hand.

The first person took my hand. Nothing. "Nothing. Um, norm?" I waited a beat and then with more certainty, "Norm."

I held the hand a second longer and then let go. Pretty sure it was Piper; I could sense a wolf seed in her, about three years off.

The next hand gave a tingle, but it was so slight, it really wasn't there. I gasped. "Oh, my gods, Bevin, under a year for your wolf."

He spoke loud enough to be heard over the music. "Sorry, not the game we're playing now."

We kept the game going, though I figured I'd proven my point.

The next one took a few seconds, but I was getting a

feeling of who as well as what. "Mom, wolf."

"Dad, wolf." A bit faster.

A different tingle. "Sarah, panther."

"Fred, wolf." Faster.

"Pebble, wolf."

I rolled my eyes under my blindfold. "Dad, wolf."

"Norm." I so wanted to sniff, but I couldn't. "Tom? Yes." Holding on to his hand until I was certain, I answered my own question. "Tom."

"Wolf. Dad, stop jumping the line."

"Piper, three years out."

"Cindy, norm."

"Can I stop?"

Someone removed my blindfold and I recoiled from the light. I blinked a few times before my eyes finally adjusted.

"That was amazing," Dad said, "you could identify animal, length until they would come out, and person, all within a few seconds. Do you have to prime the handshake, or is it always on?"

"Don't know, Dad; this is new for me, too. But I think it's always on. Panther likes the game."

"Three years?" Piper said. "That's more time than you gave before. How sure are you?"

Grabbing her hand again, I narrowed my eyes. "Two years, eleven months," I said with a challenging smile and a wink.

She just mouthed "wow". She grabbed her phone and typed.

Bevin just looked up at me. "Did you really just tell me under a year?" He came over and forced his hand into mine. I closed my eyes and breathed in deeply.

"Yep, next spring sometime. Hopefully, it will be over spring break and not during classes."

"Or, knowing my luck, during finals," Bevin mumbled.

The room started to reel around me.

"Okay, lunch time," Mom said.

She put her arm around me to support me as we all tramped upstairs for lunch. After lunch, Piper and Sarah left with their families. Even with them gone, the house felt full.

Mom called Owen to get him caught up with all the gossip. I called José.

He sounded shocked about everything that had happened. "Bevin will find someone; he's so beautiful." José sounded so sad for our friend. "I wish he knew how beautiful he was—inside and out."

I shook my head. "It's hard when you've never felt comfortable in your own skin. I can't imagine feeling like you were born wrong, and then trying to fix it…but it can't really be fixed for years. He's trying, but it's hard. How can you believe someone else will accept you when you have a hard time accepting yourself? Cody just pushed all his buttons. That jerk!"

"What will you do about him on Monday?" José asked.

"I don't know. Cody's been hanging out with us, but he can't think that we would ever choose him over someone we've known all our lives. At the same time, Bevin doesn't need the drama. I'll go ask him when I get off the phone with you."

"Not right away, chica. I'm going to give Bevin a call and talk to him first. He needs more friends. I've been falling short in that department. Give me an hour, then go and be his in-person friend."

I agreed, and we said our goodbyes.

CHAPTER 25

Monday morning, Dad had the news on in the living room while I sat and drank coffee trying to wake up enough for school. This early, most of the others were still asleep.

The announcer spoke in a brusque, neutral voice as he announced his findings to the camera. "The elderly couple was found dead on the stoop of a local family's home. A neighbor was walking her dog early this morning when the dog began barking uncontrollably. The police were called. When they went to question the family, they weren't home."

My hand shook as Bevin's house flashed on the TV

screen behind the reporter. It was blurry, but I'd spent enough time there to know it. "According to the police records, the family is staying with friends and have been since Saturday. More to come when we learn of it. Suzanne, back to you."

Dad paused the TV when the images of the dead couple from a framed picture flashed on the screen, and sat next to me. Putting down my coffee before it spilled, I tried to breathe around the icicles building throughout my body. "Are Fred and Bevin in trouble?"

"No, they've been here the whole time. They can track Fred's phone if need be, but this pulls him into an ongoing investigation. He has a solid alibi, but the police want to question him."

He shifted his gaze from the TV to me. "Do you know who the couple is? Any relation to your life?"

I studied the picture of the victims on the TV, but I didn't recognize them. "No. The only connection here is that they were left on my friend's doorstep. Poor people."

"It looks like they weren't taken slowly," Dad said clinically, checking an image on his phone, a growl in his voice. "My company grabbed some images from the police report."

I shivered. "That's just sick. Do you think it's the rogue wolf again?"

"We think so. The way the couple looks matches the other eaten victims. We think Janet found the wolf or can identify him. He must know she survived, and now is trying to scare her off, scare the family off, or somehow get the family in trouble, maybe warn them to keep quiet. We aren't sure which. Things are going to get very dangerous before they get safer. I don't want you going anywhere alone."

Moving to the counter, I grabbed a bag of bagels and slid one into the toaster. "Before I started healing Janet… her injuries. It would've been enough on a human. If the rogue doesn't know about other werewolves, he wouldn't know what was needed to kill one."

Leaning against the counter, I watched as Dad gathered fruit and yogurt from the fridge. "I had a similar thought. But he's now had practice. I don't want his next test werewolf to be anyone in my pack."

Jumping as the toaster finished, I spun and prepared my bagel with cream cheese and jelly. I took a bite and thought about the situation. "How would they know Janet survived?"

Sipping his coffee, Dad leaned back. "They—he—may have been watching as we collected her. Listening and learning."

Unhappy with the idea that this rogue wolf was collecting information on us, I snarled. *How dare this unknown wolf terrorize us and limit our movements.* "Bevin is here, so we can walk to school together. Is that enough?"

"No, I'll drive you in. We'll pick up Sarah on the way. Piper's dad will drive her to school. Everyone will be getting picked up afterwards. Don't play around with this rule. No more walking until this wolf is found. I want you to be especially careful. You were right. All of the original victims centered around you and your group of friends."

He turned off the TV. "This latest one as well. I'm not sure how or why, but there is a connection between the rogue and your group of friends. I'm not going to rest easy until we find the connection and the wolf."

"Is someone driving Estrella?"

Quirking a smile, Dad nodded. "Of course, pumpkin."

I opened my mouth then shut it, unsure about the maelstrom of thoughts in my head. Dad placed his hand on mine. "What? What are you worrying about?"

"Dad, have you, Tanner, or Greg checked into Cody and his dad?"

Dad just searched my face. "We know what we're doing, hon." His voice hardened. "Focus on school right now, and let us do what we're good at. That said, though we're planning on looking into Cody and his dad as people close to you, new to the community, and potential suspects, they aren't our only lead. For now, don't let your friends know. If they are the rogues and know you figured it out, it will be more dangerous for you and your friends. Just be careful, and smart."

Once everyone was up and had eaten, Dad got us all safely to school, as promised. Trying to avoid seeing extra people, Bevin and I slipped off to AP bio right away. I sent a quick text to Piper letting her know where we were and why.

I said, "Well, this worked out fine, but we still don't

have a good plan for the day. What are you going to do in the classes you have with him? Not to mention lunch."

Bevin played with his pen and I could smell the nervousness wafting off him. "I don't think he'll try to sit with us at lunch. In English, we're assigned seats pretty far apart. Study hall, I'll go to the library. Gym…I'll figure something out."

It's good he's making plans; I hope it pulls him away from the guilt and grief over his mother.

"Did you and José come up with ways to navigate school around him last night?"

"Yeah. Before Cody, José and I had been talking regularly. I forgot how much I missed our nightly talks." His scent turned from nervous to something earthy and citrusy. A sad hope. Maybe thinking of what he'd missed.

"I think you're wrong about lunch. I mean, hopefully he won't sit with us, but if he does…do you want to do anything about it, or do you want to play it off as 'whatever'? Can you play it off like 'whatever'?" My brow rose as I let my challenge fall. His gaze floated off as his thoughts drifted and I placed my hand on his arm to pull him back.

Bevin focused on me and shook his head. "I don't know, we'll cross that bridge when we get there."

And that had been the answer I'd been getting since we'd woken up. Until he was face to face with Cody, he probably didn't know what his reaction would be.

Sighing, I couldn't blame him. *I wouldn't be able to*

predict my reaction in his place, either. And maybe Cody will stay away and it won't even be a problem.

I wasn't the first to arrive at lunch. Piper and Sarah had found a table off in the corner. I got my food and joined them. Bevin arrived next. We had saved him a seat between me and Piper in the corner. If Cody joined us, he would be stuck between me and Sarah on the outside. As it went, Cody wasn't at school. All this planning for nothing.

"A practice run," Sarah said, in her ever-positive view of things.

"He must be sick," Piper said, as we enjoyed our drama-free lunch.

Near the end of lunch, Estrella came over. "Have any of you seen Thompson? He usually sits with us, but I haven't seen him since first period today."

"Nope," I said, "why would we have seen him? I only met him twice, and one of those times he was unconscious."

Estrella fidgeted, glancing down at her feet. "Right, yeah, sorry. I'm just worried about him, that's all." And with that, she went back to her friends.

At the end of the day, Uncle Jackson waited to drive us home. No one had seen any signs of the rogue.

At home, Pebble told me and Bevin about the comings and goings of the adults and what she had heard of the searches. She was a great sister spy since no one noticed her sitting there listening to their every word.

Janet still hadn't woken up. Instead of returning to

work, Fred stayed by his wife's side. I asked if I should try to help again, but Dad said no. I needed a few more days to build up my strength.

Tuesday was a repeat of Monday. Lots of psyching ourselves out for nothing.

At lunch, I took a detour over to where Estrella sat. "Any word on Thompson?"

She shook her head. "I called his house last night; he never came home." She pulled out her phone as if he may call right then. Giving it a small shake she shook her head. "No texts, no calls." She sounded distracted.

I furrowed my brow. "That's weird. But he was here during first period yesterday?"

"Uh-huh." She looked around the room, checking out all the students at the different tables. "And now I can't find January. I was with her two periods ago, and now she isn't answering my texts." She gazed at her phone again, now off. Then her head shot up, face taut with fear and the sweet fear-scent around her. "Jade, what's going on?"

Grabbing her hands, I met her gaze. "Estrella, go to the office, talk to them. Tell them about January right away. Tell them about Thompson as well. I'll call my dad."

When I got to the table, I filled the others in on Thompson and January.

"Both of them are missing today?" Piper asked, eyes

wide, though the rest of her had gone still with nerves.

Leaning forward, a chill of dread flowed through me. "As far as Estrella knows."

Sarah's brow wrinkled in thought. "And she called Thompson's house and he wasn't home last night? Did his parents call the cops?"

Piper stiffened, hands fisting at her sides. Her voice lowered. "Oh, my gods, could the rogue have claimed them?"

The air quivered with tension. Everyone froze. I took a deep breath. "No idea." I pulled out my phone. "I need to call Dad and let him know what's going on here, this is too much."

Once I got off the phone, I told them my dad said we needed to meet at the lockers and walk out together.

It sounds paranoid; but at this point, a little paranoia seems wise.

Mom had relented on the 'no TV during family meals' rule. The news played as we ate spaghetti with meatballs with a side of garlic bread. The anchor, a perky blond with a no-nonsense attitude toward her male colleagues, was informative and fun to watch.

I froze mid-bite as the main report began. "Two students from Stolzburg High School have gone missing in the last two days. Fifteen-year-old Thompson Smith on Monday, and Fifteen-year-old January Jones just today. Both disappeared from the school within twenty-four hours of each other. The police are warning all parents and students to be wary of anyone they don't know. The school will be upping their security, and the local police will be patrolling…"

I stopped listening as images of Thompson and January filled the screen. A phone number flashed asking for any information. My hands shook. *What is happening?*

Wednesday morning, Thompson was found, dead and mauled, in front of Bevin's bedroom window. Like a cat leaving a gift for its owners. It was the second time a body-drop happened in front of the same house, which meant the police were going to be looking even closer at his family.

Since Bevin and his family were staying at our house, he didn't find out until the police came to talk to his dad. By now, they knew where to find them—even if the rogue wolf didn't seem to know.

School was a somber affair. We started the day with an assembly. Bevin sat between me and Sarah, with Piper on my other side. Bevin's sadness about Cody scented the air. We'd talked about the two body drops at his house on the way to school and were both sick over it. He needed his friends.

When I looked over at Sarah, my eyes nearly popped when I realized Cody sat on her other side. There were too many people in the room to be able to smell anyone approaching us. At my look, Sarah whipped around and saw him, I felt her body stiffen and then relax; poker face.

"Hi, Cody, long time no see. Where have you been?" she asked.

He ducked his head and his voice trembled. "I felt really bad about my fight with Bevin. I was trying to think up an apology gift."

"You missed two days of school to think up an apology gift?" Sarah asked, dubious.

Cody looked up, his eyes wide. "Well, when it has to be a special gift, it takes time to make sure it's perfect." He leaned in and I caught his scent; it was off, aggressive. I frowned. *Drama boy wants to put on a show for us.*

"Did you come up with something?" Piper seemed determined to keep things peaceful.

"I think I did, but I'll know for certain later on today," he said with a somewhat twisted smile.

My eyes slid to Bevin. He didn't say a word. He followed the conversation but didn't add to it. I could almost taste the spice and earth of his anger and pain. Taking his hand, I gave it a squeeze.

Once it began, the assembly lasted an hour and a half, full of teachers, principals, and social workers talking about the grieving process. They let us know that they were there for us, and that if any of us had a question or concern, we should find one of them, even during class.

A few students were invited up to talk about Thompson, a popular kid about whom they had only nice things to say.

The freshmen class would be in classes today, but most of the classes would be discussing nonacademic matters. Like last time, the sophomore, junior, and senior classes would have classes as normal, with a shortened assembly schedule for the day.

When we were finally dismissed and allowed to leave, I let Bevin pass me and head out with Piper, saying I'd meet him in AP bio. Sarah passed me, giving me a hard look then a narrow glance towards Cody.

As I got up, I stumbled over my bag and Cody caught me, grabbing my bare arm.

Werewolf.

"Thank you," I mumbled. I grabbed my bag and headed to class.

When I got to class, I took out my phone and texted my dad.

`Cody.` I sent an image of shaking hands, a dog's face, and a shocked face.

He texted back. `Secret!`

Bevin got out his notebook and saw me put away my phone. He jerked his head at my phone. "What was that about?"

I made sure to tuck the phone away and got out my own notebook. "Umm, just forgot to tell Dad about Mom's appointment tonight."

"Your mom has an appointment? I was with you all morning. When did she tell you?"

The teacher's voice cut through our conversation, saving me from further discussion. "I know that we were supposed to have a test today, but since class has been shortened, I decided to move it to tomorrow. Pull out your books and study quietly alone. Not talking…I'm looking at you Collete and Jordan; you also, Jade and Bevin. I mean it, no talking. Prepare for tomorrow's test. If you have a question, raise your hand and I'll be around."

Everyone in the class seemed bummed but me. I felt saved by the zone of quiet.

As my morning progressed, I contemplated more and more about what it meant that Cody was a werewolf. Was he our rogue? Was he leaving the dead people at Bevin's house? Had he attacked Bevin's mom? It was too much of a coincidence. I couldn't see any other answer.

By the time lunch rolled around, I had so many questions bouncing around my head. I had to calm down. I was making my way to the table when Estrella grabbed my shoulder. "Jade, I don't know what to do."

Spinning to her, I gave her a hug. "My parents are working on this and have some leads. Tell your friends to travel in pairs."

With panic in her voice, she protested, "But Jade, what about January? She's still missing."

"I know, hon, I know. Everyone's trying to get her back."

"Two of my friends are dead. What if I'm next?"

I wrapped her in my arms and squeezed. She was crying

and I didn't know how to help her. I didn't think she was in any danger, but I also didn't know. I stood there rocking her for a few minutes while the whirlwind of the lunchroom spun around us.

Panther nudged me, reminding me of who and what I was. Reaching down deep, I found a bit of calm, and shared it with her. She finally managed a full breath as she relaxed a fraction.

Bevin came up to us. "You two okay?"

Estrella sniffed. "Hi, Bevin. No, I'm scared." Bevin wrapped her up in a hug much as I had done. He whispered some words to her, swaying with her and rubbing her back.

Eventually her tears ran out, and he backed up and looked her in the eyes. "José would be proud of your strength. You are the world to him. You can do this."

She smiled and nodded before wiping off her face and heading back to her table.

Bevin turned to me and slipped his arm around my shoulder. Sarah, Piper, and Cody already sat at the table, eating. Before I could sit down, Piper raised her eyes and said, "Bevin, I'm struggling with a chemistry problem, could you help me?"

He nodded and sat next to her. It was a tossup which of us was better, and he had been tutoring her this year. That left me to sit next to Cody. His head dropped and his face contorted into a scowl for a few seconds, but then he smiled and grabbed a few fries.

Sarah searched my face and, as my alpha, I felt her probing me. Throwing up blocks, knowing there were things I wasn't ready for her to learn, I tried to keep things light. Narrowing her eyes, she finally asked, "How is Estrella?"

Drooping, I grabbed a fry to drown my sorrows in grease. "Not good. Two of her friends have been attacked. She's convinced this jerk is somehow focused on her and her group. I don't blame her, it's scary."

One side of Cody's top lip twitched. "Why would she think it has anything to do with her?" He sounded neutral but his scent informed me of his disgust.

I furrowed my brow, trying to look confused. "Well, two of her friends were killed, one is missing. I would say it puts her somewhere in the middle."

Sarah looked at me sharply, confused. I couldn't do anything about that now.

Cody's scent became more peppery. "Is she connected to the other deaths? And what about the dead people at Bevin's house?"

We all froze. Though the reports had been out that dead people had been left at a house, nothing had been said about whose house. I nodded. "You're right, Estrella must be mistaken."

Everyone else looked at me. I took a quick breath. "How were everyone's classes?"

Though the answers were short, everyone answered, following my lead. They didn't know what was going on, but they all trusted me.

As the bell rang, Cody turned to me with a smile and said almost hungrily, "Can't wait to see you in history class, Jade."

A shiver slid down my spine.

CHAPTER 26

Early Thursday morning, I just finished brewing a pot of coffee when the door opened.

I froze and stared.

Only pack members should be able to get in, but these were weird and scary times. I didn't think anyone would walk in unannounced. Andy walked around the corner, saw me, and froze. Submissive wolves made up the heart of the pack, and along with Aunt Allison, the pack had Chris and Andy, who were also a couple. Chris had petitioned the pack to allow Andy to be bitten once they'd become partners, even though he was technically older than normally allowed. Packs often did a lot to keep their submissive wolves happy.

"Jade, you're up," he said softly. He smelled worried. Being a submissive wolf, he probably picked up the tension from everyone in the house. A normal person wouldn't have been able to hear him, but we weren't normal. I thought for a few minutes and realized I hadn't seen Andy in days. He had missed all the drama around here.

"Where have you been?" I asked as I slid off the stool and ran up to give him a big hug. Well-being swept through me, centering me and easing away the tension. *The power of the submissive wolf.*

Moving into the kitchen, he gave me a confused look. Normally, a pack member could be gone for weeks without anyone noticing. Smiling, I reached over to squeeze his hand. "You've missed some major drama around here. Didn't Chris tell you?"

He shook his head. "I've been on radio silence. Then again, depending on the drama, you may be as well. You wouldn't know, because who would you tell?"

That was true, though I had told José. *Should I have not told him?* I'd have to ask Dad about that later. However, he almost lived in town and this affected his family, he had every right to know. Estrella probably called him every night, too…and Bevin.

"Want to trade stories?" I asked. He looked dubious, as if he had the better story, and he didn't want to risk getting in trouble. "I'll give you a teaser: we're hoping Janet will survive."

His eyes widened, and he took the mug of coffee I offered. "My story is long; you first," I demanded.

He sighed. "I went to Santa Fe to look for John Fortune and to get his story. He is a werewolf. He's *not* our rogue. Hell, he isn't rogue at all. He was a work partner with Pebble's dad. They had a scheme to steal money, said they'd bring him in. The plan was their daughter would be staying with friends. He said no and Pebble's parents tried to kill him, turned him against his will. He was pissed. When he saw them trying to escape the area, he followed them and killed them."

Andy poured some cream into his coffee and took a long drink. "Only afterwards did he see they had their daughter with them. He claims he didn't bite her, and I believe him. He ran, hoping authorities would find her and help her. He didn't know she was a werewolf. If he had, he'd probably have taken her with him and tried to help."

"Why were they trying to escape?" I asked, getting caught up in the story.

Getting up to search for food, Andy spoke into the fridge. "They had embezzled a bunch of money from their employer and were on the run. With only enough clothing to look like they were going on vacation and would return; they figured they could frame John, but he had evidence to use against them. When he showed them the evidence, they tried to kill him. Instead of killing him, they changed him." Andy plopped back down with a bottle of soda.

I rummaged in the pantry. I held up a bag of bagels. Andy nodded and then continued his story. "He was freaking out about being a werewolf, followed them to confront them, and killed them. He doesn't know what to do now. I'm going to talk to your mom and him about him moving down to Florida and joining that pack. He needs a pack, but I don't think ours is the right one. The other pack locations have snow and from what he said I'm not sure he's ready for that."

Once he finished talking, I stuck bagel slices in the toaster. "Wow. That is so not the story I expected you to tell. He really isn't the werewolf marauding up here. If he didn't change Pebble, then who did? Her parents? Damn, now I'm really curious."

Andy worked on pulling the label off his bottle. He shook his head. "No, he seems like a decent guy, and mostly in control—---considering how he was changed. He didn't handle his initiation into becoming a wolf well, but he didn't cause Pebble's werewolf status. That must have come from her parents or whoever changed them."

"I wonder if she would tell me, if I asked," I mused, looking deeply into my coffee for answers. *But would that be the right thing to do—stirring up past trouble now that she's settled in with us? I don't want her having any more nightmares.*

"I don't see how we could get her to remember, she's only five." When I continued to look into my coffee he said, "Your turn, missy. I need to know what happened, so I can help our pack." He pinned me with a piercing and demanding stare.

Smiling, I quickly finished preparing the bagels. I then spent fifteen minutes explaining about the werewolf attacks and about my new ability. I told him about trying to save Janet and almost killing myself in the process. I laid out my theory concerning the reason for the attacks and my pick for the rogue werewolf. The end of the tale focused on Estrella, and her friends, including January, who still hadn't been found.

By the end, he just gaped at me. "Damn, girl, you are up to your eyeballs in this. I was convinced I had the better story; but I not only got a better story out of you, you made me coffee and breakfast."

I smiled at him and gave him a big hug. "Welcome home," I said brightly. "Now, I should go shower and get ready for school; who knows what today will bring."

On that ominous note, the front door slammed. Dad walked in. His shoulders hunched and he had bags under his eyes. He looked tired and haggard, ready to drop.

He looked at us. "Andy. Did you get caught up?"

We both nodded. "Good, saves time. So, Jade, that Cody boy is a werewolf."

I nodded again. Dad and I hadn't had time to discuss what happened. He'd gotten my text, but apparently he wanted a full confirmation. "I went to their house. The whole place stinks of bleach. Lemony bleach." He collapsed in one of the living room recliners. "No one has been there for a few days. I searched for him and his father. We need to find both of them. Text me if he's at school again today."

I sighed. "Okay, on that note, I'm off to get ready."

Since Dad was in no mood or condition to drive, Andy drove me, Bevin, and Sarah to school. We didn't talk much; everyone was stressed and tired.

Though I wasn't allowed to tell my friends about Cody, I did tell them that my dad wanted to talk to Cody's dad. If we saw Cody at school, we should text Dad right away. Wary of seeing him, they still agreed. The day went by smoothly until lunch when Cody showed up.

"Hi, Cody," I said brightly when he joined our table, as if I hadn't a worry in the world.

He just looked at me, clearly expecting a less welcoming greeting. "Hi," he said suspiciously.

He sat down between me and Sarah, the only spot open to him. He looked like he wanted to sit closer to Bevin, but we had been making sure that wasn't possible all week. We had this seating trick down.

We returned to talking about Thanksgiving, which was just around the corner.

"Will you have to rent a table for the house, or is it going to be a bunch of smaller tables? Or are you going to rent a hall and have it out of the house?" Sarah asked.

She had never had Thanksgiving at the pack house. She

was so curious. I could tell she was ready to burst.

Piper perched on the edge of her seat, curious enough to burst, as well. Her face alight and her blue eyes shining. I had to force myself to remember where we were and not get lost in how pretty she was.

"You act like you'll all be celebrating together," said Cody. Peering around the table into everyone's faces, he seemed to be looking for something. Acceptance? Inclusion? His expression morphed into one of confusion and suspicion.

I shrugged, trying to play it cool. "Probably. My family always invites a big crowd. Bevin's family has always been part of our celebration. Since I'm dating Piper, her family will get added to the list, and Sarah…"

"Is your best friend, I know," said Cody, cutting me off.

"Actually, she's been that since kindergarten and has never been invited. I was going to say, she is dating my brother. Maybe *that's* what finally did it." I gave him a devilish grin.

I knew that Cody could guess the real reason. Being a werewolf, he could probably smell it on us, but he didn't know I knew, and no one else knew it about him.

Damn, this was going to make my head hurt. I wished at least Sarah knew, then she could play with this information, too.

"So, Sarah, can I text my dad a confirmation on your family?" We all knew that it was a yes, but I needed to text

Dad about Cody, and everyone knew that, too.

"That's a go on Thanksgiving for the Baller family," Sarah confirmed.

I took out my phone and texted Dad. `That's a go.`

Cody watched my every move, but he wouldn't be able to find fault.

Dad texted back a thumb's up emoji.

My phone lay face up on the table and everyone saw the message.

"Coolio," Sarah said. "I'm all legit and everything now. What happens if I break up with Owen?"

"You mean, in the next two weeks, when you have literally no contact with him for him to mess things up?" I asked. "Well, then you can come as my friend, I guess. We just won't tell my dad, or Owen…he would be crushed."

We all laughed at that, even Cody.

Bevin had been quietly watching everything, seeming to not want to get noticed by any of us, though it was probably just Cody. I quickly grabbed his hand under the table and gave it a squeeze.

"Did you hear that my uncle Andy has returned?" I asked the table at large.

Since Andy had driven me, Sarah, and Bevin to school, there was no way they didn't know, but I needed to say something to get everyone talking.

"How big *is* your family?" Cody asked.

"Well, he really isn't my uncle, he's more like my mom's

gay best friend, and it's easier to say uncle." I smiled. "He went out on a fact-finding mission for my dad's IT company, found out this guy they were looking for was really above board, which is cool. He just got home this morning."

"Where was the person from?" asked Piper.

"Santa Fe," I said breezily.

Sarah froze and stared at me, and then laughed.

"Above board, really?" she asked.

"Yep, totally and completely. He may join the Floridian branch of the company."

"Sounds like a really successful adventure," said Bevin, looking interested but smelling confused. "Going to be joining Tilly's branch of the business? Interesting. I'm guessing Andy has great stories from the southwest! Did he bring you back any gifts?" Tilly was the alpha of the Floridian werewolf pack.

"Damn. I knew I forgot to ask about something."

CHAPTER 27

By Friday, the school day was back to normal, at least inside the building.

It had been four days and January was still missing. There was a tree by the main entrance that kids and teachers covered with flowers in honor of the deceased boys and missing girl, along with handwritten notes and pictures. As I passed the tree with Bevin and Sarah, we saw Estrella wrapping ribbon around the trunk with a few other freshmen. Her eyes were puffy and I could tell she'd been crying. She and all her friends wore black.

I looked down at my jeans and grey sweatshirt and

then over at Sarah. "Should we be in mourning? I could have worn black."

Sarah followed my gaze to the gaggle of freshmen and then shook her head. "Nah, you didn't know them. You're fine."

On Thursday, Tanner had been waiting for Cody to leave school and had followed him home. He found out that Cody and his dad had rented a hotel room instead of staying in their apartment. He reported the address and room number to Dad. Tanner grumbled, asking why we cared about some punk kid who had hurt Bevin, or the punk kid's dad, but our resident bounty-hunter was good at following directions, even if he didn't understand them.

In AP bio, Bevin leaned over to show me his phone. "Just look at all these messages." Cody had sent him myriad texts asking if they could talk. Apparently, Cody really wanted to get back together.

At least he hasn't pushed to sit next to Bevin at lunch.

My eyes bugged out. "How far back do those go?" I grabbed his phone and scrolled, too fast to read. Staring up at Bevin, I handed him back his phone. "There are dozens of messages."

He nodded. "I know. It's insane. Like he's obsessed. I have a bad feeling about him now. I really think we should try to avoid him. Can we find a classroom for lunch? Yesterday sucked."

I closed my eyes. *I don't want to run and hide. I don't want him to win.*

He continued talking as if he sensed my reluctance to change our routine. "I've been talking to José and he agrees with me. I need to stay away from Cody; he's toxic, and I really don't need that right now." Bevin's gaze darted around the room as if Cody may jump out of one of the cabinets.

I grabbed Bevin's hands and squeezed them, wanting to impart some strength. "I don't disagree with you, but I also want to make sure he's in school. Dad has been tracking him. If we hide, and Piper's right that he's nuts, what trouble might he cause? At least with us he seems decent, or at least stable. He shouldn't be with you alone, but in the group, maybe he's a little bit better?"

Cody showed up for lunch, but after grabbing food, headed out the door. We weren't sure where he went, but Bevin's shoulders dropped as he relaxed as soon as he disappeared. I decided this was the best for my friend.

Pulling out my phone, I texted Dad. `Cody is here again. Can you check his apartment, just to be certain?`

His reply was fast. `We've already checked, but if it means that much, we'll check again. We'll also check the hotel where the two are staying, see what we can find. Again, I don't want you to worry about this stuff. I want you to go back to class and focus on your education.`

I sighed. *As if that's a possibility today.* I replied `I'll` try. Love you, Dad.

In history class, we learned of a huge exam coming up the following week. "Do you want to come over next week and study again?" Cody asked.

"Maybe we should study at the library," I hedged. "That bleach smell gave me a headache for days."

"Sure," he said, hanging on to our friendship and the chance to study. I could smell how desperate he was that this study time would happen. "Let's plan on studying on Tuesday night. Okay? Maybe even your place?"

"Sounds good, maybe the others can join us. But I'd rather study at the library," I repeated. I didn't want him at the pack house. "They can study other subjects."

"No!" he snapped.

I jumped.

He took a deep breath and then gave me a pleasant smile. "Sorry, I just want to focus on history, and if the others are there, they'll use you as a tutor for their studies. I've seen it happen with you."

I was nodding in agreement when I paused. *Wait…my friends don't actually do that. And when has he seen my friends and I studying together?* I was about to ask him when the bell rang for the end of class and he ran out before I could say a thing.

I sighed. I had a few days to figure out what to do about this study session. No reason to worry about it yet.

When I got home, Dad smiled at me.

"What?" I said, feeling like he was about to give me a gift.

"We brought the cops with us when we searched for that missing girl at the apartment and the hotel room. You were right honey; we found her. They had her. The police have an APB out on Cody and his dad. Unfortunately, it went out after school was released, so they weren't able to grab Cody at school."

My emotions were on a roller-coaster ride with this news. Dad continued. "The girl, January, is fine. She was a bit bruised, but mostly unharmed. They had her tied up at the hotel. She's at the hospital getting checked over, but she should be home by tonight. She said they kept asking her about things she liked and didn't like. If she thought things were gross or acceptable. It seems they wanted to find a reason to kill her. Thankfully, they couldn't find one."

"Does Estrella know yet?" I asked.

"I don't know; do you want to give her a call?"

"Yeah, if you don't mind. It was one of her friends, and she's been really worried."

Dad nodded.

I went to my room to make the call. She hadn't heard, and she started to cry when she found out her friend would be okay. One of her friends would survive this ordeal.

Then I called Sarah and Piper to let them know. I'd tell Bevin at dinner.

I felt lighter than I had been in weeks. It was the first good news since the beginning of the rogue wolf attacks.

CHAPTER 28

Saturday started off early.

Waking up before the sun, I decided to run outside on the bike path near my house. It was cold, but I was tired of the gym.

Not to mention, it smells.

Stolzburg was famous for its biking trails. Wisconsin had converted most of the old railroad lines into wide pathways across the state. The path I chose passed near our property and dipped south, so there weren't usually many people on it. I may have found a few determined souls, but not many.

During my run, the sun rose, warming my soul. I knew

I wasn't supposed to be out alone, but no one was out to confuse scents and I figured I knew the scent to beware of. I was also already running; I doubted Cody could keep up. After eight miles, I turned to head home.

About six miles from home, I reached the point where the bike path wound through a forested area. There was a small lake to my left and not a person around. I could feel myself relax…

Honk!

I leapt a foot in the air, coming to a sudden halt. Raising my eyes, I found a group of geese standing in front of me…a gathering? A pod? *Wait, Bevin and I looked this up when Brooke's group harassed me last year.* A gaggle…a gaggle of geese. I jogged in place. There were over a dozen geese on the path. I took a few steps forward and three of them ran towards me. I backed up. Geese were mean.

I was not prepared for this sort of attack. The trees provided thick cover and I only wore exercise shorts and a crop top. The clothes were old, and nothing I cared for. One more turn to make sure no one was around. I stripped down and let panther flow over me.

Feeling secure in my superiority, I padded over to the geese and let out a roar. Hissing, the geese attacked en masse. I back-peddled…as fast as I could. Once I was a good way down the path, they stopped and watched me with their beady eyes.

I took stock of my surroundings; to the left stood a tree,

a sturdy limb hanging over the path. After a running start, I jumped, landing on the tree's limb above the geese. They let out a chorus of honking sounds. Leaping past them, I ran home along a game-trail that ran parallel to the bike path.

I looked in the back door and saw my parents drinking coffee. Mom gave me a quizzical look. I found my human form and came inside. "Clothes, please."

Mom couldn't hold back a chuckle as she threw her robe at me. "How is it you were in panther form?"

"Geese."

Dad raised his eyebrows and nodded. "That tracks."

Mom just shook her head, brows furrowed as she gave me some water and a banana.

"Thanks. I'm off to shower."

Dad pointed at the papers on the dining room table. "Don't take too long, we need to discuss your being out alone. After that, we're going to plan a hunt."

After a shower, I returned to the kitchen for coffee and food. Dad cooked breakfast. Mom sat next to me while I ate eggs and bacon. "He seemed so stable at school at the beginning. Could he have started out that stable at school and still be the rogue out killing and eating people? I wish I had my touch ability when I'd met his dad."

Mom took a drink of coffee. "I don't know, dear. If so, you may become the new expert on rogue werewolves. You've had more exposure to Cody than the rest of us. He not only integrated himself into your group, he knew you were a wereanimal and covered up his scent. He attacked what he thought of as your enemies. If he wasn't trying to date Bevin, I would say he was trying to attract you, dear."

I shivered. *Ewwww.*

"The thing is, he really did like Bevin. I could see it, and smell his attraction. Every time he messed up, his fear of losing Bevin was so obvious even a norm could tell. Piper and I talked about it. His physical reactions couldn't have been faked unless he's some sort of psychopath," I said, thoughtfully.

Mom nodded in understanding. "Maybe he did. Maybe he went in wanting to get close to you, found out you were a couple with Piper, and that worked to his advantage, especially since there was still Bevin for him." She shook her head. "I do feel bad for Bevin. I wish his first boyfriend had been someone nice—not a crazy rogue werewolf that will probably have to be put down."

I heard a gasp and looked up to see Bevin walking into the dining area.

She sighed. "How much of that did you hear?"

"Most of it. I listened from the hallway. I figured I would get more of the truth if you didn't know I could hear what you said. I guess it's true, you get what you get for eavesdropping."

Bevin came up to the table and plopped down in a chair. Dad brought him coffee and a breakfast sandwich. He smiled at him in appreciation. "Thanks. This year started off so good, but as bad relationships go, I should win a cookie or a ribbon. Or something."

We chuckled; it was true, a murdering rogue werewolf was an epically bad ex-boyfriend.

I put down my mug. "Look, Bevin, I'm really sorry about not telling you Cody was a werewolf as soon as I figured it out."

Dad cleared his throat. "You would've been going against my direction—alpha direction—if you had."

I scrunched up my face. "Yeah, I know, but sometimes, doesn't friendship trump even that?"

Dad stared at us, eyebrow raised. "Not in this case; it was too dangerous. The more people who knew, the more people who could've let on that we knew. Hopefully, Cody still doesn't know that we know, and that's important."

Bevin grabbed my hand before I could get to my coffee. He gave it a squeeze. "I do get it. And somewhere deep down, I'm really not mad, it's just all building into a huge ball of hurt that's hard to deal with." He let go of my hand and ate his food. When I searched his face, tears shone in his eyes. He shook his head slightly, silently asking for space.

As more of the pack joined us—Tanner, Clare, Jackson, Greg, Chris and Andy—we discussed what we were going to do.

Dad, having finished his kitchen duties, joined us at the table. "Tanner..."

Tanner put down his mug of coffee. "Clare and I have been searching for the two of them but haven't found anything yet. The police have also been looking for them in connection to January's kidnapping, we've been keeping tabs on their progress, and so far, they've come up empty handed as well. It looks like Cody and his father cleared out of town after school. We think Mr. Ants picked Cody up, and they drove…somewhere." His gaze shifted to Clare.

She shrugged. "They didn't return to the apartment or to the hotel room." She pointed to areas of the map. "We're watching the other hotels in town and the roads out of town. Escape for them won't be easy, but if they've holed up somewhere, finding them won't be easy either."

"Can we join in the search?" I asked, gesturing to me and Bevin.

"No," Dad and Tanner said in unison. Dad stared directly into my eyes. This wasn't my dad talking; this was my alpha. "I expect you to stay here and follow the rules, do you understand?"

"Yes," I said meekly.

Tanner searched my face, then Bevin's. "This duo has obviously been after you for some unknown reason. I want you both here and under pack protection."

Getting frustrated that so many people had been hurt and I couldn't help, I tensed my muscles as if to fight. "If they've been after me, doesn't it make sense…"

"No!" a chorus of people said before I even finished my statement, none louder than my parents.

Bevin laughed. "Nice try, but did you really think it

would work?"

"Well," I whined, "if I were out with Tanner and Dad, would the rogue even know how much hurt he would be in if he approached me? Not to mention, I have Cody's number, I could text him to meet me somewhere. He would probably realize it was a trap—but I bet he would still show up." Everyone just looked at me. "What? He would. He asked if I would study history with him on Tuesday. Now, if he got there and he didn't sense me in some way, deal's off, he would run. I have to be there for you to catch him."

I turned to Dad. "Right now, they are up on kidnapping charges. But they don't know *we know* at least one of them's a werewolf. They still think they have that piece of information over us. We need to be able to use that against them."

"Damn, she talks a good game," said Greg. "Did you teach her that?" he asked my dad.

Dad glared at Greg as Jackson said, "Nah, she gets that from Hazel."

Huffing out a laugh, Dad stared at me quizzically. I'd presented a decent argument, but he still didn't seem convinced any of it was the right way to go.

"I'm not going to risk my daughter on this freak and his son," he finally said.

"You won't be; he's shown he doesn't know how to kill a wereanimal," I reminded him. "Janet was only hurt because she wasn't expecting an attack. You've taught me to fight. If we pick the spot and the pack is ready, then that's that. We've trained. They don't even know we have a pack; they may be aware there are werewolves around, but what's the likelihood he knows we're a full pack? He's never even been here."

I picked up my fork and used it to emphasize my points. "Moreover, Sarah doesn't smell like a werewolf and neither do I. We probably confuse him. It's probably why he attacked Janet. She was probably the first werewolf he'd smelled, and he didn't know what to do. He attacked, thought he had done enough, and left her to die. He's an idiot."

"Either you're smarter than we've all given you credit for, or you've thought about this a lot," said Greg.

"Actually, she's just as smart as a lot of us give her credit for," said Tanner. "She's stupid smart, always has been. It keeps getting her into trouble." He growled.

"It gets me out of trouble as well," I noted.

He shrugged in tacit agreement.

Dad looked pained at everything I'd said. Mom looked resigned. *Does she recognize her own determination in me?*

Mom rummaged in the kitchen and finally put a PB and J in front of me. I stared down at it and then up at her. She gave me a piercing look. I picked up the sandwich.

While I ate, the adult pack members planned. These werewolves had come into our territory. They had attacked innocent people, including kids and packmates, and people from our community.

It was time for them to go—one way or another.

With the general sigh of agreement, I started asking

the questions that would flesh out our plan. No one wanted me to be part of it. *But at this point, I'm the best person in the pack for getting our targets out into the open.*

After a few more minutes, Clare brought over a container of yogurt. I gave her a quizzical shake of my head. Her brows rose. I acquiesced.

My first idea had involved a group of friends getting ice cream. The problem was, it involved more than one of the younger pack members and it could lead to more innocents being harmed if norms were around.

Gradually, the table filled with food. Different pack members seemed to be trying to entice me. Bits of chocolate. An energy bar. A cheese stick. Everything was high-calorie. *As usual, I'm the last to figure out Mom's game.*

With a sigh, I tried to eat as much as I could. Even if this plan was a bust, Dad would find something to do with all of these calories. He stayed in perpetual training mode.

Despite being November, the sun shone brightly and the temperature hovered in the mid forties. I decided that studying in the park would make sense: it was quiet, and no one else would likely be there this time of year. The pack liked that plan best.

I sent a text to Cody before we went any further. If he was going to be suspicious and say no, there was no reason to plan any more.

Hey, want to study history in the park? The house is really loud today and I'm

freaking about Wednesday's test. I think
if I wait to study, I'll just fail.

I was shocked when, a minute later, Cody responded
with, Sure, where?

Park near the school, quiet. Structure
that will protect against some wind.

Then I sent him a map of the location. Ten-thirty?

He texted back: Perfect, ten-thirty, and
none of the others. They will distract
you. Nothing will get done. Just thinking
about you! With a wide-eyed emoji.

At that, Mom raised an eyebrow. "He wants you all
to himself?"

"Yeah, I thought that was weird, too. I wasn't going to
go for it. I don't know where he gets the idea that when
I study with others, I'm tutoring and not doing my own
studying," I said.

"You do help others, but if you need to study, you make
it clear that your studies are your first priority. You've never
been a push-over. He tried to manipulate you. Interesting."

"Well, I better go get ready."

I gazed at all the leftover food and felt my eyes glaze
over. "No more of this. I think my belly has extended a foot."

At that I heard the blender in the kitchen. I turned and
Tanner stood at the counter with an evil grin.

Eyes wide, I stammered, "Are you making…"

He nodded slowly. "My famous chocolate shake. Recipe's

a secret. While you all were talking, I prepared it. You can take it with you while you get ready. Unless you really are too full? I mean, I'm sure someone here will sacrifice."

"No," I said, so quickly most of the room laughed. "I always have room for one of your shakes."

Holding my stomach, and trying to stifle a pained groan, I went to grab the huge travel mug he filled. I immediately took a sip: bliss. Painful bliss, but bliss.

I took it with me as I went off to change for battle. I wanted to be wearing comfortable but warm clothes. I didn't want to be confined in a coat. I wanted to be able to protect myself.

I grabbed my bag of books, intending to get there early and appear eager to study. I left the house at ten o'clock. Dad drove me close to the park, but dropped me off two blocks away. I dialed his number and turned on my speaker phone so he could hear what went on and slipped it into my pocket. I approached the park as nonchalantly as you please. I could sense the pack around me, monitoring my path.

I looked through the gate to see if Cody had gotten to the park ahead of me, but there was no one there. I went to take a drink of my chocolate shake when I felt a hard knock on my head.

The ground approached fast. I dropped the shake and put out my hands. Another impact struck my ear. I saw nothing more.

CHAPTER 29

When I came to, my head pounded.

I wasn't on the couch; this wasn't my normal blackout. I smelled two werewolves. Neither of them were family. I needed to wake up more to figure out who I smelled. This was the first time I'd woken up someplace other than lying on the couch, the floor, or my bed.

This is really bad.

Falling back on everything Mom taught all of us from early on, I tried not to move or draw attention to the fact that I was awake and took stock of my situation. I tried to keep my breathing even and steady.

I was seated in an upright position. My arms hurt, strapped to the arms of an uncomfortable chair and tied down tightly. My legs were secured to the legs of the chair, the ropes cutting into my flesh. The bindings were so tight I didn't have to shift to know there wasn't any wiggle room.

I managed a quick peek; my head was already down with my hair forming a curtain hiding my face. A thick rope wrapped several times around my torso. Not as tight as the leg and arm restraints, but it was secure enough. I was good and caught.

My brain cataloged the smells coming in. I identified Cody and his dad in the room. Correction: I could smell two males in the room. Without all the body sprays he normally used, I wasn't as certain as I wanted to be. I took a deep breath and was pretty sure I smelled the wild of wolf. They were a bit far for me to be certain, but if they'd just come a bit closer…

Was this Cody's actual scent?

I heard one of them speak. "Do you think they followed us?" I recognized Cody's voice and the cadence of his speech, so at least one wolf. There was a pause. Footsteps shuffled around. He sounded so different now, younger, like a child whining. "I didn't see anyone as she walked to the park, but the police came and took the girl. Jade must've known the police were looking for us."

"Of course it was a trap." I recognized Cody's dad's voice. "Smell her; she isn't human. Whoever she works for, or worked for, is after us."

So, both of them are werewolves. I guessed it, but damn, it's no relief to be correct.

"Do you really think she works for someone?" Cody asked, sounding confused.

"When will she wake up?" Mr. Ants—no, Nathan—asked. *He doesn't deserve my respect, the jerk.*

Cody continued with his young, whiny voice. "You hit her pretty hard over the head, Dad. Why so hard?"

"She is a creature, a monster. If we don't treat her roughly, she will not understand we are in control now. She has to understand she has a new master. She is ours to play with," he said.

He sounded and smelled so eager, I almost shivered.

"Where did you learn that?" Cody sounded awed.

Figures. Every kid's dad is his hero. Even when they're vicious rogues.

"It's basic wolf philosophy, son," Nathan said.

Lies. I suppressed a growl of disgust and anger. *He's just making stuff up at this point; trying to act and sound wise. He has no idea what he's talking about!*

Cody made a frustrated sound. "But she isn't a wolf. Smell her, she smells so weird. I can't figure her out."

There had been some walking and shuffling, but the movement stopped. Nathan sounded angry. "Are they all were-things? I thought only that Sarah girl was one, and you said she wasn't a wolf like us." He smelled distrustful.

"I don't know what she is—or what Jade is—but I smell something furry on both of them. Actually, I do smell some wolf on Jade. But there are other things, too. Maybe she spends a lot of time at the zoo, and it taints her scent enough for her to be this strange-smelling. I know her aunt works there and she spends time there regularly."

Interesting theory, I'd have to write that one down, if I got out of here. No—*when* I got out of here.

"So, when will she wake up?" Nathan asked again. His spicy scent changed into an almondy anxiety.

Don't these wolves know how to use their noses?

I could hear sniffing, closer to me. My body wanted to tense, but I tried to stay relaxed.

"Her scent has changed a bit; do you think that means she's awake?" Cody asked.

"I don't know. You're supposed to be the smart one, boy. You know the girl; you figure it out." His sanity swifty dissipated.

He came up right beside me and sniffed. "I think she's awake and listening. Her scent is different from when we got here."

I heard Nathan approach. My hair was pulled back from my face and my head dragged up. His voice came out as a sneer. "Open your eyes, girl, or I'll stick this knife in you."

I wasn't sure if he spoke the truth because he wasn't sure. I wasn't ready to test him. I opened my eyes slowly. They were gummy from being knocked out. The sudden light hurt, so it took a few minutes to get my eyes fully opened and focused on the two of them standing in front of me.

Cody held my head up by my hair, his eyes glittering. His scent of excitement filled my nose. I almost sneezed. His dad leaned against a table a bit further back with a wary look on his face. They both watched me. My phone lay on the ground in pieces. *Darn it!*

There was no reason to struggle. If I got loose, they would just knock me out again and tie me up tighter. I would be in worse shape than I was in now. If I didn't get loose, they would believe they had a good tightness on the ropes. I wasn't about to give them any real information about me. Instead, I played scared, which wasn't too far from the truth. I hoped they didn't know how to read their senses beyond when things changed.

I opened my eyes as wide as I could. "Wh-wh-what are you doing? Wh-wh-why am I tied up? Cody? I thought we were going to study." My dry throat made me sound more afraid than I really was.

Cody gave my hair one last strong yank before dropping the locks and moving back. "Nice try, Jade, you are a... what? What in the world are you?"

I looked at them with huge saucer eyes, trying to channel Piper at her most innocent.

Cody gave a condescending smile. He was back in school-mode. Great. "You aren't a werewolf—you don't smell right—but then again, you kind of do. So, what are you, Jade?"

I tried to look terrified. "I…what, huh? I don't know what you're talking about. Werewolf?" I tried to lean forward a pinch. "Are you on something? That's all make believe."

Hopefully they would believe that some people who smelled like werewolves hadn't changed yet and didn't know what they were. If they didn't, I was screwed.

I was in trouble no matter what. How had they snuck up on me? Was anyone out looking for me? Had Dad seen the attack?

"She really smells confused, Dad, or frustrated. I think that's what that minty smell means." Cody said. "Could she not know what she is?"

I had to let my questions flow. The more I questioned my situation, the more I smelled confused, the better off I'd be.

They didn't need to know what was confusing me. I continued to look at them with my eyes as wide as I could make them. I tried to get my hands to shake and my breathing to hitch.

Dad had only been a block behind me. He would've heard the blow to my head. I wondered how much else he'd heard. I was sure the pack had been tracking my phone. I wondered when my captors had destroyed it. Why bring it here in pieces? Maybe they'd been dumb enought to wait until we were here to search me. I shivered at the thought of them patting me down and going through my pockets.

"She's really smelling scared and confused," Cody

almost purred.

"Well, hell. There goes our theory," Nathan said.

Channeling Piper, I made my eyes as big as I could. *Can I get myself to cry?* "The-the-theory?"

Would Mom or Tanner be able to track me down? They had the best noses. How many were out there following us when I had been caught? What had they hit me over the head with? It had hurt. *Ouch!*

"Calm down, little lamb, and we won't eat you." After a pause Nathan added, "Yet."

That got my heart beating faster. What? I shifted my focus to Nathan. "Eat me?"

They both laughed.

Nathan, who had been hanging back, seemed to feel bolder. He moved up to me. "We were trying to figure out why you smell so weird, you and that friend of yours, Sarah. Right…Cody?"

He paused slightly before he said Cody's name. I wondered what that was about.

"Yeah, Piper and Bevin smell like normal people, but Sarah smells different, and Jade, well, you smelled her, Dad. She just smells weird."

"Do you think *you* are a werewolf, too?" I asked Nathan in a soft, but scared-sounding voice. I was still trying to convince them I thought the idea was insane.

Cody's dad chucked, "Oh, little lamb, you are going to be so tasty. So sweet. Your fear will be the best seasoning when you see us transform into big scary wolves."

My eyes got big again. I relaxed my face for a bit, letting my jaw drop. I took in a shaky breath. "B-b-both of you?"

Well, damn. I knew we had one rogue werewolf that ate people, but both of them? *I might have to try to get away after all.*

I reminded myself the pack couldn't be far. They had all been too close when I was abducted.

Cody licked his lips as if he could taste me already. Gross. "Look at her, Dad, she is so scared, I think we've blown her mind. Can we play chase with her? I bet she would be tastier if we could chase her down and eat her in the woods. We're far enough out that there's no way anyone would hear her screams. Just think how tasty her fear would be then."

He almost swooned in anticipation—just like I would over a triple-meat pizza.

I froze and stared with my head cocked to the side. Was this the same Cody who had been hanging out with us for these few months? The one who had been dating Bevin and seemed so nice, at first? Now, this psycho wanted to chase me down and eat me in the woods.

"Who are you?" I didn't have to feign my complete disbelief.

His dad watched my face, no doubt recognized the emotions crossing it. I couldn't hide them all. "I think she's shocked that her friend now wants to eat her," his dad said, smiling crookedly.

Not good. I have to control myself or they will lose control.

Cody sneered. "Her friend. I don't think I was ever her friend. She was just too stupid to realize I was using her and those idiots hanging around her. Do you think she knows how much Bevin hates her? God, he thinks she's a self-absorbed brat. He kept saying he wished the wild beast would take her."

No, he has to be lying. But, gods, those words hurt.

Cody smirked at me. "The only reason I dated Bevin was because I knew, underneath the clothes, it was a girl. God, they thought I liked boys, can you imagine? I hoped to get her out of the clothes and see what she had strapped down. I bet she was hot."

My stomach twisted. *He's still lying.* I almost sneezed with how thick the lie was. Cody paused, looking unsure for a second; perhaps his lie confused even him.

I shot a glance at Nathan who leaned against the wall, watching us as if Cody and I were the best show on TV. A small smile played across his face when he noticed me looking. If they were trying to make me mad, they'd succeeded. I couldn't think straight.

Turning back to Cody, my eyes narrowed as I stared at this person who I once called a friend. "You are disgusting. Why did you even join us if you hate us all so much?"

Cody laughed, all cocky again. "Wouldn't you like to know. You know what's going to happen, Jade? We are going to untie you, but not all of you, just enough to strip off your clothes, clothes aren't tasty. We'll leave your hands tied. We'll even leave them tied in front, to give you a fighting chance." He laughed at his little joke. "Then after five minutes, when we're wolves, we'll chase you down and eat you. Not just some of you; we will eat every last inch of your body. We will chew you down to the bones and suck out the marrow. When we're done there won't be anything for the authorities to find. What do you think about that, *Jade?*"

He spat out my name in the end. He had so much hate for me.

Why? And why do I even care?

My reply came out almost breathless. I was no longer acting. "What happened to you? Why can't you be human, Cody? Why can't you treat me like a person? Why couldn't you have treated Bevin like a human being? Why do you have to be such a horrible beast?"

I hated that I was crying. In my head, I knew none of what they threatened would happen, but the longing he exuded at the idea of killing me was overwhelming. The hunger in his eyes as he described eating me made my stomach turn. I was still full of the food my loving pack had fed me. I still had the energy, but he came close to causing me to lose it all.

Cody snorted. "People always ask why people can't be nicer to each other, treat each other like humans. But has anyone ever thought that maybe they have the wrong idea?"

Scowling, he paced the small room. "History is full of

people treating other people like crap, killing each other, maiming each other. I would argue there's more basis of proof that people, in general, are villains to each other more than anything else. So, I think you are wrong."

He stopped moving and turned, bending at the waist until he brought his face close to mine, mere inches apart. "I believe how I'm acting is perfectly human, and not at all like an animal, not at all like a beast, or a monster. Animals don't kill each other for sport or game; that is purely a human endeavor." He pushed a finger into my chest. "You are the one who isn't acting human, so stop judging me, Jade, stop bloody judging me!" He practically frothed at the mouth by the time he finished talking.

I gaped in disbelief. "So, by stripping me naked, tying up my hands, and barely giving me any time to run, you are acting human?"

"More human than you," he said, really getting into his theory. "History is about people killing each other for power. By showing my power over you, I am being human." He backed up a few inches. "If you can survive me, then you will show me that you are the better human. If you were better at history, and not such an idiot, you'd probably know all this already."

Well, I hope he remembers those words in about ten minutes; they're all he'll be eating. In the end, he wasn't going to be the one with the power.

He cut off my bindings and clothing. He told me if I

fought him, he would cut me. I didn't doubt him or his father who observed, grinning, as his son threatened to abuse me.

I'll have my chance out in the wilderness. I don't need to bring on the fight early.

Once he had me naked, I closed my eyes and ignored his ogling. "Too bad you're gay, though; I bet, given some time, I could change your mind."

Though he said the words, it didn't smell like he meant them. *He must be putting on a show for his dad.* I moved forward. *Stop looking at me like I'm meat.* He tied my hands.

"Okay, little lamb," Nathan said, "you have the time it takes for us to become werewolves. When we are wolves, you are dinner, so you better run, little lamb."

They pushed me out the door hard. I fell on my face. They laughed and closed the door most of the way behind me. The irony of my speed wasn't lost on me. *I could probably run out of these woods in five minutes and make it to safety.* But that wasn't my plan.

I crawled around to the side of the building. I couldn't believe they did everything I needed to make becoming a panther easier. I shut my eyes, breathed, and let her out. She was ready and waiting and the transformation was quick and smooth.

When I opened my eyes, I had big black panther paws. With a yank, I tore the rope, tied tight enough to hold a weak girl. I leapt into the closest tree that faced the door and waited for them to emerge. I had been practicing this.

I got into position. I found my calm, and I waited. *I will be a statue, I will not move, and I will not give away my position. I trained for this.*

This time meant life or death.

CHAPTER 30

I waited ten minutes before they nosed the door open. *Amateurs.* Two small and scrawny gray wolves emerged into the autumn afternoon. Snuffling, they followed my trail around the side of the building. They froze and whined when it disappeared. I could imagine their thoughts: *What happened to her? She just disappeared. What?*

If they had been part of the pack, they would have used their noses and found me up in the tree in about three seconds. But they didn't. They didn't know how to do anything but look confused.

They touched noses. A decision must have been made

to split up because one of the wolves ran into the woods. I closed my eyes and took a deep breath, letting the air bathe my tongue. Cody's scent dissipated. He ran off while Nathan sniffed around the structure.

My foot wanted to slip but I kept my body still. Opening my eyes, I saw Nathan on the far side of the structure, retracing my steps from the door. He smelled the door handle and my path. When he got to the bindings, he lowered himself to get a good smell.

Playing back Dad's training in my head, I glanced around, but Cody was out of sight. Taking aim, I pounced, landing on Nathan's back, and bit down on his head, twisting until I heard a snap. Ignoring the visceral shiver of disgust that ran through me at that sound reverberating through my body, I used my claws to tear out his throat, just in case.

My heart beat fast, but I stood over him, making sure he was truly dead. A dead wereanimal will shift back to human. It took maybe ten more minutes, but he finally shifted. When he did, I had my confirmation.

Oh, gods, I just killed someone. A zing of panic shot through me, but I swallowed it down. *This is what I trained for and it was him or me…and he was the monster.*

Stealing myself, I knew the job wasn't done until Cody was down, too. I bounded back up the tree to wait. I heard noises and smelled wolf. No, not wolf, my wolves. *Pack.*

I chuffed, the pack signal for, 'I'm here and I have an

enemy down.'

Dad trotted up to the structure and saw the dead human; he looked around until he spotted me. He gave a double yip. The signal for 'all clear'.

Hopefully, that meant they had found Cody.

I leapt down. Two more pack members bounded out of the woods to stand vigil over Nathan's body.

Dad and I walked away from the shed together. I heaved a panther sigh. *As werewolves went, that pair was dumb. As rogue werewolves, they're average.*

Once I oriented myself, I ran for home. Dad stayed with me the entire way. As we ran, more and more pack members joined us. We ran silently. In the middle of the day, any noise would attract the wrong kind of attention.

The hunt for the wild animal hurting the townsfolk continued, and we didn't want anyone pointing a finger at us. What would happen if someone saw a black panther? Worse, what would happen if they saw a black panther running with wolves?

When we finally got home, panting, it was nearly dark. I found a few buckets of water and clothes. I drank, changed, and collapsed on a chair in the backyard.

Sometime later, Mom said, "Come on, Jade, come inside. We all want to hear the story. And you need more food."

I groaned. She wasn't wrong; I was hungry. "What time is it?"

Ruffling my hair, she smiled down at me. "Eight at night."

I sighed. I didn't want to move.

She held out a hand to me. "I know, you've missed a meal. Let's find you some food and tell stories."

Smiling wearily, I followed her. I did love to tell and hear a good story.

Sitting at the kitchen island with a sandwich, Dad went first.

He had dropped me off and settled down to monitor my phone. The attack we expected occurred a few minutes later. When Dad heard me fall, he immediately called in to his office to trace my phone. It was illegal, but owning an IT security company had some benefits.

The tracking worked until about halfway to the structure in the woods when reception was lost.

Meanwhile, Jackson and Tyler, in wolf form, followed the car. When it stopped, Tyler retraced his path back and led Greg, in human form, to the area. From there, they set up an attack plan with humans and wolves.

They saw me get pushed out of the small shack, naked and bound, but before they could collect me, I found my panther form and leapt up into a tree.

When Cody ran out as a wolf, Tanner and Clare followed him in wolf form. They easily herded him towards Fred, who had a secure truck ready for him. Strangely, I felt relieved Cody was still alive. When Nathan was alone, Jackson planned to come collect him, but I took him down too quickly. He was dead before anyone else knew what happened. I cringed a little at that part.

Once they secured Cody in the truck, Dad continued, they brought him home to interrogate him, confining him in the garage for the time being. No one had interrogated him yet. They waited for everyone to return home first.

My story was just as quick to summarize. Why they targeted me was still a mystery, but it was clear from everything we knew that I had been the target from the beginning.

As I told the story, Bevin squirmed in his seat and his face grew red. At the end he came over and said, loud enough for everyone to hear, "I never said any of that crap, you know that right? He was lying, it was all made up, all of it. You're my sister, I love you, and I have never even been mad at you or wished you ill…well, maybe a little upset, sometimes, but you're my sister and that's allowed."

I wrapped my arms around him in a big hug. "I know that. He's messed up in the head. He joined our group hoping to get close to me; I believe that much. He used you to do that." I held his hands. I wanted him to really hear me. "At first, he used you, but I think he really fell for you. The wolf within took over and screwed with his head; made him a killer. His dad's craziness didn't help. I think if he'd been allowed to just be himself, Cody would have really cared for you."

Dad, still in alpha mode, put a hand on Bevin's shoulder. "No one in the room thought any of those horrible words about you were true, son."

Bevin nodded quickly, trying to show strength, though a tear escaped one eye.

His dad came over and, swinging an arm around his shoulder, moved him from the center of attention.

Mom came over to me. "Jade, I have to ask. You killed a rogue wolf today, are you okay?"

I was shaken up, but all in all, I was okay. I knew I shouldn't be. I killed a man in the shape of a wolf. But after killing all those people, he wasn't really a man—he was a monster.

I didn't want to answer too quickly, so I thought before looking up and nodding. "He was horrible, Mom. He killed kids. He wanted to kill me—but not until I was truly afraid. That was what they both craved. They wanted to taste my fear before they killed me. That was the draw for them; it was sick. I can't imagine what they would do if Nathan were left alive. They were truly monsters, through and through."

I turned to where Bevin sat with his dad. "I can't help thinking about when Cody challenged me about if I really thought no one deserved to die…am I a hypocrite?"

Bevin came back over to me and hugged me. He knelt in front of me, like his dad often did for him, holding my hands. "No, you tried to save your own life. It was self-defense. That's very different."

Mom gave me a big hug. Sarah came over and joined in. Then Aunt Allison, whose submissive wolf helped to center me. Others came over to show their support. I had had a bad day, I had made a hard decision, an adult decision, and the pack wanted me to know they supported what I had done. We were pack.

Afterwards, my dad went to the garage to pull Cody out of the truck and put him in one of the cages we kept in the garage for rogue wolves. The garage stood on the back of the property and was soundproof.

I followed him, as did Mom and Tanner. Everyone else stayed back.

Someone must have given him clothes, because when Cody was dragged from the truck to the cage, he had sweatpants and a shirt on. Thank goodness.

Although he looked human, I could smell his wolf. "What is *she* doing here, and how is she still alive? We looked for her but she disappeared!" Cody said, spitting at me. "You all smell like damn werewolves. She said she didn't believe in them, but you're all damn werewolves; she lied to us." His wolf was in control. His eyes wild, he searched the garage and our faces. "Where's my dad, and what the hell's going on? Why am I in a cage, and what the hell *is* she? How did she get away from us?"

He was still fixated on me. We watched as he continued to rant and rave. He didn't change what he was saying much, just kept going around and around about me, his dad, and his disbelief that I was there.

When he slowed down, Dad finally asked, "How did you get to be like you are?"

Cody just stared at him, like he had grown a second head. "You dumb or something? What do you think? I was bitten by a damn werewolf."

My brows raised and I nodded to myself. Wow. This was not going to end well. He had lost all semblance of any ability to communicate rationally.

Dad looked at me. "A little help please, unless you're enjoying the show."

I sighed and took a few breaths. I had to be calm to give calm. His ranting filth about me wasn't helping.

Tanner came up behind me and rubbed my shoulders. He whispered, "He is nothing, and our pack knows you, respects you, and loves you. You can do this. His words are air, that blows past you, never harming, never hurting. Let them go."

Shocked, I just stared at him open mouthed. Tanner never seemed to be my biggest fan, but his support calmed me down.

He gave me a half-grin. "You've got this, girl."

Trying again, I grasped hold of the calm; I closed my eyes and took another breath, and I let the epsilon essence flow out. It enveloped the garage. Cody stopped rambling. I heard a thump.

Cody suddenly sounded like a different person, scared and confused. "What am I doing here? Who are you people? Jade, is that you? What's going on?"

My eyes snapped open and I stared at him in disbelief.

Was this the real Cody? Had I put his raving wolf to sleep?

He huddled in the back of the cage near the mattress. I could smell his fear. Taste how confused he was. This wasn't an act. He smelled like a completely different person than the boy who had been in the woods with me.

I took a step forward but was still far away from the cage. "Cody, what do you remember?"

"I got your text to study. I was surprised, but happy. I was heading to the park with my Dad and…I don't remember, he did or said something. Where is my dad? Is he okay? What happened?"

I smelled the lie. He knew, but now he felt bad about it. In his calm state, he was different; now that the rogue wolf was no longer in control, it seemed he couldn't face what had happened. *This is a real Doctor Jekyll and Mr. Hyde moment.*

We all exchanged glances. No one knew what to make of him.

I took a deep breath. *Stay calm.* "Cody, do you remember attacking me with your dad and taking me out to the woods?" I didn't want to finish that statement, "to kill me." I didn't even want to think it.

His eyes widened to the size of saucers. "That wasn't really me, Jade, that was all my dad. You have to believe me. Jade, you have to let me out of here. I can explain." He grabbed the bars of his cage. "Please. Where's my dad?"

This is too creepy for me.

Not sure I could be of more help I opened my mouth,

then closed it. Cody reached out a hand to me. "Is Bevin here, can I see him? I need to talk to him. He isn't answering my texts. Jade, I miss him."

Trembling, I turned to Dad. "I can't stay for this. I don't know what is going on, but I can't stay. This is too weird, and I'm too close to the center of it all. I'm sorry. If you need me for anything, just let me know."

He looked at me and nodded.

Tanner took me by the shoulders and said, "That's a real grown-up way to look at it." He gave me a hug and pushed me towards the door.

I gave Mom a final look. She watched Cody intently. "We'll figure out what's going on. You go back in and be with your friends. It'll probably get ugly in here before we can figure anything out."

When I got back into the kitchen, everyone wanted to know what was happening. I really didn't know what to tell them because I had no idea. I told them what I had witnessed, but overall, it wasn't helpful.

I sat at the kitchen table, Sarah on one side, Bevin on the other. At the end of my retelling, Sarah gaped. "He really just changed into a different person?"

"Yeah, it was like after I calmed him down, he believed it was all his dad. He didn't believe he had any part in any of it. It isn't true. When his wolf side takes over, he's awful. It's like Dr. Jekyll and Mr. Hyde," I said, repeating my earlier thought.

I shivered at the memory.

Bevin moved over so that our arms touched. "That's creepy. So, after you left, do you think your parents and Tanner were trying to rile him up to get the Jekyll out of him again?"

I bumped my shoulder against his. "Yep, that's what I think. I think they want to get him to tell them what the plan had been. Why they had been so fixated on me. I really don't get it. Why me?"

Estrella, who sat in the living room, but obviously listened in, looked up. "If they were so fixated on you, then why did *my* friends get killed? Everyone says this is about you, but no one close to you died." Her voice was raw with pain. It couldn't have hit closer to my heart.

"Estrella," said Alejandro, her father, "that isn't fair. Jade had no control over those…those horrible people and who they attacked. Making her feel guilty won't help the situation."

"But everyone is assuming she was the only target, but so many of my friends were hurt, not hers."

"They were protecting her," Bevin said quietly.

"What?" Estrella demanded; she got louder now that she had a stage. "Why?"

Bevin wrung his hands, continuing to speak quietly about an old memory. "When Cody and I walked home on Halloween, he told me that Clinton was a homophobic jerk who spouted hate about us even after we saved Thompson. My guess is, Cody picked him up and offered him a ride home. Cody probably started a conversation about how Jade saved Thompson, and Clinton said something awful about us, and that was that."

Bevin looked up to Estrella. "Cody took him to a park after that. As for Thompson, he was a good kid. He was kidnapped, and much like January, Cody and his dad questioned him. Unlike January, he eventually gave answers that showed he was against Jade being a lesbian, me being transgender, and him being gay. He just needed an excuse that worked for us, and against Thompson."

"But Thompson wasn't that way. He was in the closet. Cody lied," Estrella accused. A tear rolled down her cheek.

Bevin gave a small shrug, sounding tired. "That doesn't surprise me. When you're held by scary freaks long enough, you either tell them what you think they want to hear, or they hear what they want to hear."

Estrella just gazed at us, lip in a sneer. "So, he tried to get closer to Jade, but why?" This was said in a condescending voice any popular person would use when the new kid chooses the nerd over them.

Jumping to my feet, I faced the girl. "What is the matter with you? Stop being such a self-centered snot! Not everything in this world is about you, Estrella. I wish, I wish none of this were about me. I wish you hadn't asked me to help your friends so they hadn't gotten on Cody's radar, but you did, and they did, and here we are. So get off your freaking high horse and realize we're all trying to survive this horrible situation!" My chest hurt as I tried to get air in after my tirade. Tears flowed from my eyes. *Gods, I'm so tired of all of it.*

Frozen in place, Estrella's mouth hung open, and even gaping, she was still lovely...it just wasn't fair. She took a breath, then slowly closed her mouth as an imperial brow rose. "You're right. I'm sorry. You can't have known why this person would choose you to obsess over." Slowly sitting, she turned her back to me.

Knowing I would have to apologize in the morning, I sat back down. Bevin slid his arm around me in a tight squeeze.

Alejandro let out a huff of annoyance. "As much fun as all of this is, answers will be found in the garage, not in here with the two of you. I suggest we all just relax and not take out our stress on each other."

With a sigh, I rested my head on Bevin's shoulder. "I'm sorry for snapping, Estrella. I know how much pain you're in. I wish Cody hadn't targeted your friends, and I wish I'd gotten to know them better after meeting them."

She swiveled back to me. "Yeah, sorry, Jade."

Bevin looked more and more sad as the night went on. His heart was broken. He couldn't help it. Cody was the first person who had shown interest in him, and my story had let him know that part of the monster in the cage was the person who had been nice to him. And in his own twisted way, had cared for him.

CHAPTER 31

Waking before the sun, I had the house to myself. With so many living at the pack house, it was nice to have a few minutes alone to find my center.

In the kitchen, I made coffee and sat to enjoy a full mug in the peace and quiet of the still house. While drinking my second mug, I also ate a banana. As I fully woke up, I realized the back door was cracked open a bit. Confused, I went to investigate. And then I heard the whimpering.

Oh, no, not again!

Pebble!

I ran.

I found her cuddled in some blankets in the treehouse. She was in wolf form, again. Whining. Lying down, I curled around her. Curling my hand around her paw, I let wolf take the lead.

Little sister, what's wrong?

I can't sleep, the dreams keep coming, they won't stop. Can you help me, Jade? Can you make me calm?

I can, but we need to figure out what's happening to you. Can you show me your dreams?

Please, no, they're so scary. Her voice was so timid and weak, it was hard not to say yes to her.

If I'm here with you, little sister, the bad things can't get you. Was that true?

She gazed up at me, uncertain. *Are you sure?*

I am sure. My wolf was certain.

This was a dream, and dreams can't hurt you, right?

Her round face turned up to me with trusting green eyes. *Okay.*

She trusted me. Us.

Suddenly, we were somewhere else. We were in her room, but not her room here at the pack house. Somehow, I knew some things, but not everything. It was weird. It was as if I knew the things she knew in her dream.

It was dark; a night-light provided a meager glow, enough to see the walls were a pale yellow and the bed was a tiny kid's bed, close to the floor. It was so small that Pebble barely even fit. She was lying there trying to sleep, but her breathing was too irregular for it to be actual sleep.

"*Where are we?*" She didn't answer. Sounds barely registered. My voice fell to the floor like a feather, soundless, weightless, and completely unnoticed.

Pebble sat up in bed and moaned.

She is hungry, I heard a small voice say. Pebble's wolf nosed my hand, explaining what I saw.

Pebble hugged herself and began to rock. She raised her eyes to the door and shook her head, as if having an internal debate. Her throat worked as she trembled.

She is not allowed to leave her room at night, her wolf explained.

I tried to move towards her, to comfort her, but this wasn't a dream but a memory, and I couldn't change what happened in her memories.

Did she at least know I was here?

After what felt like a long time, she slowly rose to her feet and padded to the door. It creaked as it opened. She searched the hallway. Shoulders relaxing, she slowly turned to her right and disappeared.

Blinking, I stood in a dark kitchen. Pebble stood in front of the refrigerator and opened it, light flooding the small room. She flinched back, shutting her eyes against the bright glare. Shaking her head, she opened her eyes and took in everything available. She settled on two grapes and a slice of cheese. Before she could close the door, I saw a shadow in the hallway.

I couldn't make out anything about this person who

came towards my Pebble. But I suddenly understood; this was the memory about what got her kicked out of her last foster home. The shadow was the foster family's oldest kid. He snatched Pebble's shoulder, yanking her away from the refrigerator. Her arm hit the door, slamming it shut, robbing my sight. I heard the two grapes hit the floor. *Plip, plip.*

"What are you doing out of bed, little girl? It isn't eating time."

I could just make out his fingers digging into Pebble's arm. In her fear, she turned her head and bit him.

You go, girl. Wait, werewolf. No!

The boy yelped in pain.

A rough voice came from another room. "What are you doing in there, son?" Thunderous footsteps approached. I had to remember this was all coming from the filter of a young girl's memory.

The boy whimpered, his voice distorted by her memory. "Dad, she bit me. I'm bleeding, I'm bleeding…"

The older man entered the kitchen and grabbed for Pebble, and in her terror, she bit him. Crying out, the man shook her. He hissed, the voice that of a beast. "Little brat! Make a sound and we'll beat you. You deserve it after biting us like a filthy animal."

He grabbed her from behind and dragged her to a cold, damp place. The basement. The lights turned on, and I saw the back of the man who dragged Pebble down the stairs, hauling her to the bottom of the stairs by the back of her nightgown.

Shocked, I couldn't take my eyes off her as they barely lifted her. Her toes dragged, step by step. I gaped as they brought her over to a cage big enough for a man, with nothing in it to keep her warm. Stunned, I saw them toss her in and lock the door. She hit the far side, sliding to the floor. And I heard her cry to herself as she curled up in the corner of the cage. A cage like the one in our garage. A cage like the one Cody was in right now.

Next to the cage, the man and teenage boy stood staring down at Pebble. The man eventually left, but the boy watched her with a naked satisfaction. Eventually, he turned around to go back up the stairs and I saw the face of the kid who had caused all this torment. However, I already knew who these two people were. The two monsters. I wanted to hurt them for hurting my sister. I wanted to hurt them again.

That was enough to shock me out of her memory within a dream.

I floated within her, talking to her through my wolf.

Little sister, I told her, as I lay there next to her, wrapping her in my arms. *Those bad men will never hurt you again.*

CHAPTER 32

I ate a bigger breakfast when I returned to the house. Thinking things through, I got on my phone and started texting. I wasn't the only person in the world who woke up stupid early. Once I finished eating and got the information I needed from texting, I went to check on Janet. She was still unconscious. Fred was awake in the room.

"Fred, I have an idea, but I may need your help. Can you put your hands on my shoulders, just in case?"

"Yes," he said quickly. He didn't know I hadn't talked to anyone about what I was about to do, and if he'd guessed, his desire to have his wife wake up was greater than his rational thinking.

I sat down next to Janet's bed, took her hand, and closed my eyes. Both animals perked up, but I wanted panther. We carefully entered Janet's body, her mind. We searched. There was nothing wrong with her physically. All her internal organs and muscles were healed. Aunt Allison and Fred kept her moving so that her muscles wouldn't atrophy, lying here.

I searched for her wolf and didn't see her. She hid. We kept going.

Hello? I called quietly. No answer. I kept looking.

I wasn't really sure what I was doing, but I had to talk with Janet and find out why she wasn't waking up. And for that, I needed to talk to her wolf.

It felt like a lot of time had passed, but I hadn't taken energy from Fred, so it couldn't have been too much time.

I kept going. We kept searching.

There, finally, I found Janet's wolf.

Sister wolf, why do you hide from me? I asked.

Nothing.

I wasn't sure if she couldn't hear me, or if she ignored me. It was like I spoke to Janet who had been lying in bed.

My panther approached slowly and when we got to the wolf, we gave her a little nose push, a shove so to speak. Again, I tried. *Sister wolf, why do you hide from me?*

Time passed. I don't know why I expected a different result, but eventually her wolf backed out of her hiding spot and turned around.

Why are you here? she asked.

I hoped to find you. You seem lost.

I am not lost, I am dying.

Confusion washed through me. Janet was completely healthy. All she had to do was wake up. *What do you mean, you're dying?*

That wolf attacked me. I couldn't keep myself alive, so I must be dying, her wolf said in very clear wolf logic.

But we helped. You survived. You are not dead. You must come back out into the light. Your partner is sad for you. He waits. Your pups also wait for you. If you stay here and let yourself fade, then your family will fade with you. You cannot let that happen.

But that wolf almost killed me! she screamed at me. Afraid. Sad. Alone.

But it did not. You are pack. You are not alone. You are not dead. We found you. You would have helped us. We helped you. Fight. Fight for your life. Fight for your family.

But that wolf...

That wolf will not hurt you again.

How do you know?

Tell me about that wolf. Who was that wolf? How did they get the drop on one such as you?

I was out looking for my pup. My son. I called for him. I stopped by his male friend's house and his sire told me to go away, that I was not wanted, and neither was my "freak of a kid." I was so mad, I left.

The wolf grew more animated. She laid back her ears and her tail drooped. *I was focused on my anger, not my surroundings. That was foolish, with a rogue on the loose. I stormed off to find my pup when a blow came to my head. I turned. The pup, the sire, the mad pair. I don't remember much more. They thought they had killed me. They knew I was a wolf, but they didn't know how to kill me.*

I killed the father. I let my memories flow. In this place they became like a movie. She watched, fascinated as she saw Nathan and Cody take me, trap me, and then my reversal of the trap on them.

The wolf liked the movie very much. *The son is in a cage in the garage,* I told her. *I do not think he will survive. I wanted to talk to you first. I wanted your story. Will you come out of hiding? Your family needs you. Your son needs you.*

My head pounded. I was getting weak. My wolf pulled on Fred.

Yes, I will stop hiding.

I must go.

I know.

Slowly, I backed out. When I opened my eyes, I was dizzy but steady. Fred looked a bit woozy as well.

"Did you figure out what was wrong with my Janet? Was it worth it?"

Before I could answer, a moan came from the bed.

Both of us looked towards Janet as she moaned and

groaned. A few minutes later, we heard a soft, "Fred, are you here?"

Despite how weak he looked, he jumped up to give her a hug.

"I'm sorry for hiding," she said.

Fred looked at her and then at me, confused.

After a few minutes of hugging and letting Janet finally wake up enough to know where she was, I ran a few basic tests. She remembered most of my talk with her, and she felt better. She was glad everyone was safe, and she wouldn't be going comatose again.

Once I knew she was stable, I quickly texted Bevin and his sisters to let them know their mom was awake, and then I went back to the kitchen. I needed more food.

CHAPTER 33

Shortly after I started eating, Dad joined me.

I told him about Janet. He was angry I had risked myself, then thrilled that I convinced her to wake up. After that, I said, "I want to talk to him."

"Why?" Dad asked. "Yesterday didn't go so well."

"I have new information. I want to get to the bottom of this and I want to get there now. I need concrete answers."

I think the desperation in my tone convinced him. We headed out to the garage. When we got there, Tanner slept on a couch on guard duty and Mom paced. Two pack members stood guard so that if he had to go to the bathroom, they could take him out and bring him back safely. The safety was as much for him as the guards. The pack wasn't happy with Cody, and mistakes could happen without two guards.

Cody lay in the cage, asleep.

Seeing the set-up the pack had in the cage, I realized I was wrong that the cage was the same as the one from Pebble's memory. Our cage had some blankets in it and a pad so Cody could sleep in some amount of comfort.

"What are you two doing in here?" Mom asked, frowning.

Dad shrugged. "She needed to speak to the boy again."

"He's asleep," Mom said, looking tired and worn out from a long night.

Watching Cody, I caught his lie. "No, he isn't. He's listening to us, waiting, trying to figure us out, but he isn't sleeping. His breathing isn't regular enough."

"Are you sure?" Dad asked.

I just nodded.

"I could bring out a knife and threaten to stab him with it like his dad did to me, but unlike him and his dad, we're not monsters." That word tasted like a swear word and I didn't like speaking it aloud.

With that proclamation, Cody snorted.

"So much for your act," I said plainly.

He sat up and stared at me. It took him a few blinks to adjust to the light. "Do you really believe you aren't a monster?" He smelled genuinely confused.

"Yes," I said, "I really think that you are an inhuman beast, and I'm human."

He glared at me. "You put me in a cage and left me here all night!"

He apparently woke up angry. *He's ready to break.*

I lifted my chin. "At least you have a bed and blankets. That's more than you gave Pebble when your dad put her in the cage."

His look of confusion took me back. Everyone else in the room froze. They had no idea there was a connection between Cody and Pebble.

"What are you talking about?" he asked, utterly baffled. "Who's Pebble?"

I could tell from his scent that he wasn't playing; he really had no idea what I was talking about. *Interesting.* "I'll paint you a picture, and then you can explain yourself to us. You lived in a house with your family: your mom, your dad, your younger brother, and a bunch of foster kids."

As I told the story, he froze. His eyes got big, and he just gaped at me, terrified. "Of course, at that point in your life you weren't Cody Ants, only son to the grieving father, Nathan Ants, were you?"

Answering my own question, I shook my head in disgust. "You know, you told me your mom had died a couple of years ago, and then your dad said she had died when you were young. I was curious about that. Now I know you're Conroy Ashton and your mom is very much alive. I guess it all makes sense, doesn't it? You two should have figured out a better story."

You could hear a pin drop; everyone listened. "So, your parents got a new foster kid, one whose parents were killed in a violent crime. Penelope Anne. You liked enforcing the rules. Your dad was tough on you and you could be tough on the kids. But when one bit you and was taken away, you decided to, what? Follow her up here?"

I took another step forward. "What then? You figured out my family had Pebble, so you decided to get close to my group. I was your 'in.' But then you found out I was with Piper." I smirked. "Did you know you were gay before you met Bevin?"

"I never liked that freak," Cody yelled, his denial an obvious lie.

"Cody, Conroy, whatever, you are in a room full of people who can *smell* when you lie. I could tell when you looked at Bevin you got excited. You were so into him you couldn't hide it from either me or Sarah. We could taste how much you lusted after him. If you weren't really into him, we would've known right away. There is no way to hide the attraction you felt. You may hate yourself for what you were feeling, but, dude, why hate yourself for falling for such a great person? I can see hating yourself for being a bit too rough with little kids, putting them in cages and enjoying that…"

I just let that last part sit there. *All the little kids. Not just*

Pebble. That was her biggest fear. She knew she was safe, but she knew that Cody wouldn't stop with her. She knew that if he escaped, other little kids would be hurt.

Voice shaking, he asked, "How do you know all of this?"

"How do you know all of this, Jade?" Mom asked, her brow furrowed.

"Some of it I got from Pebble, the rest I got from Kira. I texted her this morning to ask about the foster family."

She pursed her lips and nodded in understanding.

I looked over to Cody. "How do I know all of this? Penelope Anne, Pebble, is my sister now. How could I not know?" I asked him, looking hard at him so he couldn't look away. I wanted him to know that I saw him. The real him.

His eyes bugged out. "But I stayed out of sight. I made sure she never saw me. My first day in town, I saw the two of you give that homeless guy money; that was the only reason I even knew who she stayed with. After that, your family kept her so secluded, I never saw her. More importantly, she never saw me. I made sure she never saw me, never saw us." He was so shocked he couldn't stop babbling. "If she saw me, I would understand you knowing all of this, but she never saw me. How could she know that Cody Ants was Conroy Ashton, her foster brother? How do you know? I just don't get it. How?"

He yelled these last few questions. His confusion wafted off him in waves, mixing with his terror. We knew too much. He knew he couldn't survive a bunch of werewolves who knew this secret. I didn't think he realized we were a pack yet. He was just afraid of us as individuals.

Not as stupid as his dad.

"So, that's the last piece," Dad mumbled to himself. The last piece of the puzzle we all needed.

That was why he had been focused on me. That was why the homeless man was the first victim. That was the connection we had been looking for. It hadn't really been about me; it had been about Pebble.

"Why were you after Pebble?" I asked.

"What pebble? You keep talking about a pebble. What are you talking about?"

It suddenly occurred to me he never knew the nickname. "What do you and your dad want with Penelope Anne?" I asked slowly and clearly.

His face twisted with rage. "That baby is a monster. She bit us and turned us into horrible creatures. She has her due coming to her—and we're going to give it to her!" His voice got quiet and dangerous. "Once I get her out of this house, she'll be our last victim before heading home."

I laughed. I tried to stop, but I couldn't. Here he was, in a cage, surrounded by four werewolves, and he still thought he was going to get to Pebble. Did he think he had a chance of ever seeing her again? He, who had killed how many people, was upset that a little girl had bitten him out of fear. Bitten him to protect herself. He was beyond psychotic, he was delusional. I laughed so hard I doubled over and a sharp pain began in my side.

My laughter only provoked him. He scowled. "What's so funny? Why are you laughing at me? Why?"

Mom came over and patted my back, trying to calm me down. It just all seemed so funny all of a sudden. Cody, or Conroy, and his dad had been bitten by a five-year-old girl and their genius plan was to come after her to kill her in retribution. When she was obviously protected, did they give up? Nope, they went after other innocent people. *Why, you ask? Because they're crazy.*

Slowly, I got myself under control, though I was still shaking with mirth. Finally, I could stand up. Taking a few calming breaths, I finally managed to speak. "Does your mom know what happened to you?"

"No, Dad told her we were heading out for a semester to look at colleges. She's so dumb, like that's how high school works. Like I would even consider college; what a waste of time and money."

The sad part? He's smart enough for college if he ever decided to apply himself. I shook my head in disgust at the waste.

He looked around again. "Where is my dad, anyway? I've answered a bunch of your questions; when are you going to answer mine?"

I tilted my head and quirked a smile. "How much do you remember about yesterday? Do you remember deciding to chase me down and eat me?"

His eyes sparkled; he remembered. We were dealing

with the dangerous rogue, the scary version of the werewolf, the one who loved pain and other people's fear. *Good.* "I have no idea what you're talking about, *lamb*."

"Right, well, when you pushed me out the door, then came after me, he didn't survive. I guess, in your theory of power, I have the power and am the better person."

His jaw dropped and the room reeked of his gingery shock. "You bested my dad?"

I was about to answer but was stopped by the sound of Dad and Tanner chuckling.

Dad shook his head. "If you're shocked that my Jade bested a newly turned rogue werewolf with no training, then you're more foolish than you look, kid. There were several wolves watching, ready to help, but she had taken care of the problem before any of them had a chance to even let her know they were there."

He laughed again and shook his head, like that was the best joke he'd heard in a while. "It took her less than three minutes, and that was because she let him sniff around first. You two really do give werewolves a bad name. She would have taken you both out if we hadn't been there to save your sorry life. You and your dad best Jade. What an idiot." He shook his head in disgust.

"What *is* she?" Cody asked. "She doesn't smell normal, and no one will tell me. I've asked."

Tanner sized him up then lifted an eyebrow. "Better than you."

Everyone glanced at me and I shrugged. "I'm a werewolf."

His eyes popped. "But that isn't how you smell. That isn't how Sarah smells either. That can't be right. Besides, you said you didn't believe in werewolves." He started to get agitated again.

Not feeling the need to tell him more, I shrugged. I didn't think he was going to survive the day. I gave him a condescending smile. "Your nose isn't trained. I'm surprised you can pick up anything. I just want you to know that Pebble, er, Penelope Anne is going to live a long and happy life."

Shifting on my heel to leave, I stopped. "You know, if you had come here and asked for help instead of getting the taste of human meat in you, we could've helped. You could've been a decent person. I saw that in the few weeks I knew you. But instead of becoming a good person, you chose the path of the rogue werewolf."

With a shrug, I turned to my parents. "I think I'm done here. I'm going to go make sure Pebble gets in from the treehouse and showered. I told her she was safe now, but I want to make sure she heard my words. I want her to know that all the little kids are safe."

They nodded and I left.

As I walked away, Cody yelled after me that I was the monster for killing his dad, I was the monster living here with all the other monsters. I was the monster for loving girls. He yelled anything he could to hurt me. The thing was, at that point, nothing he said was going to stick. Like air, it just blew right past me.

I just walked out and shut the door.

In the end, I heard Cody's death was quick and relatively painless.

CHAPTER 34

Piper and I ate lunch at her place. It was quiet.

Piper grabbed a second piece of garlic bread. "My dad said he was taking the police out to the shack today."

My heart sped up. "Dad said that they removed any traces of me, but it still freaks me out. I don't want to be connected to them in any way."

Piper gave me a warm smile. "My dad knows CSI well. He went over the cabin with Tanner. They tried to pick up any traces of you last night. The two of them act like brothers sometimes; it's crazy thinking about their first meeting."

I laughed. "Is that true?"

"Yeah. They challenge each other in these things, trying to trip each other up. I think they tried to see who could find the most 'Jade' evidence when they started and then again last night. That's how they know it was clean enough to bring in the police."

That made me relax.

"Do you know if they found a way to connect everything to Cody and his dad? I know that there's evidence for Thompson and January because of the kidnappings, but I haven't heard about anything else."

Piper thought for a few seconds. "I think they found Clinton's coat in Cody's car. So that puts all three of Estrella's friends in their court officially. I don't think there's anything they can do about the others. Not with werewolves still a big unknown."

I sighed. "Well, hopefully if the deaths stop, the curfew will go away soon, too."

"How do you think they'll explain the wild animal angle with Clinton?" Piper asked.

Shaking my head, I couldn't think of a way to spin that. "No idea."

Helen came in from the kitchen with a tray of freshly baked chocolate chip cookies. They were still warm. She had obviously been listening. She patted my shoulder. "I heard your dad speaking to Tanner and Clare. They said the police think Mr. Ants owned a farm somewhere between here and Joliet. There were probably animals that he kept locked up and used to attack people."

I squinted in disbelief as I reached for some chocolatey goodness. "That's ridiculous."

"I know, dear, but that's easier to swallow than werewolves."

She turned and went back into the kitchen. I heard a timer go off. More cookies, yum!

Piper grabbed a cookie and took a bite, getting chocolate on her cheek. "How is Pebble doing? Is that foster family still in business?"

"Pebble is doing great. I got to tell her that the young kids were safe. The family was a harder issue. Kira tried to get an investigation after she heard about the cage. The problem is, there is such a huge need for foster families that the word of a five-year-old isn't enough to get the investigation as a high priority."

Piper looked ready to run down to Joliet and throttle some people. I put a calming hand on her arm. "But," I continued, "when they learned about the family having two murderers, the investigation jumped up in priority. From what I understand, the kids were rehomed to new foster families and Mrs. Ashton's license was revoked. Once again, I got to tell Pebble about one less bad person out there harming little kids."

Piper's brows furrowed. "In all honesty, if Cody and his dad are dead, the worst of the family aren't really there to harm the kids. Was closing that home necessary? Playing devil's advocate here."

I huffed a small laugh. "I've thought about that question a lot. I think so. Mrs. Ashton had to know the little kids were getting harmed. Letting it happen is bad, too. That house was just not a safe place."

The following week, I sat in the basement with Sarah, Bevin, Owen, and José. We lounged on the couches, eating pizza. José, who had been lying down on the couch, gazing up at the ceiling, scooted up to a sitting position. "I can't believe I missed all of it."

Bevin stood and plopped down next to him. José threw an arm around Bevin, who said, "At least you're here now. And you have off until Sunday."

Owen and Sarah cuddled on the love seat. Owen's eyes shone. "Five days away from campus. Five days to hang with my girl. Heaven."

Piper wasn't here tonight to cuddle with, but I was too happy to have the gang together to mind. I turned to Bevin. "How are your sessions with the counselor?"

He tensed for a second, but then relaxed as José tightened his one-armed hug. "Good. I've opened up about Cody and what he did. How he was using me to get to you."

I got up and moved to sit on Bevin's other side. I slid my arm around him, and he wrapped his arm around my shoulders. I dropped my head to his chest.

I could smell Sarah's concern. "He really liked you… you know that, right? I know he was a freak in the end, but it wasn't always like that. It wasn't just Jade he wanted. Every time he looked at you, we could smell his attraction and his lust."

Nodding, I stared up into Bevin's face. "I think if he hadn't gone rogue and his dad hadn't ruined him…" I shrugged. "I don't know…"

Bevin shook his head and his chest rose as he took a deep breath. "He was broken before he ever moved here. I've thought about it, and I've talked to my counselor about it. It hurts…a lot…but I'll survive. I'm starting to learn that I've been with me my whole life, and I should trust me more than I trust someone who doesn't know me as well. I am a good person."

José turned to him and kissed his cheek. "You, my friend, are one of the best people I know."

We all smiled at that. Bevin blushed. Then, eyes calculating, he turned to Sarah and Owen. "I guess you two stayed together long enough for Sarah to make it to a pack Thanksgiving."

Owen's brows furrowed in confusion, making me laugh. He shot me a questioning look.

Relenting, I explained. "We told Cody that the only reason Sarah was invited to Thanksgiving was that you two were dating. I'm pretty sure he was convinced it was the only reason she stayed with you."

Sarah punched Owen's shoulder. "Oh, it's absolutely the only reason."

Pebble came skipping down the steps wearing footie

pajamas and holding a package. She ran up to me and put the package on my lap, then she turned to Owen. "Now?"

Owen laughed. "Well, pipsqueak, I was thinking when the pack was here, but now is good, too."

I glared at Owen but felt Pebble's trepidation. I took a breath and gave her a smile and a quick hug. "What is this, sweetheart?"

I smelled her fear turn to excitement. "It's a gift…for you. For helping me with the…for helping me."

I lifted her onto my lap. "Wanna help me open it?"

She nodded, and together we peeled aside the wrapping paper. Inside was a stuffed goose. I just shut my eyes for a second, unable to respond. Owen let out a loud honk, and Bevin and José laughed.

I closed my eyes and spoke through clenched jaws. "I swear. How did you find out? I didn't tell anyone."

Sarah, who had been trying to be supportive and not laugh, snorted before collapsing in Owen's lap, laughing.

I sighed and looked around at my friends. Pebble wasn't sure what to do since I didn't seem happy. I gave her a big smile. "Thank you, love. Will you put it on my bed before heading to bed yourself?"

José interrupted. "Oh, no, it stays down here. Pebble, it was a wonderful gift. Come give Uncle José a hug before going back upstairs."

Pebble made the rounds and then scampered off.

"Talk. How did you find out?" I grumbled.

Owen, getting his laughter under control, spit out, "I heard Mom talking to Aunt Allison on the phone. She thought she was alone. Best story ever. You know I had to share."

I flopped back on the couch. Bevin leaned back with me, still shaking with mirth.

We continued to talk and joke until, one by one, we all fell asleep.

The next morning, we woke up early to help cook. Sarah's and Piper's families arrived early to help.

Pack Thanksgiving was amazing.

The kitchen table held the deserts. The dining room was set up as a formal buffet with four turkeys, three hams, and more sides than anyone could get through. There were potatoes, salads, veggies, stuffing, cranberry sauce—both from a can and freshly made. The list went on and on.

A long table was put in the pack meeting room for all the adults. A table was set up in the basement for the kids.

Everyone came hungry.

Everyone ate their fill, and with werewolves who can eat a lot, that's saying something. In the end, the food looked barely touched. Finding places to put all the leftovers was the real challenge.

After food, there were games. Board games, card games, electronics…the works.

The evening lasted late. No one went for the black

Friday sales. Thanksgiving was about family and food, not shopping and the crazies.

December started to get cold, but our family got an early gift.

Everything went through for the adoption, and Penelope Anne officially became Penelope Anne Stone.

Pebble Stone to her friends.

ACKNOWLEDGEMENTS

I want to thank the people who make me laugh every day and continue to encourage me to write despite the number of my words they are forced to read. Wes Imrisek and Angela Grimes take my stories and make them more. They see my vision, a bud of a story, and help me create the garden of words you see published today. My son, Gavin, brainstorms with me about every concept I need to work through. He grumbles as any good teen would, but his great mind has a whimsical way of turning my thoughts in new directions. The rest of my writers' group, Haydee Milner and Lawrence Henry, help to refine my thoughts and ideas, making me a better storyteller. And of course, my friends and family, as always, are rock stars who encourage me every step of the way. None of them seemed to think it weird that a dyslexic math teacher wanted to start writing about a wolf pack.

ABOUT THE AUTHOR

Huckleberry Rahr is a mathematics instructor at the University of Wisconsin-Whitewater. She spent many years teaching math around the Midwest and in Papua New Guinea with the Peace Corps. Her parents instilled a love of reading from a young age.

She grew up with lesbian moms who had a huge collection of women authors with heroines as the protagonist. Her favorite genre was fantasy and science fiction, that is, until she discovered urban fantasy. What her mom's library lacked were books with characters that looked like her family: diversity in background, gender identity, and sexuality. She decided if she couldn't find that series, then she would write it.